A Brief Excursion
and Other Stories

D1563632

»»»»»»»»»» 《《《《《《《《《《

Antun Šoljan

A Brief
Excursion

and Other Stories

TRANSLATED FROM THE CROATIAN
AND WITH A FOREWORD
BY ELLEN ELIAS-BURSAĆ

NORTHWESTERN UNIVERSITY PRESS
EVANSTON, ILLINOIS

»»»»»»»»»» 《《《《《《《《《《

Northwestern University Press
Evanston, Illinois 60208-4210

Printed in the United States of America

ISBN 0-8101-1635-9

Library of Congress Cataloging-in-Publication Data

Šoljan, Antun.
 A brief excursion and other stories / Antun Šoljan ; translated from the
Croatian and with a foreword by Ellen Elias-Bursać.
  p.   cm. — (European classics)
 ISBN 0-8101-1635-9 (pa. : alk. paper)
 1. Šoljan, Antun Translations into English. I. Elias-Bursać, Ellen. II. Title.
PG1619.29.O4A24 2000
891.8'2354—dc21   99-45330
                                                         CIP

»»» CONTENTS «««

We see Antun Šoljan in photographs from a commemorative issue of *Most / The Bridge* at two moments in his life: the younger man, sailor and adventurer, edgy and smart; and in his later years, his eyes jaunty and irreverent, his lower jaw eroded by years of throat-cancer treatment. It is in these two roles, youthful seafarer and aging satyr, that he ruled Croatian literature as a poet, playwright, novelist, and essayist.

The stories and novel in this collection bring us Šoljan's razor-sharp wit, his attention to his peers, his fascination with barren coastal landscapes, and his shrewd political and social dissection. Several of the stories turn on poignant, elusive beauty—frescoes, love, a trophy, music—which, though it inspires and motivates the characters, invariably slips away in the end. Despite his playful references to world literatures and cultures throughout his writing, Šoljan cultivates an unrelentingly anti-intellectual voice that keeps teasing the reader for taking things too seriously, while somehow never letting us forget that writing is a life-or-death fight.

In 1957, when his first stories were published in book form as *Special Envoys* (included in this collection are "The White-Haired Pavlićes" and "Special Envoys"), Šoljan was twenty-five. Already he had been in and out of German and English studies at Zagreb University, had translated a volume of American poetry, put out the only two issues of the journal *Medjutim*, and coedited *Krugovi*, the literary journal around which he and his peers revolved.

The late 1950s and early 1960s were a golden age of experimental writing all over Yugoslavia. Miroslav Krleža's groundbreaking speech in 1952 defending the integrity of art from the pragmatic claims of socialist realism won some room for a modicum of innovation in the otherwise stringent, repressive atmosphere of postwar, prereform socialism. An irrepressible explorer, in Columbus-like fashion Šoljan chose English and American literatures as his new world, translating Nelson Algren, Lewis Carroll, F. Scott Fitzgerald, Joseph Heller, Ernest Hemingway, Norman Mailer, George Orwell, and William Shakespeare. In defiance of the plodding dictates of official rhetoric, he mapped frustration and failure, banter and humor.

In 1961, Šoljan issued a closely knit cycle of stories, entitled *Traitors,* as a novel (included in this collection are "The Garden of Nightingales," "Traitors," and "The Third Team"). The experimental narrative of his earlier writing grows more complex here: flashbacks, political satire, and a first-person narrative with a voice much closer to his own.

In 1964, Šoljan spoke at the graveside of Antun Gustav Matoš on the occasion of the fiftieth anniversary of the poet's death. His demand that his generation of writers live up to Matoš's excellence and aspirations for Croatian literature was viewed as controversial, and the wrath of socialism was brought down upon him.

Šoljan says of this time:

I wrote *A Brief Excursion,* it is true, in a single breath, in a week, while I was sitting at home, weathering a political tempest I found myself in the middle of. It doesn't matter which—I was in political hot water every so often. This was only one such instance, a little more fierce than the rest. I avoided venturing into town so that my acquaintances wouldn't have to look the other way, cross over to the other side of the street to stop from saying hello. I was beginning to feel just a touch abashed about existing at all. I was living in a social wasteland of sorts, which perhaps coincides with the landscape I use in the story.

As far as I can recall, as I wrote it I did not have consciously in mind a political statement of some sort, an allegorical image of the road our generation has taken, and even less our path to socialism, which, in my story, ends up smack in the middle of nowhere, or, as vigilant ideologists soon noted, a negativistic attitude or (which to their minds was more or less one and the same thing) nihilism. It was rather that landscape I kept seeing. That devastated landscape, bound to my private, at that moment not very cheerful, frame of mind dictated the setting for *A Brief Excursion*. (*Prošlo nesvršeno vrijeme* [Zagreb, 1992])

The novel, a picaresque tale of a group of art historians in search of fabled Istrian frescoes, appeared first in the Zagreb journal *Forum* in 1965, then, immediately thereafter, in Belgrade's *Prosveta*. Beset by claims that the novel was a threatening allegory exposing the futility of socialism, *A Brief Excursion* was not published in Zagreb again until 1987.

With the speech at Matoš's graveside and the controversy over publication of *A Brief Excursion*, Šoljan acquired a reputation as an antisocialist dissident, a reputation his tenure as president of Croatian PEN from 1970 through 1973, when he spoke out in support of Croatian writers jailed during the anti-Communist, pro-secessionist demonstrations of 1971, only made stronger. In the unusual hybrid of Yugoslav politics—repressive, yet not as repressive as the Eastern bloc countries—Šoljan was banned from holding interviews for radio, television, or the papers, and from making pronouncements of any kind on current politics. He often served regime-supported critics as a dartboard whenever they were inclined to take a shot at him.

He did, however, continue to write and to publish. In 1975 he published a collection of short stories, *A Family Dinner and Other*

Stories (included in this collection is "The Tour"), and in 1976 a searing political novel, *The Port*. Politically critical prose was a popular genre in Serbia and Slovenia in the 1980s, and there had been a few titles in the late 1960s, again in Serbia, but, besides Šoljan's, only two or three novels of this type appeared in the Croatian literature published during socialist Yugoslavia. His fourth novel, *The Second Men on the Moon*, appeared in 1978; its picaresque structure was much like that of *A Brief Excursion*.

Throughout the 1980s Šoljan published plays and translations, but it was only with the multiparty elections in the spring of 1990 that his status changed abruptly from that of éminence gris to that of an active public figure. His political commentary appeared regularly in the Zagreb papers until his death in 1993.

I owe a debt of gratitude to Christopher Edley III and Peter Elias for their careful reading of the manuscript of the translations. Special thanks go to Nada Šoljan, the writer's widow, for her thoughtful comments.

Ellen Elias-Bursać
May 1999

A Brief Excursion
and Other Stories

A Brief Excursion

I'll start right off by saying that my friend Roko is a madman. A person might think that anyone with such a chickenlike breastbone, scrawny arms, colorless, wispy hair standing on end, anyone who had lenses on his glasses so thick that he was always shoving them half-blindly into the face of whomever he spoke to, or into any number of dangerous electrical installations or kinds of equipment with spinning gears, could not possibly allow himself the luxury of being a madman to boot. But my friend Roko was one of those legendary maniacs protected by the gods.

He'd walk along the street, staring at pigeons on roof gables and, oblivious, he'd stride straight across a foot-wide board bridging an excavated ditch. He'd drop some change (he was always dropping things) and it would roll off among the high-voltage electric lines on some construction site, and he would lean right over—blind to the huge black skulls on signs that warned of the danger—and retrieve his property unharmed (because at that moment the gods switched off the electrical current all around the world), and with his innocent blind gaze he would glance at you, startled, wondering why you were standing there, staring at him aghast as if you had seen a ghost.

People who knew him from earlier on told me that during the war he had just barely escaped being shot—one of those hastily assembled firing squads with which they had begun thinning our ranks at the start of the war. Just at the instant when the blurting machine guns spoke in their simple language to the lines of the condemned who were dropping around him and on top of him like sheaves of wheat, he leaned over to retrieve his glasses, which had fallen into the mud among the feet of the strangers whose fate he only seemed to share; he, too, fell under the weight of the others who were dropping, and he searched, crawling and groping in the mud, for his glasses. He poked about among the corpses in the mud and blood for what was maybe half an hour, maybe an hour, and when he finally did locate his glasses (needless to say, undamaged), he stood up, put them on, and walked away. He walked away. The people who recounted this event tell me that for him the most grisly moment of the entire shooting episode was when he finally did manage to put his glasses back on.

How they know this, I've never been able to figure out. He never spoke of it. I asked him, anyway. "What can I say?" he answered, shrugging his shoulders. "I have no basis for comparison. No one ever shot me again." Coming from him these words sounded like a cheery, yet entirely ordinary, comment. Some they shot again and some they did not. "Why would anybody shoot me, anyway?" he wanted to know.

I have to tell you again that Roko was a madman in order to explain the nervous vitality, the incurable restlessness, the irascible drive to action, any action, the insatiable thirst for chance that, without the slightest provocation, without any visible logic, would dictate his unpredictable moves. He was simply unable to stay put for long: he had to keep constantly on the move.

Because of this, many had the impression that he was a shallow man and untrustworthy, prone to switch loyalties, or at least that he was what we would call "a person with a mind of his own," somebody you would be better off staying well away from. He had never cared much for what other people thought of him—he followed his whims no matter who he was with—and that certainly contributed quite a bit to his reputation as a lunatic.

But despite his renown for being a fidgety, headstrong man, he tended to draw people. There were always crowds around him. Was there in his inborn nervousness some sort of magnetic charm, an alluring promise that something might "happen"? Or was it that things in his proximity always seemed, indeed, to be "happening," and that this intrigued people more than he himself did? I don't know. I only know that I almost never saw him by himself. The people around him were, admittedly, new (they rarely returned to him once they'd dropped him, as, after a while, they all did—they couldn't keep up with the tempo), but still, new people are, nonetheless, people.

He behaved toward all the people surrounding him, the new and the old, in the same way. Now, when I think of it, it seems to me that he was one of that rare breed who treats everybody the same regardless of gender, faith, race, or social position. All those who came in contact with him were aware that before them was a unique, a remarkable, personality whom they should indulge in every way. At the same time, his most mysterious and alluring aspect was that it always seemed, no matter how headstrong and capricious he might be in his wanderings, that he was a man with a purpose, a purpose that we were never able to divine; a man who with his every action was following the dictates of some elusive, cruel star.

Whether borne by an almost greedy curiosity, a passion for testing fate, a physiological drive for novel sensation, or by an innate tendency to live dangerously, he always followed that absurd comet shining beyond his thick spectacles, and with unfailing instinct he sniffed out discomfort, trouble, danger, complication, conflict, from which he invariably emerged, like a phoenix, unscathed.

People did not like him—after all, why should they?—and they all knew it, but still they dogged his every step in all he did, though the fixes he got them into had far more dangerous consequences for them than they did for him. From the swampy backwater of their own lives, his life probably seemed like sheer high-altitude ozone. We, all of us, seemed to be drinking thirstily at that source of energy and vitality, in a tireless quest for change, to find in his destiny something that was lacking in ours. Maybe we believed that with his help we could free ourselves of the nasty feeling that all we did, all we possibly could do, was meaningless and paltry. We always wanted to believe that he had a goal. He never spoke of it. But wouldn't anyone assume that a person working as purposefully as he did must have a goal?

It seems clearer to me now as I tell this that he flung himself mindlessly and recklessly into everything he did. He tried his hand at whatever was risky. He ventured into the new and the unknown. All he embarked upon bore for him, though only for him, no consequences whatsoever. Maybe this is the very thing he was after, nervous, hysterical—an act that would bear consequences. Maybe he, who was mad, blind, clumsy, infantile, frail (and all of it more than the rest of us), was protected by that star of his.

I'm betraying him now for the third time—writing this way about a friend does stink of betrayal—and I'll say that he certainly was crazy, because despite everything, or maybe precisely because of it all, he invariably gave the impression of being a happy man. In a slightly bizarre way, of course. He was a version of the happy fool, the third and youngest son, mad Ivanushka, but also the enlightened prophet, the inspired seer, the disguised Messiah. He never complained about a thing. He never seemed worried, never was out of sorts.

He traversed the unending repertoire of his misadventures in such a way that it seemed to everybody that things could have turned out far worse than they did, that the outcome was the most auspicious possible under the circumstances. From each tangled labyrinth of complications he extracted himself, always with losses, which for the rest of us might have been tragic and lethal. For him these losses seemed practically like uncovered pirate treasure he had stumbled upon thanks to the special grace of Fortune, which had taken him under its wing. He wore his scars like medals.

In him, for the first and last time, I saw a genuine, and genuinely different, feel for happiness. For all the rest of us happiness meant one and the same thing: a sequence of more attainable goals, a shallow, winding staircase fading into rosy mist. His happiness, or at least so it seemed to us, was something extrahuman, a granite torch above the mist. Or maybe—as we unconsciously sensed in the constant pulsing of his hysteria—it was true, irrational happiness of naked life, pure happiness, something along the lines of happiness on its own terms.

No one, I believe, could have sustained his fate except him. Somebody else in his skin—if he could have survived it even briefly—would be a Job, he would stir general compassion, and people would have long since placed him under the aegis of social welfare as a sterling exemplar of somebody plagued by misfortune; but in that role Roko flourished, just as ice roses bloom only in frosted windows.

He had two big advantages—he owned nothing (had no home, no relatives), yet he was never alone. I never heard where he had come from, no one could boast that he was from their part of the country, no one could claim him their brother. I never learned where he lived. But he was never alone.

Were we friends for him, or was it that we needed him as much as he needed us? I do not know how he perceived us. But he was always connected to a crowd of people by a series of quixotic, complicated bonds that overlapped, augmented, clashed, snarled, and only he could steer through that tangled mass of relations with which he had, as with everything else, as with his whole life, only a string of misadventures, scenes, troubles.

He greeted all of this with joy, with boundless energy, beaming with a happiness which even today I cannot fathom, which I probably never will fathom as long as I live. He always had time for others, always had strength for others. Again, I wouldn't call it personal sacrifice or selflessness. Those words do not apply here. He, I think, had no choice. Maybe he had no other self except in others. Maybe he had no luck but bad luck.

After all, who can say? He never was alone because there were people always there, always dumping their troubles on him, always letting him guide them through the labyrinths of his endless adventures, somewhere where they never would have gone otherwise.

Maybe all those people—I count myself among them—had the feeling that somebody had to be like that. Maybe not so much that they themselves needed him as that he was needed for some general, elusive purpose, some spirit of the times, some primary life principle, some values beyond their ken.

They did not, however, admit to this. They would never admit to it, even in their dreams. We had mostly torn down the principles: values as such were dead or they were, rapidly, in those days, dying. When people spoke of Roko, they dismissed him with a shrug and a sneer of condescension: "That lunatic! The man does not know when to stop." Yet they were eager to recount his latest escapades.

So it was that the Roko I knew became, in time, a legend that devoured him whole. None of us today, I or anyone else, knows anything about him but his legend. In that legend, as things always go, he is in some ways larger, but in other ways smaller, than himself. He himself is missing altogether, as are many of our other friends from that time. That is why I have written this introduction: I know that in the lines that follow I did not succeed in reviving the man we used to know. That man and this world here are meant for you, dear reader.

∞

It was at some point during the first years after the war, when it seemed to all of us that the world was starting anew, from primeval magma. Bravely we tried, with everybody else, to believe that everything could be discovered over again, instilled with new meaning, and that an entirely new drama could be played out here, on this bit of turf. It seemed that the earth itself disclosed for us the white hillsides of its body and permitted us to roam them and poke about like tiny, but fertile, bugs. There seemed to be so much virgin turf where no human foot before us had ever trod. We seemed to be the ones called upon to continue life after the destruction, to assume the legacy, to crown the centuries with a glorious synthesis, to bring them to fulfillment. One of us even said, as I recall, that "somebody was drawing on our suffering to complete the world."

We had the impression that something, at last, was really happening.

The wartime question of "Where are we?" and the postwar "Where are we going?" had lost their edge (we were getting more and more diverse, each of us in a different place, all of us moving every which way); that was when we had begun to wonder once again "Where are we from?" and the thesis "We should backtrack along a part of our path to get the momentum to move ahead" became the watchword of the day. We wouldn't always begin from zero, would we, always back to the beginning, as if nothing had been there before us?

I remember that it was precisely at that moment that Karaman wrote about the medieval frescoes of Istria, and it just so happened that a combined team of young archaeologists, art historians, reproduction painters, and photographers set out almost spontaneously for Istria, without much in the way of preparation, with very little funding and no definite plans, the way, after all, so many things happened back in those days. Before us hovered the fuzzy notion that, if possible, we meant to discover some new frescoes, to scout out what could be done to preserve and categorize the old ones, to alert local governments to the treasures in their midst, to write the occasional dissertation, and so forth. I no longer know who organized and financed all this (probably some fund for this or that), but, like so many other youthful and enthusiastic jaunts, it soon turned into a jovial collective summer holiday on the shores of Istria. If you recall, my friends, that was the only way to have a summer vacation in those days.

I found myself in this distinguished coterie of young scholars thanks to my old friendship with Roko—we had known each other since back in high school and from time to time we'd renewed our acquaintance. Our time together consisted of his talking without stopping and my listening without stopping. I was a good, attentive listener, and that must have been what drew him to me; maybe he assumed the attraction was mutual. That must be why he proposed, while we were in a café once picking through reminiscences from high school (he was doing the picking, I was playing the role of head-nodder), that I work out some way to join him and a team of cultural workers on the expedition he was preparing for Istria.

In what capacity?

"We'll figure that out as we go along, don't worry," he said eagerly. "Look, I mean it, we really need somebody from the press corps. This really is, how should I put it, more of a goodwill mission than something bona-fide academic."

I was still young then and, they say, a pretty good reporter (with a few small pieces in my modest opus on farming collectives and a couple of educationally penned efforts on the uplifting of the masses, of the type "How Man Evolved from the Ape"), so I went to one of the daily papers and requested that they give me an advance and the proper "credentials," and told them that I could write them a few pieces on the frescoes of Istria, the new canned-fish factory, and, along the way, of course, a word on the Istrian collective farms. I got the advance and the credentials. It was enough for the daily that I was young, and for everything else, except the small sum of money, all I needed were the credentials.

Credentials—really any scrap of crumpled paper with a stamp of some sort and an illegible signature—at that time opened all the doors. All that mattered was that they were official. The more official they looked, the better they worked. With credentials you could get a room in overbooked hotels, food in fancy restaurants, a free ride on a train, various services from local authorities. In other words, only with credentials were you somebody, particularly when you were doing work in the "field," as we used to say. It was enough to have some sort of institution behind you for everybody to believe that the entire state was backing you up.

I remember one of our common friends who had remarkably impressive credentials, which, of course, he had manufactured himself. They were the quintessential credentials. He bound two sheets of some old school certificate between two small red covers, glued a photograph in place, and smudged it with a number of rubber stamps. Across from the grim photograph stood the laconic words: "Nothing must happen to this comrade from 0–24 o'clock." Signature. One stamp. A second stamp. In brief: comrade, this is serious. Whenever he showed this at some ticklish moment in a late-night bar, crowds would part before him the way the Red Sea had parted for Moses.

So, with my credentials in my pocket, and with my already rather jaded youth in my heart, I found myself in a little town on the Istrian coast, where every few days, under Roko's firm guidance, in, decidedly, the spirit of strictly scholarly endeavor, we went on expeditions toward towns in the interior where, apparently, one could find the ruins of little-known churches, but also bottles of rather well-known red wine: on the trail of legendary monasteries with particularly marvelous frescoes, but also on the trail of a particular and marvelous prosciutto. While it invariably turned out that these monasteries and churches were mere fiction, the prosciutto, cheese, and wine generally turned up exactly where we thought we'd find them. The written documents on the basis of which we were searching for the treasures most often turned out to be the crudest of counterfeits, while, as we all well know, the oral tradition of reporting the location of other sorts of national treasures has always been faithful and reliable.

Soon I acquired my modest place in this learned entourage, and, like all other members of the group, I became one of the playing pieces in the endless and quirky chess game Roko was playing with life. Many of these people, like me, had only gotten to know each other here, on the expedition, and our company as a unit existed only in Roko, who fused all of us together in some way. Roko watched over our every movement, every conversation, every little quibble, like a worried hen over its flock of chicks. He was the master of ceremonies, the maker of plans, the organizer of the entertainment. He was constantly rushing off in all directions.

Almost every day we set out on yet another investigative jaunt. The young scholars applied their scant and rather abstract knowledge to the objectives of our day trips, mostly in long, and ultimately tipsy, discussions about, for instance, the Croatian-Italian question in Istria, or the moral qualities of this or that professor, or the head of some distinguished institute they were relying on. They preferred shade, grass, and red wine from the plastic jugs we always carried with us, but they had nothing against some little tavern off the beaten track in a village, where in the smoke and musty smell of sulfur people played briscola, the prosciutto was sliced thin, and Istrian bagpipes warbled reedily.

Since I knew nothing of the object of their studious interest, I could not participate fully in the fierce disputes over the salient moral and professional questions, and my modest contributions on the trips usually consisted of haggling with villagers over the price of wine, cheese, salted sardines, and olives, which we later dined upon in the comfortable historic shade of some cultural monument. My newspaper reports came down to touching descriptions of the beauties of recently liberated Istria, fabricated dialogues with the salt of the Istrian earth, and several general points on what "ought to be done" for the cultural elevation of the masses using frescoes—should the frescoes be brought to the masses or the masses to the frescoes?

I must emphasize once again that it was to Roko's credit that we went anywhere at all. After the first earnestly begun but ultimately unsuccessful attempt at finding some legendary church from the tenth century, a sample of unique early Croatian architecture which we found no trace of (right by which we allegedly trudged without seeing it, as some later claimed, or figuring it was nothing but a field hut for storing tools—or maybe it really was an ordinary stone field hut which others had thought was a church; chances are that will never be explained), all of them were already weary of archaeology and art history, and surrendered lazily to the sun, the wine, and promiscuity—something that invariably happens to bookworms such as they who, after hungry years spent living in clouds of dust, give themselves over wholeheartedly to pleasure as soon as they smell a little fresh air, not to speak of prosciutto.

All of this would have shifted smoothly into a more or less enjoyable summer if it hadn't been for Roko driving us ever onward like sinful souls, or if only we had had enough of our own will and strength to defy his pressures. But people are helpless in the presence of superior energy, such as, doubtless, Roko's was. As soon as somebody desires to lead us, no one is happier than we are;

we submit to leadership as if it is the sole thing we have been waiting for all our lives. Maybe our thirst for leadership (because we ourselves can see no farther than our noses) is what made Roko the leader, or maybe it is in the very nature of a leader to stoke such a thirst in his vicinity that all else, except for the one road leading toward the mirage of his oasis on the horizon, seems like a barren desert. I don't know. I know only that from the start, with a sigh of relief, even enthusiasm, we embraced Roko's leadership.

It is difficult to say why he was the one guiding the expedition, and why he was doing it all in the first place. Was he under obligation to some government office, or engaged by some institute, or was he simply assigned to the task by a tourist or other agency? It was clear to me that it wasn't our success in scholarship upon which he was planning to build his career; that, after all, would not be the way to do so: all of our jaunts (I can call them his now without blushing) ended up, of course, without result, and as far as the scholarly aspect of things was concerned, we could have spent our summer more pleasantly without them.

We all soon had the impression that he cared less about the outcome of what we were doing than about the doing itself. Some inner edge, a restlessness, was in him, some crazy quirk of his temperament drove him to drive us equally mercilessly. One had to keep working incessantly. Whenever we set out under his leadership on the latest expedition, against our will and without the conviction that there was any genuine reason to do so, it seemed to me that somewhere in some cloudy and forgotten part of the brain we were looking for something we genuinely lacked, something terribly important (not frescoes or churches, not history); something that could not, in fact, be found, but something vital and essential of which only Roko was fully cognizant, and I would struggle to figure it out, feeling my helplessness and ineptitude and a heavy pall of weariness, pettiness, and hopelessness would settle upon me, irrational but all the more terrible as a result, and something seemed to be screaming in me: don't go, stay, there is nowhere to go. But no one could resist Roko.

You can imagine that this did not make him particularly popular among the ranks of young scholars who were helplessly stuttering, messing about, trying to evade his eyes (they may have believed he was following some higher dictates), while he laid out his ferocious plans, as happened more and more often. Each time the plans were more elaborate. Each excursion ventured further and required greater effort, as our stay hastened to its end. But his intensity and his evident seriousness ("Comrades, you know that we must . . .") created such an atmosphere that it got harder to say anything against his itinerary without him taking it as a personal insult and a group no-confidence vote against the organizer.

So every few days we would set out from our base on the coast on some new foray into the Istrian interior, and for a while we would be grumpy and lethargic, but then, gradually adapting to the conditions that had been imposed from above—as always happens—we managed to salvage what there was to be salvaged, which actually meant: to get out into the landscape and poke around as soon as possible, to stretch out somewhere on green grass, forget Roko, get rolling drunk, sing some songs, and in that way survive the tribulations of scholarship until we returned home to our base.

I have related all of this to you only so that you may understand at least a little more clearly how it happened that near the close of this brief, communal summer vacation, when Roko proposed one day (no matter how much we were expecting it, each time it took us by surprise) in a voice that brooked no opposition: "Hey, folks, off we go to Gradina," off, indeed, we went. We did not ask him to give us any reasons for the trip; it was enough for us that he said we should. That must be the principle for a good-enough reason.

Somebody says something and you see no reason to go along with it, but how can you refuse, because what reason would there be for gainsaying the suggestion?

"According to my information, Gradina is a place we have got to see," said Roko. "*Vedi e poi mori.* If you haven't seen it, you haven't seen anything. A whole entire town waiting for us out there."

Even the tone of his voice suggested that it was clear we had never seen anything—in our miserable lives—and this town had to be seen just as man needs the air he breathes. It was immediately crystal clear that we had no alternative.

"What have they got there, anyway?" some of us tried to sway him.

"Is there any point in going out there like the blind?" reasoned others. "Whoever heard of this Gradina? Aren't we being just a little naive? Chances are everything has been ransacked, carted off. Where the hell is Gradina, anyway? It isn't on our detailed map."

I have to confess here and now that I am no longer certain it was Gradina that Roko spoke of, or some similar generic name which I have since forgotten, and which later no one could remember. Just as we could no longer, later, remember the direction we took, or the man to whom Roko brought us on the evening before the excursion, who swore to us up and down that "you have paintings to die for out there," and whose stories got glitzier and glitzier and his description fuller and richer the more we foisted the wine on him, which we, naturally, were paying for.

Later many did their best to reconstruct our movements through recollection of landscape, houses, or different signs, and to determine approximately the position of the town of Gradina, but all in vain. The memories did not fit, or they could not be anchored in reality. Some even undertook to travel to some spots or ruins that were known as Gradina (there are more of them than a person might think—they found a handful of Gradinas), but they found nothing similar to the place where we went and what we saw.

At that point Roko produced convincing answers to all our questions fervently and readily. Later we tried to reconstruct his every word, but since we couldn't summon to memory the fervor and enthusiasm that lived in him, the words were cold and stripped of their real meaning, nothing could actually be gleaned from them, so we soon mixed them up and forgot them.

Maybe only he knew how to utter them in such a way as to breathe life into their hidden meaning. Maybe he alone could show how there *was* sense in doing precisely what it was that we were doing. Or in doing anything at all. Maybe his untamable energy, an intense thirst for action, conveyed that meaningful life in words and maybe there really are people to whom the hidden meaning of things that eludes all the rest of us is disclosed. Maybe Roko was one of those. Maybe in some other time he might have been a kind of prophet. What else could he have done, being the kind of man he was, in that day and age?

"People, tomorrow we go to Gradina," he said earnestly, as if all of us until that moment had waited for nothing else. "I will see to the details, don't you worry about a thing. Maybe we'll have luck with the weather. It is about time that we had a little luck."

He continued his optimistic monologue the next day in the morning while all of us, sleepy and out of sorts, were gathering around the open door of a small bus with sixteen seats, as colorful as one of those sherbet swirls on a stick. Roko and the driver had found it who knows where and for what elevated cause. The bus stood on the little square, its doors ajar like some gawky albatross. We tossed in our bags with provisions, the demijohn for red wine—if worst came to worst we could always mix the wine with water and make *bevanda*—which we never went anywhere without. None of us said much except Roko. He pranced around us, counting us, getting us in order, not allowing us to meander off, as we were generally inclined to do, to the local cafés and bars.

"Hey, people, get moving, goddamn it," Roko stirred us from our early-morning reverie and crankiness. "Come on, get into the bus so we can see if everybody's here. Can't you sit still in one place for five minutes? Where do you have to go know, I want to know? You blockhead! Wait: twelve, thirteen . . . where are those Slovenes? . . . Where are the women? You see, damn it all, it is eight o'clock and we aren't even half . . . Come on, show at least a little humor . . . Fuel? It has taken you this long to figure out we are low on fuel?"

"The wreck usually runs on cheap brandy," somebody defended the driver. "What good will diesel do?"

"What are you doing standing here like a statue?" Roko descended upon one of the others. "Stop blocking the doorway and let somebody in . . . Now you have to stuff yourselves as if you haven't had a bite to eat for days? Now you have to drink like fish?"

So we clustered together under the barrage of his words, one by one, yawning, scratching ourselves, thinking of a thousand little objections just to delay the time of departure.

Vladimir, the photographer, waddled slowly over, one step at a time, hungover as usual, and tossed somewhere into the inside of the bus a leather bag with a camera and a series of dangling leather attachments. He saw Roko, cursed under his breath, and then began examining the bus from the outside, like a horse, patting it on its flanks. He did that for a while. He suddenly liked the way the door resounded under his palm. Once more he banged it carefully, harkening to the sound, and then like a drummer in a trance he performed a whole little tam-tam on the door, an unintelligible message that rang out over the entire square. When that had pleased him, he smiled wearily, brushed off his hands, and turned, weaving, in the direction of a café.

"Where are you going now?" Roko shrieked after him hysterically.

"To take a piss," announced Vladimir laconically, right into the faces of our two female fellow travelers, who were just arriving, perky, tidy, freshly washed, and, to spite the heat, dressed from head to toe in identical gray windbreakers, casual skirts, thick socks, and walking shoes, like twins; they walked over with an elastic mountaineering spring, as best suits two well-bred city girls, now aware young women and future cultural workers who were probably born with the mentality of spinsters and who considered this their own special social virtue. For as long as I had known them they had never been apart, and no one was entirely sure which was which. We called them, out of fondness, "our two Ophelias." The air of general moral purity imposed such convent-related associations. Vladimir's mention of pissing was at that moment tantamount to scatology—the times were like that: everything natural was appalling.

They were the only women on our expedition (as you can see, the whole thing, at first, had been designed with the best scholarly foundations), and they were of the opinion, isolated as they were, that they were threatened in this crowd of men; at one moment their virginity was under assault, at another their suffragette pride. They probably figured the two were one and the same. With their presence, our expedition, despite all the advantages that the company of women usually provides, acquired only their automatic, profound disgust at every single, even the most innocent, vulgarity, so the men at least had the satisfaction of cursing from the heart, whenever the opportunity arose. As is usually the case when all else fails, we cursed: we cultivated several of the curses just for them.

Both of them were angular, unfeminine, with hair that had no shine, and both of them wore identical eyeglasses with colorless frames, just as the two of them seemed colorless; both had identical sketchbooks and in them identical clumsy drawings, and in their minds identical banal thoughts; both of them were students of art history, in which they had not made it far enough to figure out yet that the main subject of their studies ought to be the art of finding a husband. On that subject they instinctively, at this point, knew one thing only: in their mountaineering past, in comradely asexuality, they had learned that a woman, no matter how suffragette-inclined she may be, should always on a day trip take with her in a little bag a small tablecloth (white, if possible), hard-boiled eggs, a breaded cutlet, and salt. Again, they had brought with them their military gray rucksacks stuffed with all manner of things, and were carrying them, militarily, over their shoulders, prouder than another woman might be of her silver fox stole. They had done their scouting duty: these little men, left to their own inclinations, would so easily wander from the true path, abandoned to the mercy or mercilessness of the local taverns and barmaids.

"Ah, and what are we doing *today?*" they inquired in their melodious early-morning voices, as if every other day we went to the movies. "Comrade Roko, where are you taking us?"

"Out into the great, wide world," answered Petar the Archaeologist from the bus window, the rock upon which the foundation of our expedition relied. "Off into the fucking wilderness of wolves."

"Local folklore has it," somebody explained from the next window, "*tutto il mondo e una* fucking wolf-ridden wilderness."

The Ophelias snorted disdainfully and moved vigorously toward the front door of the bus.

"Don't you be getting your hopes up about the local wolves," somebody chimed in.

The drunken interior of the bus was already singing harmoniously: "Who's afraid of the big, bad wolf?"

"Go at it, fuck-offs!" somebody chided. "You sheep! Where are we going? Where is this imbecile taking us?"

"Didn't you know," explained learned Petar, "that the name Roko comes from the old Nordic *hróhr*, which means 'strong man'?"

"An imbecile just the same."

The driver shrugged demonstratively while he tossed empty army surplus fuel canisters into the baggage compartment. Roko shouted something from afar, dragging several of our fellow travelers from a café, where they had already sunk into their morning brandies.

"Have you tried the local bitters?" one of them whom he had grabbed by the sleeve did his best to extricate himself.

Holding a glass in his other hand, he tried to stop him and explain the advantages of locally produced beverages. "Apparently not. Bitters, now there's a drink! Here, please. Try a little! Just a sip. Do try! See whether you are a man or not."

You could hear the genuine drunken entreaty in the man's voice, as if this really would prove once and for all whether or not Roko was a man. But Roko was merciless. He shoved him busward until he nudged him through the door.

"Bitters!" crowed the man at the door like some bizarre rooster. "Drink the local nepenthe!"

One by one, the last stragglers appeared. Two Slovenes, brothers with red faces, both of them young experts from Ljubljana who never showed their alcohol: no matter how much they had had to drink they always looked the same. Usually they were quiet and drank systematically. They called it "working at drinking"— and in it they were reliable, the way Slovenes ought to be. They drank until the red veins on their faces turned blue, and then calmly, oblivious of all else, wherever they happened to be at the moment, they fell asleep, blessed as children.

Now they arrived with their always rather rigid, dignified stride, their eyes a little glassy, with a bottle of wine from Koper in their hands; on principle they drank no other wine. Sober they were not, but no one alive could venture a guess as to whether this was still lingering since last night or a fresh morning acquisition.

"These two no longer really drink," somebody had said of them. "They just keep topping it off."

"Let's get going, people," shouted Roko around the bus like an anxious shepherd. "The worst of the heat is going to hit us."

When the bus finally started moving, some started singing in a mood as if we were already on our way home:

> Four men sat down to drink their wine,
> Two by two, and two by two . . .

Petar was still chuckling over some joke he had thought of himself, and from time to time he would rejoinder to some invisible conversant sitting on the seat next to him: "What was that you said? *Tutto il mondo?* . . . What was it we began with: that we are setting out into the wide world! No, narrow. What was it we began with? I've muddled everything. Hey, everybody, I've made a muddle of everything."

Petar needed things to be clear.

Soon it began to fade, that feeling so natural to travelers that it seems as if they cannot even travel without it, the feeling that they have left something behind, they've forgotten to bring it, neglected to do it; something particularly important, some part of their past life which, no matter how long they travel, no matter where they get to, no matter how much everything has changed, they will need in their new life. But nothing is that important. We started gradually succumbing to indifference, that transitional hibernation of the spirit when a person is not in close contact with anything, does not make connections, merely observes images framed by the window. That is how we became transit travelers who happened, only by chance, coincidentally, to be part of precisely *this* bit of landscape, near *these* houses or these trees. It was not our lot to live *here;* we had other, more pressing goals. We had places to go.

It seemed that we had finally freed ourselves of some inner spasm, a panicked rigidity, and we surrendered with trust to the bus, certain that it would take us somewhere—travelers have nothing left but that assurance. Only two points continued to live on in our consciousness: our departure point and our destination. All else was merely a long-practiced, unshifting system of coincidences, a labyrinth of digressions it is better not to study too carefully.

I kept being plagued by the illusion that somebody was missing. From time to time it would look to me, at the edge of my field of vision, as if there were somebody sitting in the empty seat in the back part of the bus, but whenever I turned to look the apparition would vanish. Whom had we left behind? I wondered. Who else was supposed to be with us?

We looked back less and less, and soon we stopped altogether. The monotonous shaking and rocking of the bus lulled us, and then enveloped us in that semi-stupor in which one sustains relatively easily the discomforts of travel. We shook and bounced along, our jaws loose, dazed, staring with half-lowered eyelids into space. I had the feeling that from banging on the sides of my skull, my brain had softened like jellied headcheese. All conversation ceased. Even Roko said nothing for a while.

We passed through monotonous landscape (stone walls, vineyards, underbrush) and only occasionally through a town (tavern, post office, church, stone houses). I noticed something that was to stay with me for the rest of the trip: the landscape didn't seem to be changing. The towns we passed through were as like to one another as eggs; I had the impression that we were going round in circles. What else could we do? I figured we were out to do precisely that, after all: circle through the towns and go back.

"The road is abysmal," somebody moaned behind me.

"It is as though they plowed it," said somebody else from the recesses of the bus.

"Maybe it was Kraljević Marko in person," commented a third, perking up. "He chased off those Turks and now there is no one left here to maintain it."

"You cannot be serious, the Turks in Istria!?" rebelled one of the Ophelias.

"OK, so it was Veli Jože. He is the one who chased away whoever the bad guys were."

"As soon as you turn off the main road," somebody said from the front seats of the bus, "it is as if civilization stops. Not a single sign."

True, I had noticed the same thing myself: since we had turned off the road I hadn't seen a single road sign. Did that matter? I could see that Roko was sitting up with the driver, showing him the way.

"Who knows what this town is called?" somebody asked indifferently.

"Do you care? It's a town like any other," somebody else concluded.

After a little while, at some empty intersection with no road sign, while the driver was nervously shifting gears and deciding which direction to take, the bus gurgled as if something were choking it and halted. The cloud of dust that had been following us settled about our windows. A sudden hush fell.

The driver turned the key several times. You could hear the ignition whining into nothing. The driver pulled himself out of his seat and leaped out, angrily slamming the door. We exchanged glances in silence, while outside you could hear how the driver was banging the hood of the bus. Roko followed the driver out.

We got up one by one, stretched our stiff joints, and went out into the first heat wave of the day. For a little while we watched the tangled guts of the motor: the driver nervously fiddled with it while cursing under his breath. The bus stood there smack in the middle of the road. To the left and right there were smaller roads branching off and vanishing into the dusty maquis undergrowth, but with no signs to suggest where they were headed. There was no trace for a long way of a settled area, a house, or a living being.

"What now?" somebody wanted to know. His voice sounded unnatural and hollow in the silence.

"Don't you worry about a thing," said Roko to all of us with a cheery expression, as if he were about to give out Christmas presents to everybody around him. "Everything will be fixed, any minute."

That "any minute" lasted for over half an hour and nothing did get fixed. The two young Slovenian scholars, who had poked only their noses out of the bus and then sat back into their seats and continued drinking, finished their bottle of Koper wine, lobbed it through the window into the rocks by the road, and started singing: "Cinca Marinca, going nowhere fast . . . ," which clearly was irritating Roko. A little further on, on a meadow surrounded by stone walls, the women were picking flowers, just as true Ophelias ought to do, while others were impatiently poking around in the dusty grass on the side of the road with their feet. The driver wiped away the sweat and swore.

It got hotter and the impatience grew. For a while we made idle guesses as to where we might find temporary lodging. But there wasn't a thing on the horizon, no tavern, no charming country manor, no simple yet hospitable person, and that made the interruption of the trip seem even more glaring; clearly we were in big trouble.

We looked at the bus with huge hatred. It seemed to me that it wasn't broken at all, it was stubborn. As if somewhere in its gut of wires and gears, in its oily circulation, it knew that we were depending on it and that was why it had intentionally dug in its heels. Man doesn't even notice how dependent he is on things until they betray him. They betray him precisely when he needs them most. That is civilization. That is when we notice that we live with it, but that it has its own say. We are, mainly, helpless. Fellow travelers, so to speak.

The driver mentioned three mothers of God.

"There is civilization for you," I struck up a rather foggy meditation, because the sun had gone to my head. The driver understood that this referred to him. He glared at me and furiously smashed the wrench to the ground. Vladimir leaned his ear to the hood, as if listening to whether anything was working in the motor or not. He banged the chassis with his hands, chanting:

Tam-tam, tam-tam-tam-tam, tam-tam
Tam-tam, tam-tam-tam-tam, tam-tam

and finishing a complicated rhythmic phrase, he listened once more and then shrugged his shoulders.

"No one responded," he concluded.

"You have got it under a spell," somebody said.

"Me?" said Vladimir. "Roko is the one who brings bad luck, everybody knows that."

Roko stared at him, wordless.

We collected around the hood like old anatomists. We exchanged confused glances: the expedition was turning into a problem.

"What now?" asked somebody in the silence. The question was general, but we were all expecting, not without a certain dose of spite, Roko to answer. We waited a pretty long while. He looked us over one by one.

"We will proceed on foot," he said in a small, muted voice, which surprised and alarmed me. A person who knows fear can swiftly spot it in somebody else. I could see that he was scared. What is he afraid of? I wondered, and I, too, got a little apprehensive.

"On foot? Are you serious?" somebody said.

"I know the way," said Roko, "and it isn't far off."

"But on foot?" They were appalled. "We know scholarship requires sacrifice, but *per pedes?*"

"The brother Slovenes are dead drunk," somebody announced from the bus door. "They are sleeping like the dead."

"Smart," somebody approved.

"There, I can see," somebody mused, "but back, how will we get back?"

"Come on, folks," said Roko, "the place is flat as a plate."

"The only thing flat on me are my feet; I am no walker," said one of us and demonstratively moved back toward the door of the bus. "I will wait here until a car comes by."

"The last time a car came by this way," began Ivan, pretending an elderly effort at recollecting, "must have been '28 or '29, if my memory serves me well."

"For walking I have exactly enough strength to walk back to town," somebody said.

"Roughly sixty kilometers, give or take a few," said the driver.

"Well, then to the nearest bus stop."

"What will we do with the women?" they shouted. "How will they walk?"

Feeling that women's equality had been called into question, the Ophelias reacted readily: "Don't worry about us. We are alpinists."

"There's not a single alp in sight," said Vladimir. "Don't go assuming that we will make it to Triglav, in this direction. Or south to Ohrid if we take the other."

"Ohrid is not a mountain," said the Ophelias.

"We will have to spend the night, no matter where we end up."

"How about right here? I am beginning to feel like taking a nap," said somebody.

"Let's go, folks," concluded Roko. Meanwhile, he had pulled his small blue sports bag out of the bus, tossed it over his shoulder, and set out along the road. A lonely, hunched, grotesque figure. Where was he headed? something in me asked hysterically. Where? But I didn't dare listen to that voice.

"Let's get going," I said, thinking I ought to. "Roko knows the way."

I could see that many of them were hesitating, and only some of them were deciding. Soon two groups had formed: the first was making up its own mind; behind them, to the left and right, were those who had decided that they would do what the others had decided.

"Will you come with us?" I asked the driver, who was perched on the front fender and trying to wipe his hands with a household rag he had soaked in fuel.

"No," he said calmly. "I have to look after the bus until a car happens by which can fetch help. What good am I to you without the bus?"

Roko had already gone pretty far down the road.

Quite a few had decided, I saw, to stay.

"Well, then, that's it," I said to those who stayed. "We'll tell you how it went."

They waved reluctantly to us, just as we reluctantly started walking. When we had gotten twenty-odd paces off, I turned to look back once more. The bus was standing in the middle of the road watching me with its headlight eyes like some mammoth hippopotamus. Everybody had hidden from the heat by going back into the bus, and the bus door was shut. It looked as if there were no people there at all.

Panic and apathy are the procrustean bed on which the spirit of my generation was stretched. Between those two poles there has been an entire range of states we were taught to think of as actually normal. But it was as if some unfeeling and terrible hand had erased all those transitional nuances for us. We were not capable of a single instant of life in spiritual equilibrium. Why? I don't know. There are so many things I do not know about my own generation. It always seemed to me that the generations before ours and after ours had it so much easier.

I only know that I had been driven to madness, to hysterical trembling, by sudden outbursts, explosions of panic, the only thing capable of pulling us out of our apathetic struggle to get by and our listless acceptance of everything that was offered to us or imposed upon us. Were these in fact inborn prenatal horrors we had otherwise managed to suppress and control only by a total oblivion of spirit, desire, self, hope, through some form of self-protection such as apathy? Many were the times when I had pitied my friends, hated and despised myself, that we do not know how to live or cannot live without these extremes, we cannot live outside the mold of extremes in which we are enclosed, to live in a bright equilibrium with the encouraging support of reason. But I was as helpless as the next man.

Maybe because he was stirring me from apathy, or maybe because I felt I had no strength to stay the tide of panic, I looked at Petar with powerless rage, verging on hatred.

At Petar, who until that moment had been walking moodily, with resignation, down the dusty road in the heat for maybe a whole hour, enveloped, like the rest of us who had set off on foot on this long and uncertain journey, in a heavy, self-recriminating silence in which you could clearly distinguish among the individual crickets chirping in the sparse olive trees. Petar now began, in a panic, with an urgent restlessness in his voice, to repeat for the who knows what time, with growing intensity: "Where are we? You guys, do you have any idea where we are?"

No one answered him the first time. In our straggling column we looked down at the dirt road beneath our feet.

"Come on, for the love of God, have you noticed that there are no signs along this road?" he said a few paces further on. "There are no names of towns. Nothing to tell us where we're headed. How can we tell where we are?"

"So what?" somebody muttered through clenched teeth. "Here or there."

"Relax," another said. "Roko probably knows."

We tried to quiet him down, but the anxiety in our voices fed his panic.

"You guys, we've got to do something. We can't just keep going on like this, as if we are cattle. We're lost. We're lost, get it, lost! We should turn back while we still can."

We stopped in the middle of the hot open hand of the road, which, as far as we could see, stretched before us and behind us completely evenly, as did the landscape on both sides of the road, so that it seemed as if we hadn't stopped anywhere, but rather that we were still traveling along in some strange way, here, stopped suddenly in the middle of nowhere, that we were spinning along with the world in some terrible orbit, scorched like bugs on the glowing frying pan of the road.

"We're lost, we're lost, this is it," rose Petar's voice hysterically, and rebellion and the despair in his voice mingled with accusation. As he spoke, he watched Roko without blinking.

"You know the way, do you?" he said, finally. "You know where we are? You know this? You know shit. I cannot imagine why I am still following you."

Without turning, Roko kept on plodding forward. Huge drops of sweat dripped from behind his ears down onto the nape of his neck.

We argued with Petar, explained to him that the road had to go somewhere, that what did "get lost" mean anyway, here in a civilized place, where there was an average of so many inhabitants per square kilometer, and where you could always find somebody. See, people, nothing is wrong, we are not in a desert, we're in Istria, we still can walk all the way across it from one end to the other in a day, it is really small, yet it is trusty; Istria may be an orphan, but it is ours; we know where we are; what kind of a coward is he anyway, what a spineless wimp, he is scared to stretch his legs, sleeping by a stone wall or in the hay, getting rained on if need be. Nothing sounded convincing, and I raged on helplessly, feeling in my words, even as I was saying them, a fear and panic much like his, noticing the same panic in the gestures and voices of the others. I felt as if the reasons we were giving were paltry and insignificant, as if we'd refuted them before we even spoke them. Not one of us believed them. No one believed anymore in the reasons, words, of anyone else. If somebody were to tell us where we were then and where we were headed, we wouldn't have even believed we were in Istria, or in this century, let alone that Gradina did exist and that we would get there: it would be only a word, an empty shell. With the first shivers down our spines, we spun around to scan the landscape, and the sentence Petar had been repeating as if he were drunk—"We should turn back while we still can"—echoed in us louder than all words of reason as the last desperate call, as the only summons of salvation.

Just then, as suddenly as it had welled up, the panic subsided. The quarrel waned, we stopped trying to convince one another of anything, we grumbled a bit more, but we had set off slowly and instinctively in a scraggly group after Roko, who was standing the entire time a little to the side, watching us. Now he grinned and slowly began to move on down the road, holding his head cocked half at an angle to see, out of the corner of his eye, whether we were following him or not. We followed him.

We walked after him humbled, still smarting from the quarrel, exhausted and tired from the panic which had left us like squeezed-out rags, and I knew that not only in terms of myself, but in some collective way, the good old apathy was back. It descended upon us from these skies like a gentle curtain of sunny mist in which everything around us shimmered like a glittery, fuzzy, groggy mirage.

Several steps ahead, Roko stopped and glanced at us mockingly, with superiority, pointing ahead, like Napoleon at Austerlitz, and announced: "Here is your sign."

Sure enough, we saw the sign, way ahead of us at a curve. From that distance you couldn't see what was written on it. We got closer, a little abashed because of our foolish behavior moments before, and laughed at ourselves, shrugging helplessly, as if we wanted to say to one another: how could we have made such a fuss, talked so feverishly, lost control, panicked over something so silly?

The sign stood by the side of the road, at an angle on a bent, black-and-white-striped metal pole from which the paint was peeling. It was dented as if somebody had thrown rocks at it, the paint was almost all scraped off, and rust had so deeply eroded the edges of the metal that this may have in fact been only half of the sign. Nevertheless, a sign it was. Clearly old, who knows since when, now unofficial, though it might possibly still be valid. You could read it.

TURN LEFT HERE

it said.

We stopped in front of the road marker and repeated the words over and over again, each to himself. A short and indefinite shiver went through me at its enigmatic tone. It was horrible that here, in this desert, all at once, out of nowhere, such a terse sign had cropped up. "Turn left here." Where to? I wondered, but forgot the question a moment later. Why split hairs? No matter what, I repeated, it is a sign, an indication of direction, somewhere something does exist. Whoever wrote it knew what and to whom he was writing. He knew this headed somewhere.

To the left of the road a small path, only the width of a single person, wound away through the bushes. We stood for a while help-lessly circling in place, like waters swirling at a place where rivers branch off in diverse directions. The path probably used to be much wider: on the side, overgrown with weeds, you could see the tracks of tractor tires, truck tires, many passersby. Roko suddenly laughed aloud and marched into the bushes. I went after him. As if we had agreed to do so in advance, the others did not follow. Vladimir sat down by the sign, leaning his back on it, as if demonstratively wish-ing to show that the research project did not interest him.

In front of me, Roko was pushing blackberry shrubs aside, cautiously hopping over the low-growing brambly bushes that had grown over the path. We had gone hardly a hundred paces when he suddenly stopped in his tracks amid the brush, which kept getting denser and higher. He had caught sight, in front of him, of something I couldn't see for his back in the tangle of branches.

"Mother of God, those rotten bastards," hissed Roko through his clenched teeth. "Goddamn those sly tricksters . . ."

I came up and peered over his shoulder. The bushes stopped suddenly at that spot. So did everything else: the path, the traces of vehicles, even the ground stopped. Before our feet yawned a stony pit, no more than five or six meters deep, but certainly deadly enough. On all sides, surrounded by bushes, was an oval depression, and jagged stone cliffs dropped all the way to the bot-tom, almost perpendicular. The path clearly only went this far. There was no path branching to the right or left. There were no signs. The rocks in the pit were ruddy, stained with the blood of many travelers who had followed the sign this way. Or was it bauxite ore, the iron-red soil this region had always boasted of?

An abandoned bauxite mine? An old quarry? These were mere words before the abyss which lay in wait for us.

We turned, appalled, dumbstruck, avoiding each other's eyes, and went back along the same path. Roko now walked behind me. The others were waiting with questioning gazes—hope was mirrored in their eyes. I had no strength to tell them anything. I looked at the sign. It stood there by the road, an ordinary traffic sign worn by time, rusty. I was speechless at how ordinary it seemed. I knew that I could do nothing. I couldn't even hate it. There was something incomprehensible in the fact that it was so insignificant, so trivial, and yet that it held so much hope, so much disappointment.

"All right, you guys, what's up?" they asked Roko. "You look as if you have seen a ghost."

"A pit," said Roko. "The path leads straight to this big pit. It is more like a trap. How the natives trapped lions."

"There could be natives around here," said Petar. "I did hear drums."

"But as far as the lions are concerned," Vladimir said spreading his arms, "it is a bit iffy. You won't be able to scare up a couple of lions no matter what you do."

He and Petar chuckled gratefully to each other.

"Goddamn their filthy mothers," repeated Roko, still pretty shaky, as if he had looked into some deeper and darker abyss.

No one asked whose mothers, whose filth? They all knew that something nasty had happened and that it was better not to know who the perpetrators were, the reasons, the intent. They all knew that many more turnoffs awaited us, more pitfalls. But we kept on walking: at first peering every which way in excitement, anxious about what we might see and what was still to come, and then gradually more indifferent, as if nothing had happened.

Roko led us along a winding and dusty road, not allowing us to stop anywhere. We had been walking for an eternity at this point. From time to time we passed a crossroads, which would fork before us like unkept promises. We'd look with longing to the left and the right, we'd halt, feigning hesitation, feigning the need to think, to choose, but he paid not the slightest attention.

There were no signs at any of these intersections, no warnings or signs for no trespassing, names of towns, or kilometers, the roads joined and split, but he, without a trace of indecision, with some inner certainty, selected the way that must have seemed the right one to him. Without altering his step, he continued on down one of the roads as if he took this route every day. We didn't even have a chance to ask where we were headed.

We longed for a pleasant scholastic dispute on the direction we were going, on the chance for a choice, with a democratic over-ride somewhere at some three-pronged convergence of roads in the shade of a lime tree, by a green tabletop of grass. But he was in front of us at one moment and behind us the next, then among us, prancing around like a careful shepherd, and we could do nothing. Whenever somebody said a word, he would sniff the danger with a sixth sense and there he would be, prattling con-stantly like a man who in fact was talking to himself, but in the presence of dumb animals, which, in some way, he loved, but whom he knew he must lead ever onward, sometimes gently, at other times firmly. He wove his endless, fragmented monologue around us, which, as we know, is characteristic of lone shepherds on long treks with their herds. He talked about all sorts of things, but not about where we were headed, though he would sometimes mention Gradina, as if the road and the objective were crystal clear, and so it was that it turned out somehow, thanks in part to him and in part to our apathy, that no one actually asked where we were.

We kept going, going on. By one streambed that cut across the road, murmuring through a low vaulted culvert under the road, we did everything we possibly could. The stream was cool and clear, it burbled like the kitschy burbling brooks in stories, and along both sides of the road stretched pleasant, shady, grassy oases, along which we went scrambling out like crab children, as at some soundless order, straight from the road, without stopping. Some filled their canteens with water. Others threw themselves out on the grass stretching in a sweet longing for rest. One of the Ophelias immediately extracted a white cloth napkin from her pack and spread it on the grass under an acacia tree.

"Shall we picnic?" she asked.

"There must be an underground spring near here," shouted Petar from the stream. "Hot as it is, the water is like ice."

But some ten minutes later, Roko, who had not come down from the road but was perched at its edge, lowering only his feet into the grass, alone, dusty, tense, not relaxing for a moment at this rest stop, lurched suddenly to his feet and flung his bag over his shoulder.

"Come on, folks. We aren't far now," he said. "We can make it before dark. Come on. Gradina is waiting. Then you can relax to your heart's content."

On he talked until the last of us had packed up our things, and with heads bowed, looking back enviously at the grassy oasis, hunched over like camels, each of us scrambled back up to the road and moved along, swaying under an invisible and ever-growing burden.

So on we marched in subdued silence, a scraggly column, evading each other's eyes, staring down into the dust under our feet. The water in the canteens soon grew tepid and flat, and even the mere memory of the freshness of the stream turned into something a little shameful. There was nothing behind us that seemed worth our regret, or anything ahead of us to thrill to. The effort bore bitterness.

"How can you help hating him!" said somebody next to me.

I didn't even look up to see who was speaking. The voice was full of rancor, hissed through teeth, impotent. Soon that same voice was speaking inside me. We walked in long, silent hatred, through the hot scenery, which was shimmering under the beating sun.

That was how it happened (happened, I say, because you could hardly suggest that any of us was following any kind of plan, and even less whether we wanted or didn't want to—the question never came up) that around noon we walked into some town, and we didn't even notice. Suddenly we found ourselves among the first scattered houses sprouting out of the landscape before our very eyes.

The entire town, as we could soon see, consisted of two rather long, rather monotonous rows of houses strung along both sides of the road. The road narrowed and wound its way now among the faces of these houses, like a river in some sort of gorge. All of them were roughly of the same height, one-story houses made of stone that had been plastered with stucco a pretty long time ago, now crumbling, and all the doors were closed, all the windows shielded by closed shutters. The shutters were the only thing that lent variety to the town: there were dark green ones, gray ones, brown ones, black ones, even bright red ones. All of them were closed.

The heat was insufferable. The sun glared a hundredfold off the white stone dust on the road and along all the gray, smooth walls, which channeled us like a snakelike funnel. No longer could you feel even the slightest cool breeze, which had followed us while we were walking out in the open. There was no one on the road. We walked through this dead city in total silence.

"There must be somebody here," said Petar thickly. "They must have gone indoors to escape the heat."

"Maybe they heard we were coming," said Vladimir.

"There must be some sort of tavern, damn it," said Ivan. "Something must be working even in this heat."

"The famed Croatian hospitality holds true only for decent people," warned the Ophelias, "not for thugs like us."

We walked by the blind windows, turning left and right in search of some sign of life. The paint had peeled away from most of the window frames, but there were some freshly painted, and that gave us a shadow of hope that there was something alive in this phantomlike town. Then we saw the women.

They were at a window no more than three feet up off the ground—you know what those low houses look like in provincial towns. At first we felt relief when we saw the open window, even though it was the only one. But we came nearer, as if enchanted by the scene, and I could see the women close up. There were three of them, all three unexpectedly huge, and they were standing in the dark gullet of the window like a living picture framed to the sides by dark red shutters; one of them had planted her bare elbows on the windowsill, another was leaning on the shoulder of the first, and the third was standing on the other side, upright, her arms dangling, loose.

They were at a low window, so we had the impression we were watching them from above—partly because the window was so low and partly just because. I won't call it disdain or condescension, but into our attitude toward them crept, instead of the gratitude and relief we had felt at first, the kind of reckless bearing that travelers or passersby have for people who live in the place they are passing through, when they have no intention of stopping there and putting down roots. We felt that our world was inevitably passing by theirs and that we would touch each other only superficially, only in a chance moment. What, therefore, would be the point of feeling any restraint, regard, or scruple? Our laughter was rude, bold, vulgar.

The women ogled us from the window ledge, responding to our laughter with the same bold, impudent laughter, poking each other, three enormous, monumental, stalwart women in the narrow frame of the window, with expansive, grinning faces, wide cheekbones, disproportionately large, round arms, as if Kljaković had painted them; resting their meaty, muscled lower arms on the windowsill, nesting on them their capacious healthy breasts as if they were offering them up on tremendous brown platters, breasts like immense, ripe cantaloupes, in coarse, almost masculine shirts made of unbleached, homespun muslin. They took turns sitting at the prime spot on the window ledge, competing robustly for space, but you could hardly tell who was who, for all three were so like each other that they were like giant bronze triplets at the base of some monumental sculpture.

People, these women were monstrously huge! The closer we got, the more they seemed to grow. Three gigantic, warm, strong women, a little tousled, their shirts half-buttoned as if they had just gotten up from a hot bed, studied us openly, impudently, greedily, unbridled, just as their immense breasts under their shirts were obviously unbridled rolls of flesh, and they grinned at us, half mockingly, half beckoning, elbowing each other with an ironic lasciviousness, with vulgar hints of lust, three primeval, potent females of insatiable strength, who knew it and flaunted it. Three women at a low window in a nameless deserted town were beckoning to us from the tantalizing semi-darkness, from the stuffy interior with unaired bedding, they tugged at us like huge irresistible magnets to enter the moist darkness heavy with the smell of their sweat and pungent juices, from the heat and mugginess, from the curve of the winding road, from where you couldn't see any further as it was. What kind of Odysseus was needed here to stop his sailors! Like a maelstrom, the eddies carried our ship toward the low abyss of the window. How sweet and final seemed the stuffy, hellish darkness behind their broad backs!

We stopped, trembling with lust, on the very verge of the abyss. All but a few steps separated us from the women. What was keeping us from crossing over? I do not know. Everything was fine without words. What forced us at that moment to speak and disperse the sweet mist we had so suddenly surrendered to? We stopped and began making little jibes, tossing out challenges, obscenities, as if something within us were prompting us to, whispering the words to us as if pouring poison into our ears. Each of us masked our dismay at the situation with sneers, exchanged glances, shoving, all the more unsettled by the realization that the obscenities were all pointless and unnecessary, and that we did not understand the real meaning of what we were saying, but rather felt powerlessly that something was being ruined hopelessly and irretrievably by what we were doing. The women did not respond to us; instead, they kept grinning, wordless, impudent, but with a dignity animals have, a head and shoulders above our pubescent sparring with words.

The impetuosity and force of the initial experience toppled before us like a house of cards. Suddenly I felt like weeping. Why had we done this? Was it perhaps the scorn of people passing through? Or maybe it was the group mood, since there were too many of us. Maybe it was that we were ashamed of one another, maybe a person can only make such decisions on his own, maybe there are opportunities which only a person by himself can take advantage of, or maybe at the last moment we felt fear at the sight of these monumental protomothers, we were not mature enough for them. Or maybe we felt undeserving and were taking our revenge. Maybe a little of everything.

Fatefully, we stopped. Our two Ophelias, so different from these women, almost boylike, nearly sexless in comparison to these grandiose lady wrestlers at the window, retreated demonstratively a few steps to the side, and from there they snorted

indignantly at every gesture we made. But despite all the indignation, they couldn't help but look, and they couldn't help but be
fascinated by the rhythmic ritual of gestures we were performing,
like some tribal fertility dance, next to the window.

Vladimir, the photographer, pulled his leather camera bag
around onto his belly and, banging a tam-tam on it, sang in a cracking voice, before all of us, like a medicine man, grinning brazenly:

> Hey there, girl, roll your shirt up high.
> What is that black between your thighs?

and the women at the window threw their heads back with howls of
laughter, and their monumental necks shone before us like mirrors—
the fretwork of muscles on their necks wove a tangle, a marvelous
kaleidoscopic shimmer, with invitation and desire, warmth and lust.

At that moment Roko stepped in (sure, when he was no longer
really needed), and only then, when he spoke, did it dawn on me
that he had not taken part in the wordless game, and that up until
that moment he had been standing behind us, his wide-open eyes
mirroring misery, horror, disgust, or something. Was he queer? I
wondered, having no clue.

"Have you gone stark raving mad?" said Roko with agitation,
choking as if afraid he was running out of time. "Have you never
seen a woman before? You are behaving as if you are fresh out of
prison. Drop it, people. Some other time. Later. We have to keep
on going. You've forgotten: Gradina is waiting. Are you, with
these here . . . Because of these women . . . People, let's . . ."

He hopped from one of us to the next, blustering and cajoling,
tugging us by the sleeves, pointing to the road, reminding us of
our Ophelias, who were letting us know that they were insulted
and that they despised us, and only from time to time, from the
side, out of the corner of his eyes, would he glance briefly at the

women in the window, like a man who is in a hurry and who has no money looks almost with hatred at the toy store window which his unreasonable children are staring at.

Something irretrievable finally snapped in the atmosphere, and we saw that we ought to keep going.

When we finally got moving, slowly, one by one, Roko breathed a sigh of relief. We looked at the women once more, with endlessly helpless regret, and set out down the middle of the road, not daring to turn left or right, as if we feared the houses. All the other windows were closed and the shutters tightly fastened to keep out the terrible heat, and we walked in a muggy silence, turning only toward the one window that, it seemed, was still open, for a moment longer, precisely for our sake, a last chance that was being offered us, and beckoning us to surrender to its warm, saving embrace.

Maybe that window is always here, always open, I comforted myself a dozen paces further down the road, maybe we can always turn back.

"Lord almighty," said Petar suddenly, "were they big!"

"Huge!" said Ivan, giggling. "They reminded me of that joke about the swallow and the elephant."

"You creep," said the Ophelias.

"Who could ever satisfy such monsters!" said Roko. "They would break the spirit of any man."

"They must be some awful women," said the Ophelias. "Offering themselves up like that to everybody who passes by."

"There you have our world-renowned hospitality," said Vladimir.

"They are so large!" repeated Petar longingly, dragging his feet as he walked along the road, raising dust.

"Besides," said Roko, as if he were continuing a thought he had started earlier, "who knows, syphilis may be endemic around here."

The heat was unbearable. We walked a little while longer, out of sorts, retreating deep within ourselves, each of us thinking our

own thoughts, weighing some invisible, intangible values in relation to the three hefty, muscular women who were here, within
reach, and meanwhile it was not clear where we were headed and
whether we would actually get anywhere. But there was nothing
to be done. There were, as I said, too many of us: we kept close
watch on each other.

All at once, just as the image of the women had begun to fade
gradually in our memories, Petar, who had been lagging behind,
stopped suddenly in the middle of the road, blotting the sweat
from his forehead and nervously removing his eyeglasses, wiping
them with a grimy handkerchief, far behind us, somehow small,
alone, and hunched in the funnel of the road, which vanished into
the distance, and he shouted from afar in a high, strained voice,
strained maybe by mounting desire, maybe by the weight of the
decision, a voice I barely recognized: "Stop."

We all stopped and turned as one, like a herd. It seemed to me
for a moment that in some of the eyes I saw the same naked flash
of hope, a brief miserable gleam, which was repeated so often
among us and then snuffed out the next moment. Petar stood
there, focused on wiping his eyeglasses, in the middle of the road
and said, now more softly and naturally: "I have thought it over,
people . . . and here . . . no matter what you say . . ."

Roko took several hurried steps toward him as if he wanted to
prevent him from saying those last decisive words. But something
froze him halfway there.

"What's gotten into you, Petar?" he asked in a quavering voice,
stopping himself, uncertain, as if seeking balance.

"Nothing," said Petar. "Nothing's wrong with me, Roko. It's
just that I'm not going one step further. I'm going back." He gestured with his thumb behind his back.

We all looked at him wordlessly. I felt as if some instinctive
resistance was rising in us, a collective judgment. All together like

this we did not approve of his action, though, I think, each of us individually wanted to be in his place and envied him the courage or the cowardice, his weakness or his strength.

"Be a friend," said Roko. "All of us went into this together and all of us will . . . We need you as a scholar."

"Sorry," said Petar, squinting in the sun, partly from the glare, partly from the awkwardness. "I don't want to ruin the excursion, but . . . scholarship isn't everything."

"There is no point in splitting up now," said Roko.

Petar kept quiet, looking through his lowered lids. Then he mustered the resolve and cut the conversation off, curtly.

"Why not?" he asked, and obviously it was clear to him that there was, indeed, a point. He turned, and with a lighthearted, cheerful step, as if he had abruptly shed that immense burden all of us were feeling, he went straight back to the house with the three gigantic women, to a whole world that now belonged entirely to him.

We watched him as off he went, tiny and lively now, down the deep gorge of the road. That could have been me, I thought. A part of me was leaving, I felt. We were solemn for a few more minutes in subdued thought, and then on we went, and for a moment each of us had something to say about Petar, about how his action was all wrong, how it was not nice, how he never really had been one of us, anyway.

The heat beat down cruelly on our temples. The silence lasted for an eternity. We walked on through the empty winding town without meeting another living being. The shuttered windows looked out at us from the houses. At each new turn in the road we hoped that we might come out into the open, but from both sides of the road we were met constantly by yet more houses and only houses and always the same houses, so that we began to believe that we were walking around in circles.

Our progress was slow, listless, taciturn. Only Roko sustained some sort of vigor and circled as he walked among us, not daring to speak, of course, but peering baffled into our lowered faces, and it seemed to me that when he came over to me, I saw despair in his eyes at our lethargy and lack of will. He urged us on, but it seemed as if he had already had it. He encouraged us silently, but he, too, needed encouragement. I almost felt sorry for him and nearly spoke, to brighten his spirits, to say that I understood everything (though I understood nothing), but some sort of mute defiance, spite, even envy, held me back. I clenched my teeth and kept quiet, just like everybody else.

A little further down that too-long string of houses, we noticed a cellar door open wide with a steep stone staircase descending from the road's edge somewhere deep into its dark interior, and above the wide, dark halves of the oak door, with its large latch, which were flung open to each side all the way to the wall, there was an ordinary, unplaned board on which, in black oil paint in awkward, backward handwriting, were written the words: HOMAYD WINE. With thinly disguised relief, with a tremulous gaiety, with feigned, heartfelt cheer, Roko turned toward the door and in a loud, falsely carefree voice, exclaimed: "Fellows, wine! Homemade!" And like some sort of eager crab he scampered down the uneven stone steps into the dark hole, which readily swallowed him, into which we all crowded after him, pushing each other greedily, happy that for a moment we could evade the heat, for a moment we could forget the road, that in this town there was a place for us, after all, that we would see at least some living person, and, finally, that we would be able to shake off the disturbing impression Petar's departure had left on all of us.

We descended in a heap into the deep wine cellar, where it was dark and cool, and when our eyes got used to the fresh, velvety darkness, which smelled like wine mold and vinegar and damp

stone, we could make out several big barrels on lengthwise gird-
ers, and a wine press, and large oak vats bound by metal hoops,
copper sprayers with malachite-green splotches, and crude wooden
benches in the middle of the cellar, a row of smaller kegs scattered around, and some sacks, probably potato sacks, and working tools, and huge wreaths of onions along the walls, and we felt
at home, cozy, relieved.

We sat around on kegs and benches and sacks, loosened our
shoes, wiped our foreheads, and at once all of us started talking
and talking and talking about anything at all, just for the sake of
talking, so that we could hear human voices, we chattered brightly,
like tourists on an excursion, while the scrawny, tough old man,
toothless, his hair thinning, gnarled like the roots of an olive tree,
one of those little old men who seem ageless, who seem to live on
forever, the proprietor of the cellar, scampered around us with
alacrity and decanted from the barrels thick red wine that poured
out of the spigots into liter table jugs. The wine slid into the jugs
like liquid velvet—"What can you do, what can you do," he mumbled toothlessly, "we make red wine only; that is our way around
here; the *teran,* the *teran;* there aren't many of us left who make it
right, pure"—and he handed us the bottles as if he weren't even
counting them but doling them out for free to suit his guests, and
we drank the tart, cold wine full of tannin, with its thick taste, that
kind of village wine which is as thick as wine soup, for in that
region the people are parsimonious, and they'd squeeze the soul
out of the dregs if they had a soul, and the barrel was probably
near its bottom, and we drank and talked, talked and drank, as if
we were competing to see who would forget more surely and
quickly what had just happened, or maybe forget in general.

The old man scampered around us handing us painted earth-
enware jugs ("Drink, Ante," "Drink, Ivo"), "Each one gets his
own, each one gets his own," pouring wine up to the very brim,

mumbling something that was only partly intelligible through his toothless gums—something like "This is my labor, this is my blood"—and soon we were all slightly stupefied, and we prattled on all at the same time and competed to see who would praise the wine more, and the old man listened all the while and chuckled gleefully with a high, tight giggle. It was perfectly natural that there would be something in his glee of the pride of a winemaker whose work is flourishing, and something of the pleasure of playing host, which you can always find in small towns off the beaten path, but it seemed to me that in his narrow little eyes gleaming behind the wrinkled eyelids I saw the flash of something malicious, wicked. What was it?

In one enlightened, frozen moment I caught sight of this wickedness and flinched from the stab of some murky fear, but the moment swiftly passed, lost in the drunken babble and bustle of everybody else, and I may have gone on to wonder, Why malice? but I did not know what to make of it, I had already had too much to drink, and besides, somebody at that moment was telling me, or I was telling somebody, something that at the moment seemed hugely more important—though now I know that nothing could have been more important—and I could not fathom why there would be a wicked edge to the old man's laugh, and I forgot to ask.

The old man ceased his snaking around among us and his garbled mumbling for a moment to bark through the door into the darker back part of the wine cellar: "Bring out a little cheese and prosciutto, Mara, my dear. No one must leave here hungry or thirsty. How about a few olives, some almonds?"

He scurried about us, shoving his contorted face into ours, his squinting malicious-cheerful little eyes, pouring wine left and right. We were all pretty drunk by now, drinking the cold wine so suddenly after the heat from which we had come. The noise gradually subsided, and soon we were mumbling more than speaking. Mara appeared, probably his wife, a corpulent creature wearing a black peasant dress down to her ankles, a kerchief tied under her chin, her lower arms bared, and she brought in cheese and prosciutto on rough-hewn wooden platters, a bowl of olives, a bowl of almonds, and when she left the wine cellar without a word, you could hear how somewhere behind the wall she was cracking almonds with regular blows as if she were pounding nails.

Maybe it was the dull thudding, or maybe the symmetrical order of the rough-hewn benches, or maybe the wreaths of onions hung on the wall, or maybe the subdued voices of my friends, that gave me the impression that there was something funereal about the atmosphere, as if we were sitting at somebody's wake, or that we were ourselves deep below the ground in a dark and cold, stone family tomb. It must have been that the lot of us, the whole family, was taken by a similar mood: I noticed how my friends were peering around the room anxiously, as if they were afraid they might catch sight of somebody lurking behind their backs, or as if they were checking for the exits, just in case. I was horribly thick in the head.

I noticed how Roko, as always, was standing a little to the side, leaning against the wall, with a peculiar expression on his face, an expression in which sympathy mingled with sorrow, disgust with fascination. I did not dare to interpret that expression for myself. Roko was staring at one moment at his hand, twirling his wine glass from which he had taken hardly more than two or three sips. Why? I wondered for a moment. Why is he pretending? I thought. Why the pose? Now I know: he was not posing. But it is much easier to be unjust than to see things as they are.

The sudden gaiety that had swept over us as we entered the cellar and began to drink had evaporated entirely by now, the voices were still. It seems to me that it was precisely because he wanted to disperse the sense of anxiety and melancholy that had descended upon us like a funereal shroud that Vladimir began to make a scene.

Swaying shakily on his feet, he staggered over to one of the large barrels and began to beat his tam-tam rhythm on it with his hands, first lightly and then more and more loudly, as if he were falling into a trance. The chilling, muted rhythm filled the entire underground room. We looked at him with fear, frozen. No one reacted.

Vladimir got tired, he sank just as suddenly as he had begun. He was standing there for a few minutes, leaning his hands and forehead on the barrel as if waiting for some response from within. Then he pushed off from it as if he were unable to govern his own body, and swaying with his arms open wide, he staggered over to a heap of potato sacks and collapsed onto them, flinging out his limbs as if he were on the cross.

"Hey, old man, more wine over here!" he howled into the total silence. The old man came right over and gave him a full glass. The old man's movements had suddenly become useful.

"Bottoms up!" Vladimir tipped back the glass thirstily, lying on the sacks, and the wine spilled over the corners of his mouth, leaving two sharp red stripes, as if two of the blood vessels on his neck were suddenly visible.

"More wine!" roared Vladimir. "Then let everything go to hell. Bottoms up!"

He gestured wildly with the glass from which the dregs of wine sprayed around the cellar. All of us were sprinkled by a rain of tiny, dark red droplets. The two Ophelias, to mask their sudden fear, began giggling foolishly and drunkenly as if this were some sort of high school prank. They were sitting together on a bench, hunched close to one another, pressing their knees together, squeezing their eyes tightly shut behind their foggy spectacles.

"Who cares about the excursion, who cares about Gradina!" shouted Vladimir. "Here is where we ought to stay. This is God's country. Since there are no gods, it belongs to us. Is there anything we don't have here? More wine, old man."

We kept silent and listened to him. The old man poured him more wine.

"Is there anything we don't have here?" asked Vladimir rhetorically and lay back down with the wine in his hand. "Come over, my Ophelia, come here, let's shake things up. Wise up, what are you saving yourself for? Why wait?"

It was hard to tell which of the two of them he was speaking to.

"Watch your mouth," they both said, pressing even closer, squeezing their knees together, but they did keep on giggling, foolishly.

"How have I angered God?" Vladimir turned to the old man and asked rhetorically, shoving his chin into the man's face, while the old man stood next to him with the wine jug, his malicious, attentive eyes gleaming. "For what sins am I atoning that I end up having to traipse around on these roads in the heat like some religious pilgrim?"

"You aren't," said Roko so softly that it was barely audible.

Vladimir heard him. Maybe Roko never said it, maybe it was Vladimir's inner voice. Maybe that was what all of us thought.

"Precisely," howled Vladimir. "I am not. I am nobody's slave. A free man. Isn't that so? Does anyone have anything to say to the contrary? No. I have unanimously been elected a free man. Now that you have invested your trust in me, my friends, be sure that I deserve it. I will get as drunk as a pig right here and I am staying here to sleep. You can kiss my ass."

"You have had enough to drink," said Roko softly with unexpected intimacy. "Stop it, Vlado, please. We will keep going. We must keep going."

"Where is there for us to go? There is nowhere we can keep going to!" howled Vladimir, crucified on the sacks with the bloody stain of wine on his lips. He sat up abruptly, whacking his hands on his knees. "Why the devil are you so stubborn about this? Are you my father or what? You keep driving us on. But where? Drive somebody else. Drive anyone you like. But leave me alone. Haven't we just voted that I am a free man? Here, take the Ophelias. They count as points for you. They will go with you to the ends of the earth. And go they should if they won't give. Come on, Ophelias, onward to new victories. On to the convent!"

"Stop it, Vlado," said Roko again. "Let's go."

"Leave me to drink in peace," fumed Vladimir.

"Leave the man to drink if that is what he'd rather," said the little old man, suddenly. These were the first words he had said loudly and clearly. His voice screeched like a bird.

"Don't you get involved," spat Roko. "What business is it of yours?"

The old man withdrew immediately.

"Nothing. I was just saying."

Roko turned again to Vladimir. His eyes were gentle, tormented, full of understanding, as one sufferer to another.

"Don't, Vladimir, no more," he said. "You have said what you had to say, but we have to keep going."

"I am staying put," said Vladimir hysterically, with drunken insistence.

"He is staying put," said the old man like an echo, in that same screeching voice.

"We must go," pleaded Roko, desperate, on the verge of helpless tears. "Vladimir, don't, enough now."

"It's you I've had enough of," said Vladimir, suddenly, with a nasty edge to his voice. "Why the devil are you so pompous? What makes you better than me that you can lead me around here like some monkey in this heat? In the name of what? I am not going, I tell you, I will not go."

"He will not go," screeched the little old man triumphantly.

Roko looked at the old man and he looked at Vladimir, long and compassionately. We all rose to our feet. I have to say we were scared. We paid for the wine, cheese, and prosciutto, all of it very cheap, but deep in ourselves we knew that we had paid another, much greater, price for all of it, and that we had gotten something we hadn't bargained for. We muttered our parting words incoherently, looking no one in the eyes.

One by one we left the wine cellar. Vladimir stared after us, a little pale and shocked by the consequences of his words, his decisions, but the little old man was scurrying constantly around him with a full bottle of thick, red wine. Vladimir—I saw it the moment before I left at the tail end of the silent row of walkers—daintily held out his glass, and the old man poured him the thick, velvety wine.

We soon left the town behind and kept on down the road at a steady and regular pace, like people who still have a long way to travel. With kerchiefs around our necks, with knapsacks and bags, we looked like a jaunty crew on an outing. But with our ranks thinned we were dispirited, gloomy, and constantly aware of the anxious tension that crowded our every step. We knew that it was holding us together; we knew that any minute it could release us: we weren't certain which we feared more. We walked.

The last remnants of the town—the fences, the orchards, the occasional wooden shed—moved by us, and we were walking now through monotonous, dry landscape that did not change at all. The hills were each identical to the last, the stone walls and fields were so similar to one another that it seemed as if we were going around in circles. The road crawled uniformly among the rocks, gray and dusty. Nothing appeared in sight: no water mills, no white horses, no tavern with vines growing on trellises by the doorway. An uncomfortable shadow of solitude settled on our little group, incomprehensible, phantasmal like an eclipse of the sun.

The tension and isolation had disciplined us, pulled us together, bound us like a small military unit on a dangerous mission. I looked at the faces around me looking ahead, along the road. We were a little army, but we were like an army. We walked.

Suddenly, a lot later, Ivan shouted: "Look, a house!" and I felt the relief in his voice. The others came alive, stirred, and began to rise to their toes.

"Where? Where?" asked the Ophelias, stretching out their necks like a harmonious pair of giraffes. "Now where does he see a house out here?"

"There's the house," said Ivan. "And there's another. And there behind it is something that looks like a church."

We walked on, but the marching rhythm had been disturbed. They all wanted to see the house, but no one saw it, no matter how they strained their eyes.

"It is out of sight now, behind that hill," announced Ivan. "I saw it only for a moment, but clear as day. We'll be getting there pretty soon, you'll see."

There was assurance and real joy in his voice, so much so that I was startled.

"So what?" said Roko, uninterested. "Just a stage on our journey."

"Well, at least we can have a drink of water," said Ivan, and an incomprehensible joy still kept sparking in his voice. "At least we can get a sniff of it."

We walked on, much more lively now. Ivan was nearly bounding along and he hummed:

> I came back from the great wide world,
> But this time I brought you nothing, girl.

But no one chimed in to sing along. Ivan sighed loudly and said, surrounded by the dusty underbrush, rocky landscape, and brambles that had followed us this far: "What a gorgeous place! What a gorgeous place!"

"Devil take you and this kind of beauty!" said one of the Ophelias.

"Do not take God's name in vain," I chided her automatically. But I, too, was startled by Ivan's enthusiasm. Roko was now walking quite far in front of us; the Ophelias were beginning to lag a little.

"You see," said Ivan, "there are places that give a person something. Places that are grateful the way women are grateful. The more you offer them, the more they give in return. This is a place like that."

"If we take your analogy with women a step further, then every place . . . ," I said.

"No," said Ivan. "That is what this place is like. A place that owes things to you with this noble, old-fashioned courtesy for the attention you pay it. The place feels noticed, honored, and it returns the honor to you in kind."

"To a rather modest degree, I'd have to say." I waved my hand to take in the countryside.

"It gives what it has to give," said Ivan with an affected humility. "We must value that, because it is giving what it has. Maybe all that it has. A house in the distance. A stone wall. A little field."

"Every place has some damned thing," I said stubbornly. "There is a house and a little field in every goddamned place."

"There are different kinds," said Ivan. "Take Paris, for instance. I have been all over the world, but it was clearest to me in Paris. What did Paris actually have to offer me? It did not deign to notice me at all. It did not return my attentions, if you see what it is I'm getting at . . . Now, it isn't that I was indifferent to Paris. I was not. Quite the contrary. Who could be indifferent—*sous le pont Mirabeau coule la Seine et nos amours,* and so forth, or as one of my uncles, a globetrotter and old rapscallion, used to say:

When I was in Paris
I saw the Mona Lisa

and he'd always end it with the vulgar part of the song in a whisper in a close duet with my old man, so I don't know those last words to this day. Maybe I did come to Paris ignorant and naive. But I sure was not indifferent. Still, Paris was indifferent to me. That is one whore of a place. It takes you in the way a whore takes her clients. Everybody trampled it like a plucked hen. It takes in everybody the same. A whore, I tell you. It flirts, true enough, but it flirts impersonally, commercially, with anyone who comes along. It picks your pocket completely asexually, to get your wallet. Whore."

"When a perfectly decent woman won't make time with everybody who comes along, then they call her a frigid goat," complained one of the Ophelias behind us because we weren't including her in this interesting conversation, as you could hear from far away. "But as soon as she so much as extends her little finger to somebody, then there she is, a whore."

"I cannot bear this a moment longer," announced the other, faced with crushing injustice.

Carried away by his theme, Ivan paid them no attention.

"This is a place, you see, which is like a woman in love. It knows you are there. It takes you into account. It waits for you gratefully, because it knows that you are coming to see it and nothing else. It accepts you. That, my friends, is not flirtation; that is love. It awards you with its modest beauties, but it gives them only to you. A person can get rich that way. It isn't the money, or the knowledge, or the slyness, or anything that make you rich—it is the love and the belonging. Only a place can give you that. Only a place like this."

"You are talking nonsense," I told him instructively.

"Really? Am I?" said Ivan benevolently, not letting me spoil his ecstatic mood. "Maybe because this is my place."

"What do you mean, 'yours'? Every place has the potential to be 'yours.' You just have to discover it and, say, adopt it."

"Not so," said Ivan. "I was born here."

By now we were arriving at the house which Ivan had seen from afar along the road and which had been hidden from our sight (we hadn't noticed it, we weren't born here). We approached it silently. The house was twenty-odd meters from the road, in a state of disrepair. The farm buildings out back were dilapidated. There was no glass in the windows, the stucco had crumbled away, and whole sections of the roof were missing tiles. The fields around the house were overgrown with weeds. The low stone wall along the road had collapsed in spots, on it the board gate was askew, sagging, blackened. Somewhat further down the road we saw two or three more houses and a chapel. They all seemed abandoned, forgotten. As if they were from some other time.

Ivan, his eyes open wide, licking his lips, looked the place over. So what if you were born here, I thought. Devil take your birth if you were born here. If being born somewhere means to be born and bound to that place, devil take being born.

"Everything has gone to hell," I said, and it seemed to me as if my mixed feelings were obvious in my deafening voice: there was something curmudgeonly in me because I had never had the feeling that I'd been born anywhere in particular, and I felt a little sorry for Ivan, who seemed to place so much faith in this birth of his.

But Ivan would not be dissuaded.

"Nothing has gone," he said. "It may be shipwrecked in the shallows, but it is still here."

There was a blackened board on the half-collapsed wall with a large, clumsily written inscription:

FOR SALE

Inquire at the neighbor's

and one twisted, rain-washed arrow pointing toward the houses in the background, where the neighbor presumably lived.

We stopped and read the sign lethargically.

"What now?" asked Roko, retracing a few steps. "What the devil's gotten into you? Why did we stop?"

"A stage," I said.

He pawed the ground like an impatient old nag. The Ophelias sat wearily in a ditch between the road and the wall, groaning and stretching their dusty legs.

"There, you see, it is for sale," said Ivan, as if somebody had contradicted him previously. "It can't cost much."

"That's for sure," I said, laughing.

But Roko didn't see anything funny in it.

"Are you crazy?" he asked. "Have you gone stark raving mad? You don't mean to buy that ruin, do you?"

"Why not?" said Ivan to himself. "It can't cost much. I may be poor, but I certainly have that much."

"What are these retrograde capitalist ownership interests doing cropping up in an upright socialist citizen?" I asked, still laughing.

"I was born here," said Ivan, waving his hand around the countryside in a general way, as if he were trying to remember precisely where. "Here, somewhere, it doesn't matter."

He put his foot through the gate, which was overgrown with the weeds in the yard. In he went and walked slowly around the building, peering around the corners, studying the farm buildings, knocking on the walls like some character from Gogol's

Marriage. Then he hopped over the stone wall toward the field and waved to us.

"Wait for me," he shouted from far away. He set out toward the houses, which you could just make out across the labyrinth of stone walls.

Helplessly, Roko watched him go for a few minutes, and then screamed out with all his voice: "Imbecile! Idiot! Maniac!"

Ivan paid him no attention. Roko shrugged wearily.

We sat in the ditch next to the Ophelias, in the small patch of shade cast by the little wall. Roko dropped his face into his hands. The sun was no longer beating down so hotly, and it was pleasant to sit for a while on warm grass, on friendly soil, after having trekked for such a long way.

"How long will we be stopping here?" asked one of the Ophelias.

"I cannot go on," said the other.

"If we'd only gotten somewhere," said the first. "I could write it up in a paper. But as it is? Where were we—nowhere, what did we see—nothing!"

I leaned against the stone wall, carefully, so that none of the stones would roll off onto my head, and almost fell asleep to their grumbling. Incoherent shouting from the house started me awake. Roko took his hands from his face. His face looked tired.

It was Ivan. He ran toward us, leaping over stone walls and shouting something. He staggered and panted as if he were drunk. Leaping up onto the yard wall, he froze for a moment with his hands raised like a statue and exclaimed to us with exhilaration: "Ladies and gentlemen, a new homeowner greets you. The die has been cast. I am staying."

On he went, babbling something incoherent in a joyous fervor. Down he bounded from the stone wall and through the weeds, out of which, with each step of his, rose a puff of dust, and with arms outspread he flung himself toward the house. The door fell before his charge in a cloud of dust. From the house we could hear cracks, thumps, crashes.

Roko got up and staggered, his legs stiff, over to the house window, a window with no glass or frame. He peered into the dark inside, where we could hear the crashing and smashing coming from. After a brief interlude he returned and sat down next to us. We looked at him.

"He bought the house," he said darkly. "For twenty thousand dinars."

"For twenty thousand he could have . . . ," I began, but then I couldn't come up with anything he could have done instead.

"He is staying," said Roko. "He gave everything he had on him as a down payment. He doesn't even have enough money left to pay for a bus ticket back."

"What will he do here?" asked one of the Ophelias. "Live?"

We thought about it.

"He'll live," said Roko finally, "like everybody else."

The Ophelias were suddenly restless; they turned to look around at the fields, houses, bushes, as if only now they had grasped where they were.

"This is appalling," said one of the Ophelias. In her voice you could hear, for the first time since we had set out, some tinge of genuine emotion. I couldn't help but shiver. I didn't dare think why.

We sat there quietly for a little longer, listening to the commotion from the house. The Ophelias began discussing something with agitation. They whispered and glanced over at the two of us.

"We have decided that we are not going any further," said one of them after a while. "We are heading back."

Roko shrugged helplessly.

"You see, only the four of us are left," explained the other. "What will people say?"

"What does anyone have to say about it?" I asked.

"Or rather, what will they think?"

"There is no one here to think anything. You can see that there is no one here."

"Well, all right," said the Ophelia proudly, as if she were completing the syllogism she had been gradually developing. "What would they be thinking if they were?"

"That is most certainly terribly important," I said to her gravely.

We saw Ivan as he left the house staggering tipsily, brushing the dust off his hands and clothes and laughing, my God, was he laughing. He lurched forward with several wobbly steps, and then, still grinning, he sat down on the ground as if his legs had given way, and sitting that way, he looked over at us and grabbed up two handfuls of weeds, and waved them at us as if he were exhibiting the fruits of his first harvest. Then he tossed them away and immediately scooped up new ones, and his eyes and gestures spoke: everything you see, all, all, all of this is mine.

I felt a stab of envy. He was so happy.

He got up, came over to the wall, and, rolling up his sleeves like some sort of hearty farmer, leaned against the stone wall with his hands. The wall swayed a bit, but it didn't wobble enough to ruin the drama of the moment.

"I am staying," said Ivan with pathos.

"We're going back," squeaked the Ophelias. "We will by no means allow them to gossip that we were out here in couples."

"Not that anything, God forbid, would ever happen," I said.

"Why did you drag us along on this . . . this adventure?" whined one of the Ophelias. "It all turned out so futile and . . . and pointless."

"You are not gentlemen," accused the other. "You ought to see us back to the bus, and then go where you please."

No one paid them any more attention.

"Listen, why don't the two of you stay here, too? What is the point of going back to Zagreb?" said Ivan heartily. "It won't be bad. There is a well behind the house. There are three rooms. In the words of the poet, there is a chest and a bench and a table."

We didn't answer him.

"Be my guests," said Ivan again. "You will be right at home. There are other abandoned houses here, don't forget, there over the ridge. We will find something for you, too. Why wouldn't you stay? Stay. What keeps driving you on?"

"I don't know," said Roko, surprised, with a sigh.

"It would be good," said Ivan. "If there were more of us, we could found our own city."

Roko looked around groggily.

"Maybe there was a city here once."

"Yes," I said, "you can tell by the layout of the foundations."

"All the way to there. A pretty big city."

"There probably were quite a few houses, judging by the cellar holes," I said. "Big houses."

"And the church was pretty sizable," said Roko. "Who knows whether there is still a bell in the tower?"

"There's not," said Ivan.

"There might have been nearly ten thousand people here, and more," I said. "You know how people lived in crowded conditions in those days."

"Sure, like in Osor. Probably more."

"The main street probably went here. Squares. Literature. Then the plague. Then malaria. Maybe some biggish war."

Ivan looked first at one of us, then at the other, uncertain, cautious.

"No, no, my friend," said Roko, as if he were not going to be lured out onto thin ice by Ivan's propaganda. "A man here would always have the feeling he was living in a cemetery. Imagine how big a cemetery, too! Vast! You'd be living on the graves of others. On top of skeletons. The vineyard we could cultivate here, *notre jardin*, would grow out of corpses. The topsoil, my dear, is full of bodies. As it is everywhere else, yes, always, yes, but here—here the soil is all of it solid corpse."

"Appalling," said one of the Ophelias.

"Maniacs! Who can believe a word they say?" said the other.

We were truly cackling like maniacs, Roko and I.

"We couldn't live here, no way," said Roko and turned to me for my confirmation. "Isn't that right, that we could not?"

"No way," I said. "Where can we live, now that I think of it?"

"You cynic. He is a cynic, don't listen to him, Ivan," said Roko still in that same high, false voice. "We can, what do you mean we can't? But not here."

Ivan shrugged his shoulders, his spirits crushed.

"Whatever you want," he said softly, like a man whose resolve cannot be swayed. "As far as I am concerned, I will stay and try."

We sat there for an awkward, uncertain, yet painful time, looking at each other, divided already into three small groups. The invisible threads that had joined us until now were snapping as we watched.

Only a spider's web, I thought. An invisible cloth, a mere illusion.

"Well, then. Roko and I will be moving on. See you one of these days," I said to them the way a person speaks to strangers. The Ophelias waved with their handkerchiefs, growing more distant in our perspective, as is proper in all true farewells. Ivan stood motionless by the stone wall until we had gotten beyond the next bend in the road.

Suddenly it seemed to me, in a panic, that Ivan, standing as he was by the gate to his new estate, was the last man on earth I would ever see. I stopped, breaking out in a tortured sweat. I knew that the expedition had fallen apart and that we were the only two left: where would we go and why? In front of me Roko's back swayed steadily. Behind me stood Ivan, quiet and unwavering in his decision. I could still choose, it occurred to me in a flash.

But incapable of making a decision, I waved back helplessly and accepted the road. Roko turned and smiled at me. His smile was fixed, like a doll's.

Crisscrossed by the already slanting afternoon sunlight, Roko and I continued walking along the dusty road. We went along in parallel, side by side, rather rapidly, in silence. The countryside around us was constantly the same. We seemed to be walking along a moving stage, in the direction it was turning. The scenes didn't change at all, as if we kept nearing a turn into some other world but not quite reaching it. Were we going round in circles? I wondered. Was all this in vain? There must be some goal, I would convince myself then, some logical explanation, there must be something like an end to the journey.

From time to time Roko would send me a sidelong glance under his glasses, which would gleam dully with ruddy sunlight whenever he turned his head. What was he watching? Was he checking my constancy and loyalty? I had no way to respond to his querying glances, and I continued steadily onward, wordless, clenching my teeth. The space between us was crammed with doubts. You have been leading since we started, my silence said, don't ask for support and encouragement from *me!*

Is it possible, I wondered, that a moment of weakness has stirred in him? Or is he merely looking over to check whether I will last to the end? Maybe he will suggest that we, too, give up, that in the end the two of us go back? I was anticipating this with a touch of hope (*that we still can turn back, if there is time*) and a touch of fear (*has all we've done until now been pointless?*).

But between the two of us an increasingly impenetrable barrier kept growing, and he was obstinately silent and trudged on, and I, to be able to keep following him, mastered my little urges, knowing how superfluous and petty it would be to ask and how all that mattered, once we had set out, was to endure on the journey no matter where it ended.

We walked like that for maybe an hour, maybe longer. The sun was already starting to set when the road before our eyes began to narrow, disperse like a cloud, vanish first in a few and then in more dense clumps of dry grass, in ditches and cracks. It was difficult to walk. We hopped over the holes, sidestepped the collapsed heaps of earth and stones, snagged by the brambles that grew on both sides of the road with intertwining thorny branches crossing our path.

The road grew less distinct from the countryside it was passing through. So it is with many old roads, I mused. You could tell that no one had used this one for ages. It was obvious that the road would soon vanish altogether. It was becoming obvious that the road was leading nowhere.

Strangely, I was no longer so anxious. Who cares, I thought, might as well see what there is to see! What, after all, does it mean, getting lost? Every place is *somewhere*. I gave myself over entirely to Roko's guidance. He sped along in front of me, seeking and finding the way as mechanically as a bloodhound, more like a machine than like something living.

Some storm from long ago had downed a tree across what was left of the road. Or maybe it fell by itself, of old age, rotten in its roots. From the rotten, decaying trunk grew new shoots, and they mingled with the blackened treetop. To the left and right, the tree trunk was tangled in the brambly underbrush with its exposed roots and the tops of the branches.

"This is not going to be easy," I said.

I felt as if we had been caught in a trap. I turned, sensing suddenly that something dangerous threatened us from behind. But nothing was there behind us except the road we had come on. Darkness, behind our backs, was settling on the road.

We sat on the branch of the downed tree to rest and wipe away our sweat. Dusk was falling quickly, but there was no freshness coming from anywhere.

"If there were only the breath of a breeze," I said.

"Ah, my Sganarelle. You are the only one who has not deserted me," said Roko. "And what good does it do you? Why are you suffering?"

I was surprised. I hadn't expected to be noticed.

"What good does it do me?" I said. "Nothing. A little satisfaction at the thought that I didn't leave you in the lurch. That I held my own honorably. We young scouts always stick together, through thick and thin, fire and water . . ."

Roko rose more vigorously, as if he had shed some burden or as if he had spent his quota of thoughtfulness for that day. He studied the fallen tree before us, seeking a way to get through. He started pushing the undergrowth aside. Maybe my company gives him strength, I thought. I can be Sganarelle, if need be, if that is what is asked of me.

"And then the flash of hope," I said. "The satisfaction that I did everything that could possibly be done to make it work. If it does work. We may finally get somewhere after all."

Roko had already begun to push his way through the thicket. He stood above me on the tree trunk. I couldn't tell whether he was listening or not.

"What can be a greater satisfaction to a Sganarelle than for his master to finally find what it is he was seeking? What else would I be doing? I myself, you see, am not seeking . . . anything. I don't know what I am seeking. What is it that is being sought, Roko? You, at least, ought to know. I don't. For me all these are just names. Archaeology. But I believe that you do know. For now that is enough for me."

He was already moving away from me and had dropped down off the other side of the tree. I shouted so that he could hear me. But he wasn't listening.

I pulled myself through the passage in the thicket that he had left behind him, and on we went. We seemed to be walking at a much lighter pace. Maybe because the sun had gone down. Nothing could stop us anymore, I thought. No obstacles, no traps. If there was somewhere for us to get to, we would get there.

The flash of hope was snuffed out just as quickly as it had blazed, and again I was swimming in a sea of listless dullness, surrendering with every ounce of my being to Roko's leadership. Roko patiently found the easier ways through, scrambling through the thicket with the same dogged persistence, ever tense, his ears cocked, nervously hearing certain signs and noticing certain indications of where we were going, which were unnoticeable for me.

In one place he stopped abruptly.

"It must be here somewhere," he said.

The place was no different than the countless other places we had traversed. Maybe that's the thing, I thought, recognizing what is genuine.

"This way," said Roko, turning, "if I've got my sense of direction right."

"Based on what, I'd like to know," I mumbled, but I didn't hesitate in following him. We turned from the paltry remnants of road (Was it a Roman road? Frankish? French? It no longer mattered) into an even more futile and pathless landscape. There wasn't even the narrowest of paths, nowhere to step, nothing. Stone and underbrush.

Roko picked his way instinctively, winding through the thicket, restless, his nostrils dilated, peering constantly left and right with his thick spectacles, halting here and there to orient himself according to signs that were evident only to him. Nature, as I have said before, was merciful to him. I was the one who got my face scratched by the thorns, I was the one whose shoes pinched. I followed him through the tangle of branches, tired, helpless, without any genuine will, a little doltish. If he were to leave me here now,

I realized, I would be done for. I would lie down here, on the spot, and fall asleep, die. It seemed to me as if we were going uphill. It was getting darker.

And then, in real twilight where all I could hear was our breathing and the rustling of the branches through which we pushed our way, entirely unexpectedly, in the middle of the roadless wasteland we had been wandering through for so long, before us opened a clearing, a hillside covered with a green carpetlike meadow, and perched on the hill, like a castle surrounded by a dark honorary guard of black cypresses, stood a monastery, or rather the ruin of a monastery, its gables empty, its walls cracked, with the bare skeleton of the monastery chapel tower, a small bare ruin with dilapidated flanks circled by a half-crumbling, time-eroded wall. A fortress defying time. Small, in shambles, yet as dignified and solemn as any great cathedral.

I would like to place special emphasis on just how long we had traveled and how abruptly we arrived. Roko and I exchanged looks as if congratulating each other on our successfully completed journey, standing at the edge of the twilit coppice from which we had emerged like two wild natives, before the grassy carpet which spread out to the monastery entranceway.

In Roko's eyes, as in some sort of magical lenses, all the remaining light of the peaceful summer evening collected, flashing like Christmas sparklers. Over the monastery, in the blue-gray sky, shone the first glistening, solitary, evening star.

We started walking across the soft, mildly dewy ground of the meadow, soundless, wordless, touched, grateful, two dark shadows. Enchanted, I looked up at the star. Was it you who brought us here, shining guardian? I asked it. Are you a sign? I wished it were so. If only it were, I sighed to myself.

But I lowered my gaze to Roko and knew that it wasn't. He was striding along beside me, upright, beaming with an unreal, unfounded elation, as if at precisely this moment the work he had been preparing for years were culminating. As if now, from this moment on, everything would be different. And I knew: the star hadn't led us here. We had come ourselves, of our own volition. We were doing a job that a person should cheerfully leave to his star. Which maybe is preferable to leave to a star. Have mercy on us, I prayed helplessly, not knowing whom I was praying to. But aware that for a long time now there had been no mercy, not for anyone, not anywhere. I knew, at that moment, that we were no exception.

Now our steps echo dully from the front of the monastery and the tall crenellated walls that surround the courtyard. Roko and I walk side by side, several paces apart. I feel him more than I can see him—I don't dare turn to look at him. The even tapping of our heels marks the width of the stone slabs that pave the courtyard.

Between the slabs grows tall, swordlike, sharp, dark green grass. I step cautiously so that I won't stand on it, and feel as if my stride, because of the width of the slabs, is somewhat longer than usual— they were not laid out here to my measure. It seems absolutely essential not to step on the grass, not to miss a slab, not to speak, not to look back. The silence of this courtyard is as tangible as a cloud of dark wool. In the metallic clicking of our steps, you can sharply hear our hesitation.

Just then, at the end of the courtyard, by the monastery's facade, to the right of the broad black iron-clad door, the only opening in the smooth stone jigsaw puzzle of the wall, I see a water fountain: it is built into a niche in the wall—the water is flowing from the mouth of an eternally grinning lion. The water is flowing but makes no sound. Then suddenly, turning like a sunflower toward the fountain, I remember: why don't I hear the sound of the water? In a gentle arc it washes the curving recess of the carved fountain, gliding along the stone like a silken scarf. I remember: a flock of doves used to fly to the water. I know all that, as if from a vast distance in time I am remembering something I had seen long ago and half forgotten.

And then, in that fantastical light, half aglow still from the passing day and half already in moonlight, in the frozen moment, I know with almost crystal clarity: I HAVE BEEN HERE BEFORE AND NOW I AM RETURNING. I am half seeing this before me, half remembering it. How else could I know it all already? I cannot shake off that impression.

Only now am I prepared to see the man who is standing by the fountain, holding a wooden bucket by its rim. He stands there so calm, so domestic, doing the evening ritual of the pouring of the water, that I feel touched as if I were coming home. I begin to feel I might recognize him—but he is still far off from me, and the light is shimmering like a curtain of silver buttons.

The man turned to face us slowly, holding the bucket at his hip, his arms dangling, and he waited for us, bowed, dark in his black habit, in the shadow of the wall. He seemed even darker, slower, and more bowed than usual. Than USUAL? When? Where? Suddenly something nudged me, panicked, horrified, as if this were a ghost standing before me. I got control of myself as I moved toward him, but the feeling that we had recognized each other and that he knew me, knew me well, would not go away.

Our progress toward the fountain seems slow, as if we are wading there through molten lead. The stone slabs multiply under our feet, regular, even, numberless. And between the slabs—grass. Lord, what grass! I have the impression that we are standing in place, while the black door and the fountain with the black grin of the lion and the man in the habit are approaching us, the way things in movies approach the eye of the camera. Everything is black, white, and green. I see a lighter green mist around the fountain.

Even that inner trembling, which had overwhelmed me when I stepped into the courtyard, now stopped and turned into a naked, frozen tension. It is no longer fear, or hope, but a total void in which we are not moving so much as floating, like grotesque scarabs in the amber of the moonlight: there is nothing more that can be done. Everything is a foregone conclusion—now all that is left for us is to see and hear the consequences, helplessly. Here we are.

The bucket in the monk's hand swings like a large bell. The monk carefully lowers it, empty, to the ground, but the bucket clangs its bottom on the stone and the dull thud echoes for a long time in the kettle of the courtyard like the last chime of a clock.

"Good evening," says Roko very softly, and I hear the edge of tension in his restrained voice.

"Good evening to you," says the monk, just as cautious, humble, carefully looking at the two shadows before him which had unexpectedly emerged from the dark underbrush of night. "Coming from far away?"

"Yes," says Roko.

"People seldom find their way here."

"I know," says Roko. "We set out looking for frescoes. Our vehicle broke down so we came on foot. This is Gradina, isn't it? Have we come to the right place?"

"You are welcome," said the monk with a dark smile.

We shifted from foot to foot, awkward, indecisive.

"Is there a place here we might sleep?" asked Roko.

The monk looked us over slowly, first one, then the other. His face was in the dark, you couldn't see what he was thinking. Suddenly he coughed from the shadow.

"I am here alone," he said at last. "There are no amenities of any sort. Only benches, if that will do. No blankets, actually. And you can see that we have nothing . . . I mean nowhere that you could . . ."

"That's fine," said Roko. "We are used to it. We have been through a lot already."

"Of course," said the monk, and in his voice I heard a chuckle. "You are young still. You'll manage."

But I didn't feel that way. Not young, nor that I would be able to manage much more.

While they were talking, I looked around as if I might spot something else in the courtyard besides the bare rocks and the grass. The paving stones under my feet were smooth as glass. There were inscriptions on the slabs, smoothed, polished until they were illegible. Many have come here before, I mused, the soles of feet polished these stones. Then the rains rinsed them. Only the grass grew.

"All we need is a place to lie down with a roof over our heads," said Roko. "The dew is falling. We have been walking for a long time and we are tired."

Many must have come here, tired, dusty from the road, they dragged themselves here with their last ounce of strength, seeking only a modest corner under a roof. I looked at the stone slabs on which they had walked. Some were darker, grayish yellow, and on those the inscriptions were completely illegible, and the years under the inscriptions were carved in Roman numerals. Those were years long past. Here and there, among them, was the occasional whiter, cleaner slab—the letters carved in them were more regular and deep, the years inscribed were in Arabic numerals. Out of an inarticulate, sudden, unfounded fear that I would recognize one of them, I didn't dare to sound out a single name. If I ever had kin, I thought, they may be lying here. I was afraid that their names would remind me of all of them and of how I had lost them. The years given here were our years, the stark, narrow boxes of our lives. Here is proof, I told myself, here is proof that those years did happen. They have left their trace. We did exist. We used to come here. We used to return.

"As I was saying, there are two benches, broad ones," said the monk. "I was expecting you."

He said that so naturally, so simply, that I almost didn't catch what he meant to say. Then I was shaken to my roots. Had everything been foreseen?

"You were expecting us?" I asked the shadow. "Somebody let you know we were coming?"

"I knew somebody would come someday," he said through a cough. "I have been waiting for you for a while."

And then, as we moved out from the shadow cast by the wall, I saw in the ghostly cold light of the moon his face, wrinkled like a dry apple, his slender bony fingers that clutched the habit under his throat as though he felt chilled, his narrow chest. He was very old and very frail. He certainly must have been waiting terribly long, I thought. We had come back. But somewhere in the depth I knew, icily, that for him we had not come back—he was waiting for death to release him from the waiting. I shivered from the chill.

"Where were you? Why only now . . . ? For such a long time I . . ."

Then he coughed again. We fell silent, confused, feeling guilty for some reason. Maybe he was expecting one of his own, I thought, who hadn't come. Many hadn't come. Or had he lost his mind with the isolation? I wondered, as if trying to justify myself. But the cold ball of fear in me warned me that he hadn't. Where had we been? I wondered. What were we doing until now . . . ?

"I heard there was a war," said the monk as we came over to him by the steps. "Were you in the war?"

"Everybody was in the war," said Roko. "One way or another. Didn't you, here . . . ?"

He didn't dare complete his sentence. Had there been nothing here in this ruin at the end of the world? Maybe that was what he wanted to say. Was everything here already forgotten, the war, killing, blood, hunger, horror? Had everything passed without leaving a trace? Had it all truly vanished into thin air?

"There were times when I could hear the thundering of guns," said the monk. "Far away. And then one day it all stopped. Did you win? You must have won if you are coming back now."

"We won," said Roko.

How unconcerned he sounded when he said that! Roko, I wanted to say to him, don't you hear what this guy is saying? Are we going to tolerate this? Is this the way things really are? Has everything that was ours been nothing but some little episode, a dead end in history? We have left no trace? Why aren't you saying anything, Roko? I don't want it all not to matter, a little distant thundering and no more. We are not returning. We are not even returning as victors. We are going to go on.

"We are not returning," I shouted all of a sudden, needlessly loud and furious. "You cannot return: we paid too dearly to get . . . as far as we got—there is no turning back! There never has been. We are always going onward, do you understand? We leave some sort of sign, a rock, a standing stone, a milestone, then on. The point is: on to where? Sometimes you need to look back just to orient yourself, to know which direction you are headed. That doesn't mean we are going back. Just that we are searching. Seeking those . . . signs. Remnants. Monuments. The past. At the moment we are searching for frescoes."

By the time I said those last words I was quite unsure; the longer I talked, the more my outburst lost its ferocity. Both of them stood silently, their heads bowed in my direction, as if they were straining to understand: what was it that I wanted? Why the anger?

Roko's glasses gleamed opaquely in the dark.

The monk was mildly surprised: "Frescoes?"

"Mostly frescoes. Anything. Something."

I was defending myself from him with all my strength to create some feeling of reality. I knew that there was something wrong in what he was saying, but I couldn't pull myself together, calm down enough, to say it. I felt as if I'd go mad. This is another world, I told myself, other things hold true. But the feeling that we had returned to a place where we had been before was stronger than ever.

"Come in," said the monk with a smile. "You are welcome. I will show you the frescoes."

The monastery was a dark rectangle into which, like an emerald in ebony, was set a small rectangular courtyard, full of moonlight and grass. Roko and I stood next to the monk in the shadow of the wall and stared into the courtyard as if enchanted. Roko's glasses gleamed in the dark, reflecting the moonlight.

Did I dream of it this way, I wondered, or was it, before my eyes, like clay in the hands of a sculptor, fused with my dreams? That is how I remember him the most fondly: as a perfectly fashioned whole.

As we were still standing in the dark shadow of the arcades, the image began to melt before my eyes, so that from that first marvelous impression nothing was left but memories. Later, whenever I wanted to recall this monastery situated somewhere in the middle of nowhere, I would always try to re-create and preserve the immobile, halted illusion of the perfect harmony, symmetry, and elegance of that pure and regular island in the sea of brambles and rock. In vain, I say, because the image would begin to melt every time before my eyes as if it were being corroded by some destructive inner disease, and with horror I would have to free myself of a series of subsequent images, which like some unreal genealogical family tree exposed the collapse of an illusion. I closed my eyes before that erosion like a patient who knows that his illness is progressing in leaps and bounds but behaves as if he isn't ill at all.

Now, watching the courtyard, I wanted for a moment to close my eyes, feeling, with terror, that it had not collapsed into ruin sometime in the distant past, but rather was caving in here and now, before my very eyes.

The arcade around the courtyard could only in the mind's eye be considered an arcade: the arches cracked and buckling, the columns toppled over and scattered around in the dense interwoven weeds like amputated limbs. A pillar still protruded here and there, supporting only the sky—the vault it used to support was now lying smashed in the dust.

The monk looked at us with a mute apology in his eyes and set out along the arcade, wrapping himself more tightly in his habit. The humidity could be felt in the stagnant air. We set out after him disturbed, lost, wordless. Roko stopped, touching the stone with his fingers as if unable to believe his own eyes that its rough surface was genuine.

The capitals of the pillars were fully eroded by time, gutted by rainwater, and only here and there, on one of the ones that had fallen, could you spot half of a pockmarked face, the scaly tail of a snake, a blinded eye, the wing of a bird or angel, fragments of some lost, forgotten world. The vaults of the corridor, which used to be separated from the courtyard by arcade pillars, had collapsed in many places, and we had to sidestep heaps of rocks and dust, wading through the tall wet weeds in the courtyard so that we could continue this sad journey with the somber tour guide.

The monk walked in front of us, slowly, bowed, rustling with his habit, cautiously but with practiced movements hopping over the pillars lying on the ground, the heaps of rocks, the denser tangles of weeds. He kept coughing.

"Don't touch this," he said, showing a piled heap of rocks that was apparently supporting the wall of the building. "It may crumble. This way. Follow me. Carefully, be very careful. Watch it, there is a hole there."

I listened to him attentively, following his winding path. I had focused all my energy on that; it seemed to me that I didn't dare even once to step off the path; I knew that I must not think. Cautiously,

I whispered, cautiously I should move in this world which is caving in, full of traps for the tardy traveler.

The stone slabs that paved the floor of the corridor jutted out one over the other as if the sea were undulating underneath them. Grass and vines had spread along the broadening cracks among the slabs up to the very wall of the building, keeping it damp, taking it apart, eroding it with that hatred which all living things cultivate toward the dead, envying it its durability. In many spots in the wall there were dark holes that gave off a stench of mold and mildew.

"Careful, now," coughed the monk. "Sorry, I have no candles. No one comes through here anymore, you know. I make all my own tallow candles, you will soon see. I have grown accustomed to making my way like this, in the dark."

Behind me, Roko bumped into something and groaned. He cursed unintelligibly, through his teeth. I heard another, more insidious pain in those curses. The monk turned to wait for him.

"Did you?" he asked him, full of sympathy. "Oh dear, I hope not too hard? After all these years I can see the way with my eyes closed. I know every hole, as if it has been here forever." Then he turned to me. "This must look to you like nothing more than a shambles, doesn't it? You would be amazed if you knew how long ruins do retain a lasting form. Like buildings, ruins have an architecture all their own. A ruin, too, lasts for a long time. For years. And then one day you notice that it has changed, it is suddenly a new ruin."

"You have been here for a while?" I asked from the dark.

"A while," said the monk.

"You are alone? I mean, you have been here by yourself for all that time?"

"Yes," said the monk. "What can you do? Somebody had to."

Something in me rebelled against what he was saying and the way he was speaking with such resignation, almost fatalistically.

Why did somebody have to? Who had to? Repeating his words in myself I felt as if I, too, had been chosen, and I rebelled.

With disgust Roko tossed away some rock he'd been studying in the moonlight.

"The one thing here that is intact," he said, "is probably that well . . ."

"The well?" asked the monk. "Oh, that. The cistern. That is an old cistern."

Roko stepped out of the shadow of the arcade along which we had been slowly making our way and, wading through the deep weeds, he walked toward the cistern, which was shining whitely in the middle of the courtyard, looking as if it were coated in silver. It was a cistern of white stone, with a large, richly curving iron arch spanning it. There was still a bucket crank hanging from the arch covered in iron rust, but no chain was left on it.

"Stop," shouted the monk. "Watch out."

Roko stopped halfway there, cautious as an animal in the clearing in the moonlight. The monk and I walked over to him, wading through the thigh-high grass. My feet were wet from the dew.

"The ground around the cistern gave way and it caved in," explained the monk showing several paces in front of us. The earth under the grass sloped inward sharply, but the grass from the depths was even taller and thicker than the grass around the edge, so that you could barely tell there was a pit there. "This, you know, never really was a genuine cistern. At least so I think. They had no need of one. You saw that spring which flows at the faucet. They had their source of drinking water. That spring is probably why they chose to build the monastery on this spot in the first place."

The cistern shone white in the moonlight as if it were of polished marble. It was all carved of a single piece of stone. When we first stepped into the courtyard it had seemed so ordinary, unimposing, but now—it radiated the mystery of its presence. It was so alive. It stood there only a few steps off, yet it seemed removed and ineffable, as if there were something standing between us.

"I think that the cistern was built simply to conceal the entrance to an underground passage," said the monk. "The entrance to the passageway wasn't built of stone. Instead, it was supported by rafters. The rafters rotted, the entranceway collapsed."

He led us slowly along the pit from which weeds sprouted like foam. Now you could see that the pit had a longish shape, and the further we moved away from the cistern, the deeper it was.

"Over there," said the monk, pointing to a dark opening in the bottom of the pit. "You can still see it. The passageway."

The dark, narrow hole yawned in front of us. I felt as if it were drawing me like a magnet and threatening me with something dangerous.

"Does it go anywhere?" I asked as nonchalantly as I could muster. But I was frightened by my own voice when I heard it: so much insecurity and trembling in it, so much childish hope over a single, caved-in underground passage.

The monk looked at me gravely.

"No," he said after a pause. "I do not believe that it leads anywhere at all. If ever it did, it is certainly impassable today."

"What do you want to say by that?" I asked, even more tremulously. I felt like arguing with him, grabbing him by his habit and shaking him like a sack. "What does that mean: if ever it did?"

"Nothing," said the monk, retracting into himself like a snail. "Those were simply the words I used. It must have." He spoke gingerly, softly, as if trying to soothe me. "They built it, after all, to save themselves in case of enemy attack."

"When would that have been?" I asked. "Who were the enemies?"

"I don't know," said the monk. "Ages ago. The eleventh century maybe. No one knows for sure. Everything has been forgotten, ruined, destroyed. Who would know? Maybe it was the Saracens, or the Venetians, the whoevers . . ."

"Did anyone ever, since then . . . I mean, you know, did anyone get through it, did they go . . . ? Try, maybe?"

Once long ago it led to safety, I thought, they knew a simple path to safety. In the eleventh century maybe, but they knew. Later they forgot. We are discovering it again. *That* is why we have come. And the hope that had died out in me when I had seen the ruins of the monastery now began to burgeon, a furious little flame. They excavated this passageway, everything was saying in me, no, singing in me, to save themselves. So that means that then there still was a way. That means there is a way now, even today.

"Roko," I said to him half in jest, half in desperate hope, before the monk had a chance to respond, "if push comes to shove, we can still get out of here. Imagine, even back then they took this route. Later it was forgotten. Escaping wasn't so important, maybe. But imagine . . ."

Roko peered down there scornfully, indifferent. He was depressed, lukewarm.

"Down there?" he said listlessly. "Like rats? Where to? Besides, it was different in those days."

I got angry.

"What has gotten into you all of a sudden?" I shouted. "So maybe they did save themselves. It is good to think that they tried everything possible. Maybe they managed to escape."

The monk coughed, confused, wrapped tightly in his habit as if feeling chilled.

"I do not believe they did," he said, quite softly. "The conquerors were everywhere. You cannot elude your fate. This land was hell on earth, I mean."

I glared at him with hatred.

"What I mean to say is that I was down there, once," he said, even more muddled, as if apologizing for some youthful transgression. "I meant to see if there was any way out."

"And did you make it," I asked, suddenly limp, my anger and hatred evaporated, ". . . to the end?"

"No," said the monk. "There were too many bones in the passageway for me to get through. Too many caved-in places, too many dead ends. And where could you get to anyway? Everywhere is the same, I think. It is good here, too."

"We are hungry and thirsty, Father," said Roko, and in his voice I felt that same endlessly weighty, final exhaustion which had swept me like a murky flood. "We have traveled a long way. We are exhausted."

The monk looked at us without budging. In his eyes there was plenty of empathy but little hope. How many before us had asked him the same thing, it occurred to me, and how could he have responded to them?

"I'll give you what I have," he said gently. "It isn't much. We'll share it."

Roko was standing wearily in the middle of the weeds, his legs akimbo, as if he were propping himself up to keep himself from collapsing. With limp movements he wiped his eyeglasses, looking down at them blindly. That was the way he followed us toward the building, slowly, his head bowed, as if he no longer wanted to see anything.

Poor Roko! I thought. He worked so hard. And now, at the end of the road, everything has turned out to be pointless— all that is left for him is exhaustion. In vain we traipsed all the way here and we've got nothing to do but share our exhaustion with this old monk among the stone rubble. I knew how Roko was feeling. Pitying him, I pitied myself. But what about me?

Who was I? A mere fellow traveler. Poor Roko! I repeated, even more earnestly.

"What about the frescoes?" I said all at once, as if I'd only just remembered. I said that to prod Roko. Maybe there will still be some hope. After all, we had set out in the first place looking for frescoes. Maybe we would find something. But the encouragement in my voice echoed hollowly in the resonant square of the monastery courtyard. "We forgot all about the frescoes. Now that we are here . . . I mean, we are hardly experts, the experts gave up earlier . . . but despite all that, now that we are here, we really ought to see what there is to see . . ."

The monk wrapped himself even more tightly in his habit, continuing on his way. If he wraps that habit around any tighter, I thought, he will get so thin he may vanish altogether.

"We will be walking by them," he said curtly.

Maybe it has not all been in vain after all, I said to myself, knowing that I was only trying to comfort myself. How sorely I needed comfort! But I knew that Roko needed me even more. That gave me strength. Roko dragged along behind us, wobbling, as if he were collapsing as he walked.

"Just a little further, Roko," I told him. "Just a little bit longer, old man, hold on."

Only that way, I knew, could I muster the strength for comfort: addressing myself as if I were somebody else, somebody whom I was observing with empathy but from afar. Hold on, old man. All is not lost.

We passed through the dark, winding hallways, leaning on the damp walls. We stopped and moved again, bumping into each other in the dark, finally to stand in some more spacious place through which the brisk night air was circulating: the monk in front of us rustled along for a bit, and then he struck a match and lit a candle which flickered on the stone altar, bare, at the far end of an equally bare room. Our shadows played around on the walls, huge, restless.

"This is the chapel," said the monk humbly, like a man who is showing a cathedral and knows that he has no need of magnifying things with words, since the thing he is showing speaks for itself. "Here are the frescoes."

We were in a room several paces long with stone walls, paved in yellow-brown stone squares. My first impression was that the chapel was entirely bare, empty, abandoned. The fresh night air penetrated through the openings in the wall, on which there were no longer any frames or windowpanes. The ceiling was made of rafters, but some of them were sagging under the weight of the ceiling, while others had cracked, and some had pulled out of the wall at one end and were dangling down the wall almost to the floor, and all of them were worm-eaten and full of countless little holes. Between the rafters in many spots you could see the sky. It was a clear night, I noticed out of the corner of my eye, many stars were shining through the openings.

We approached the middle of the room. I had to duck to avoid cracking my head on a rafter which was intercepting my path at an angle. When I touched it, the rafter swung in an uncertain balance and a rain of dust and fine plaster dribbled down my neck. Obviously, the ceiling might come tumbling down at any moment.

Holding a candle in his hand, the monk, smiling, stayed the swaying of the rafter. He was totally indifferent to the notion that the ceiling might bury him. He must have gotten used to living with it. Soon it would cease to matter to us, I thought, if we stayed here. If we stayed here? I was appalled at the very thought. What was I thinking?

Roko peered around, frowning, stretching his neck toward the walls, squinting through his thick lenses, through the swaying shadows. As far as I could see, there was nothing on the walls.

"If there ever was plaster on these walls," began Roko, and then he halted and came closer to the wall at the place where the monk, not without a certain pride, had brought the candle right up to the stone. Dark droplets of moisture shimmered in the flickering light.

Then, from my place in the middle of the chapel, without nearing the wall, I, too, caught sight of a bizarre arrangement of an entire archipelago of patches of plaster on the wall. The plaster flamed in flickering colors, still adhering firmly in the places where there were seams joining the stones underneath. Slightly curving, the bulging surfaces of stone penetrated deeply, like sea waves, into the mainland of colored plaster, creating the Celebes and Sumatras of frescoes as if on a map. The candlelight played on them as on a cluster of butterflies, and it seemed as if the entire scene portrayed on the fresco was alive and moving in a quivering, fragile, marvelous dance.

Entranced, I stared at this dance of color, shadow, stone, and the many broken and unfinished lines which with their incompleteness promised worlds, a dance of marvelous details that mingled before my eyes like some kind of magical kaleidoscope—it seemed to me again, as in the yard when I had been looking at the remains of the capitals, that I was seeing before me remnants of a whole rich and now forgotten world.

Their fragmentary, incomplete beauty stirred my tenderness, and I felt particularly honored that here, right before my very eyes, remains of that world were performing this arabesque dance, to show me with that dance an image of their former glory and opulence, and to award me for my willingness to prevail, my persistence, my faith. My eyes were full of color and light, which suffused me, lighting up my darkest corners.

I didn't dare step any closer for fear that I might frighten, injure, that fragile fabric of light, that playful illusion of a world which in this way was extending its welcome, showing me that I was worthy. I didn't even dare ask what it was I was, in fact, looking at: the wing of an angel? The clasped hands of some saint? A white horse in golden array? The heroic deeds of the fathers forged in pure gold?

I was happy. I opened every pore of my being, basking in the light of the colors, which growing more radiant played their enchanted game—the warm terra-cotta of the earth and the deep blue of the sky, the gold of a chalice and the silver halos around the heads of white saints.

Never, before or since, have I seen such frescoes. Vicentius or Johannes de Kastua never painted anything like these. They were not simply frescoes, they were magic spells, marvels. I was paid back for all my seeking, all the suffering. How marvelous—the joy of fulfillment! I opened myself like an abyss before that inexhaustible cascade of light pictures.

They did not seem to be the remains of a world that had vanished, but rather its first buds, which were opening here before me for the first time and which would, right here, blossom into a luxuriously opulent springtime. I had a sudden deep need to believe in them with all my heart, with all that I had in me, all that I knew and that I felt, with my whole life, forever, to enter them as if they were a real world, like that Chinese man who simply left everything behind one day and went off into the wallpaper.

But just at the moment when I was being born again, feeling the rending of the warm umbilical cord with reality, I knew somewhere deep inside me that there was no escape from the cage of this body. My habit of long years of doubting, the legacy of disappointment, the heritage of suspicion, the burden of presentiment which always lives in all of us, spoke from me at precisely that moment, at the most supreme moment of ecstasy, in the mystical germination of my whole being. Only out of the corner of my eye did I see the monk and Roko lean toward the wall and shake their heads worriedly and shrug in that gesture so familiar to all of us which signifies "Well, what can you do?" and despair mutely as they moved centimeter by centimeter across the wall, bringing the candle to it, while Roko sought the proper interval between the eye, eyeglass lens, and the wall, like some sort of scholar with a magnifying glass in his hand. But their despairing wasn't what worried and started me from my fervor; the warning came from my own gut, it surfaced from my own dark.

At that moment I halted in midair, floating frozen in place like one of those pole-vaulters in the photographs, and a chilling fear flooded me all at once. I knew that the ecstasy had drained away and that I was left at the mercy of the dark winds which rule in these spheres: I was way up there, with nothing supporting me, in the dark.

Helplessly, I waited for the least touch of reality, that Roko and the monk would say but a word to wake me and I would come tumbling down like a sleepwalker. I was only a few steps away from them, but we seemed to be separated by vast spaces. I knew that a fall was coming. The foreboding of that fall has forever been in all of us. It has never failed us yet. That is what we call experience. It is reliable. I knew what to expect.

"Can you see anything, Roko?" I asked, subdued, not daring to stir from the middle of the room.

"Nothing," said Roko without turning, leaning over the frescoes. "Almost nothing at all. *Reliquiae reliquiarum.*"

An entire world was snuffed out before my very eyes, wisping away in smoke, fog, and nothing.

"It probably was once some version of the *danse macabre,*" said Roko, "like the one in Beram. Maybe a later copy. But who can say? You can't make out a thing."

The world faded, departing in the dusk in a phantom parade over which scythes waved—a row of skeletons, each one by its victim—and a bit further on, vanishing into the twilit transition into Hades, they merged into one, the skeleton and the victim, and disappeared, embracing. Aren't we there? At the tail end of the procession? Don't I see Vladimir dressed up as a medieval cooper or vintner, carrying over his shoulder, instead of his leather photographer's pouch, a little wine cask on which he bangs out his final tam-tam, which echoes like a terrible drum throughout this whole stark, devastated monastery? Don't I see Petar hugging those two large women without noses, rotting away with illness, their bones slowly starting to poke through their putrescent flesh? Aren't those, one by one, our friends and acquaintances who are departing the world we live in?

Don't leave me, I wanted to shout, don't go just like that. There are things more terrible than death. But my throat was dry and helpless. And I felt, as if in an awful nightmare, that all around us all was destroyed, abandoned, the surrounding countryside untended, infertile, bare, and that there was no one left, because they had all gone. They had left us. I was terribly alone. Now death began to seem like a good thing, a sociable gathering compared to this isolation where ultimate suffering lurks, which will be mine alone.

And then, raising my eyes toward the ceiling, following the light of the candle which the monk had raised above his head so that Roko could inspect the wall better, I saw at the end four huge stains under the ceiling itself, stains larger than all that was around us, dark riders whose heads disappeared among the rotten rafters of the ceiling.

"What is that?" I said terrified. "Look, what is that?"

My own voice snapped me back to reality. For a moment they glanced at me, appalled, frightened by my quavering voice; then they looked at the ceiling, raising the candle, standing on their toes. A spiderweb under the ceiling sizzled in the flame.

"Nothing," said the monk after a brief pause. "They are just stains from moisture. The rain gets in everywhere, you know."

I stepped closer to them so that I could feel their proximity. My feet were heavy as lead. Only now could I see clearly: there was nothing on the wall. People, I am telling you, nothing. An empty, bare wall just as it was when we first entered the chapel. All of it had been a deception. Those paltry flecks of plaster where you could see traces of faded color, grimy with mildew and the damp, could only be termed the material proof that there had been frescoes here by a broad-minded scholar in a mood to exaggerate.

I began to cackle like a maniac.

"Why, there is nothing here," I giggled. "People, look around you, yes, do. There are no frescoes here at all! There never were any to begin with. A painted wall, while there was a wall at all. Layers of old color, nothing else."

The monk shrugged his shoulders helplessly. Taking off his glasses, Roko looked at me with anguished, squinting eyes.

"I looked after them as much as I was able," said the monk wearily, and his voice was tight, gasping, as if he were about to break into a fit of coughing at any instant. "I looked after them, I knew that one day somebody would come. I was looking after them for you. But the damp . . . the plaster drank up the moisture. I told you, there are underground springs here, it is damp. The frescoes peeled off the walls before my very eyes. They were already pretty much ruined when I first arrived here. And then year after year more of them were gone. They peeled off in patches. Every year I saw different images on them . . . you may think me mad, but no, no, I am not mad . . . I saw the images . . . I watched them for days, years, they were carved so deeply into me . . . and now I still see what was on them . . . figures, destinies, stories that last . . . that is why your disappointment is all the more awful for me . . . but I tell you, I did look after them . . ."

We stood there in the middle of the bare chapel where there was nothing left except what was in the head of one lonely, elderly monk who would die soon, and so all of it would finally, irretrievably, completely disappear. We sat gathered around his phantomlike tallow candles. The monk was speaking, half mumbling, half weeping, as if he were praying. He asked from us something we could not give him.

"There, you see, I did not manage to save them. I did what I could. But, you see, the year came when the ceiling fell in. All by itself . . . Then the rains. I looked after them for the person who would come here and want to see them. I don't know why I did it. Maybe because somebody had to come. It seemed to me that it was terribly important for some reason that somebody look after them. I thought that somebody would come here and take over from me, preserve them after I am gone . . . and that it would go on . . . through time. Though, you see, now there is nothing left to preserve . . . now that you have come, I can go ahead and die in peace . . . at least you will tell somebody else that this exists, that there was something here, so even if you don't stay on here yourselves, people will remember, somebody else will come, they will return, and maybe all of it will come alive once again, maybe, once again, everything will be . . . it cannot be that the entire world is nothing but collapse, ruin, a morgue as it is here, somewhere there must be something that is being revived, rebuilt, preserved, there must be people still . . . It isn't all like this, is it?"

"No, it's not," said Roko very softly.

"I looked after the library, too," said the monk. "It was a large library. Many illuminated manuscripts, copies, parchment . . . but I didn't save it. From the mice. From the damp. From mold. But most of all from time. Everything is gone. Sometimes, to ease the loneliness—can you imagine how lonely I was at first? Later I got used to it, I mean—sometimes I would pick out one of the books, and it would crumble under my fingertips into dust, and instead of relief I would feel irreparable loss, a feeling that I had ruined what little there was left to salvage. But nothing could be saved.

I did it not because I thought it was possible, but because it seemed to me that it was terribly important that somebody be taking care of it. *As if* it were possible."

"Why?" asked Roko, shrugging his shoulders. The monk was breathless from talking. He probably hadn't said this much in the last ten years.

"I thought that somebody would turn up sooner or later," he continued, choking back an attack of coughs just so that he could say a few more things. "They would want to see, to hear, to learn . . . They used to come here, I heard, ages before my time . . . but who? Conquerors, rogues, adventurers. They came here while there were things to steal, conquer, carry off, and then when there was nothing left to take, people stopped coming. I thought maybe somebody would come, just the same, in poverty, humble, meek, with head lowered, and he'd come to find out what the books said. He would come to learn about . . . us. You know, I always felt that I belonged to those . . . before. About us . . . I said. Maybe if they had only been coming like that from the start, maybe everything now would have been different. I didn't know how to read or decipher it all myself, but I always thought: somebody will come. My job will be done. Now that you have come, I no longer have anything left here to do except die. Now I can die in peace."

"We are too late, as always," said Roko.

"I thought," said the monk with despair in his voice, as if it were terribly important for him to convince us of something we couldn't hear or didn't want to hear, "I thought that the people who came would bring me salvation, a justification, that they would give meaning to my life, which I have spent here in the desert, preserving all this, as much as I was able . . . I didn't end up saving much, but still . . . All that I managed to preserve was the act of trying to save it . . . I saved . . . my place in line . . . somebody will keep on with the saving . . ."

"We, my dear man, came here to find something different," said Roko, laughing hoarsely. "They are handing out places in line on every street corner."

"I thought, what else could I do? To tend to the little task for which God gave me a long-enough life and the fortitude to survive in solitude, to keep my sanity, and here . . . have I done it? . . . Tell me, yourselves . . . Here, you came from far away, tell me, you know, I am only a poor, uneducated monk, you have seen the world . . . tell me, judge, have I done what I was meant to do?"

"You have," said Roko softly, looking away. "You have done your job."

We sat down at the table to dine, still evading one another's eyes. The table was made of a coarsely hewn board, long and empty, and along it, on both sides, stood two long benches for the deceased brethren. Two candles flickered between us, lighting only the scrubbed coarse surface of the table and our faces and hands. The walls of the room were not visible. The three of us were a pool of light in total darkness.

We were sitting in the library. Aside from the one cell where the monk had been staying for all these years, it was the only room still in relatively decent shape, though even here the ceiling had caved in in places, and the shelves where books had once stood were worm-eaten, broken, and full of spiderwebs. Here, on the benches we were sitting on just then, was where Roko and I were supposed to spend the night. On one of the benches the monk had placed two folded coverlets that reeked of mold.

"This is all I can give you," he said.

He repeated these same words once more when he brought to the table a half-round of sheep's-milk cheese, a half-loaf of bread, and a pitcher of water.

"This is all I have," he said.

We sat there for a while in miserable silence, not touching the food.

"I am so sorry," I said, "that we didn't bring anything with us. As it is, we will eat up what little you have."

"Go ahead and eat," said the monk, coughing. "I don't need much. I often go for days without eating. I pick mushrooms, blackberries. You are still young. But you will grow accustomed, I said, to all manner of things . . . A man doesn't need much."

"No, indeed, a man does not need much," said Roko disdainfully, "to survive."

Much he doesn't need, I wanted to say, but when he doesn't even have that little bit. When he hasn't got anything. What then? A man doesn't ask for much, but what if he finds nothing, no food, no roof over his head, even no crummy little pictures on the wall. Nothing at all? What is the point then of surviving? Simply to survive, to get used . . . to all manner of things? To take your place in line? You have the wrong person! We aren't like that! That is why we shall go on. If there is something further, on we go. Where? Wherever. But we can't stop here, in no-man's-land.

I brought the water pitcher to my lips. There were stars swimming in the water. I looked up and through a hole in the ceiling I saw stars in the dark blue sky. I wanted to pray silently, but I didn't have the strength and I no longer knew how. I felt rage rise at my own impotence and at the stars, ineffable, uncaring. Nothing, that's what you are, star, I told it.

We believed in you, star, we followed you, in the sweat of our brows, we hoped. And what came of it? If this is the place by which all that we were and all that we have done should be measured, if we are justified by this, redeemed, if our life is weighed here, then what can we boast of, star? What entitles you to expect our gratitude, humility, obedience? If all this was in vain, this suffering, this humiliation, this creeping around in the muck, and if from all of this, in the end, all that remains are several fragmented chunks of stone and a few eroded, moldy paintings, then we can leave nothing more to you, star. Because you are indifferent, merciless, and inhuman. Was this old man here needed as immolation to your glory and praise? Were we, this minuscule and paltry crusade of ours, necessary to bring as a sacrifice? You haven't been sated during all those centuries? Oh, how I hate your greedy eye.

We will keep going, I knew, not because of it, but in spite of it.

The monk cut the bread and cheese into three equal chunks. We ate silently. The monk kept choking with coughs. We chewed thoroughly, without thinking.

"So, now what will you do?" asked the monk a bit later.

Roko banged the table with the pitcher, wiping his mouth with his fist.

"Sleep," said Roko, loudly.

I didn't like the tone with which he said that, carefree, detached after the defeat.

"I mean, after that, tomorrow?" asked the monk. "Of course, should you wish to stay on here for a while . . ."

"Tomorrow?" asked Roko, surprised, as if he were startled that the answer to that question wasn't patently obvious. "We are going back."

The monk coughed, long and convulsively.

"I knew it," he said.

"It would be best for you to come with us as well," said Roko. "What can you do here?"

The monk shook his head wordlessly.

"I am too old for that," he said. "And actually there is nowhere for me to go back to. I left so long ago, everything has probably changed. My place is here. I have gotten used to it. Here is where I'll stay. I'll wait."

"What can you do," said Roko, barely holding back a yawn. "Whatever. Maybe we meet again someday."

I found his superficiality and detachment insulting. I felt uncomfortable: something in me was rebelling. Was everything over for Roko? I wondered. Had he given up altogether? Can he possibly think there is nowhere further to go? Has *he* surrendered? I didn't dare say the words, even to myself, let alone to accuse him. But the most terrible thing for me was that Roko, it seemed, was taking it for granted that my path was joined with his. He wasn't even considering that maybe I might want to continue with what he had begun. How could he be so blithely certain that there was no going further for anyone. A certain desperate defiance began to well up in me like a black tide.

Defiance to what? I asked myself. To what? To the idea that there is nowhere left to go? To Roko? What is he to me and I to him that without him I cannot go on? That a man cannot go on alone?

"Listen," I said to the monk, "is there any sort of road that goes on further from here?"

The monk looked over at me, drained.

"A road? Only the road you came along . . . if you can call it that . . . No one comes along even that road anymore."

"I mean, isn't there something that keeps going . . . Anything at all . . . a path, maybe? Which heads further, to the other side?"

The monk shook his head.

"There is nowhere to go further," he said to the table. "Overgrown with underbrush everywhere. You can't get through."

"Obviously," said Roko, indifferent.

Finally I was all seething with rage at him sitting here at the end of the road as if nothing had happened, and staring with his short-sighted eyes at something of which I was no longer a part. Something of which I had maybe not been a part from the start. Maybe it was all a misunderstanding, our connection, our journey; maybe there never was anything between us to begin with. What, I caught myself thinking, what if Roko is not what we thought he was? I felt cheated and rejected. He sat there completely innocent, list-lessly admitting defeat, as if he were absolving himself of even a shred of responsibility.

"Why did you bring us here, then?" I shouted, suddenly furi-ous, helplessness catching in my throat. "Where were you taking those people?"

Roko shrugged his shoulders, calmly.

"Me? Taking? What people?" he asked with just a tinge of irony. "Are you in your right mind? Why would I be taking anyone any-where? I was just the organizer, how can I put it, the group leader. You all were the ones who wanted to go. Did you or did you not want to go? I didn't make anyone. All of you went of your own free will. Good God, man, I was just responding to your collective wishes; you designated me to do that. Once you start moving, there has to be order. If I overdid things a little, it was for your own good."

I stood up, gouging my fingernails into my palms with all my strength and screamed at him as loudly as my throat could bear.

"You are lying," erupted from me. "You led the people. You promised. They trusted you. They thought, the way I thought, that you really knew where you were taking us . . . why you were taking us there . . . they believed you. Why didn't you tell us everything, then?"

"What everything?" said Roko, archly. "There is nothing for me to tell. Just as there was nothing to be found."

"Why didn't you tell us that there was nothing, then? You didn't say a thing, you counted on our friendship just as now you are count-ing on our goodness, and then on top of it all . . . you deserted . . ."

Roko pushed away from the table with the whole bench. The candles flickered, and the bench squealed like desperate brakes.

"Is it up to me to tell you that there is nothing out there?" asked Roko, his face twisted, ugly, strange. "Couldn't you have figured that out for yourselves? Are you children? Am I your father? Of course there is nothing. There never is anything at the end. It is the journey that matters; the order, the discipline. Somebody always has to lead, and it just so happened that I was the one doing the leading. We can do nothing but try, to do the best we can. In the end, for who knows what time, to find out that there is nothing out there. What do you want from me now? I was just guiding the excursion—are you expecting me to bring you our goals on a blue-rimmed platter? Then what?"

"That is what I am asking you," I hissed with hatred. "Then what?"

"Nothing. Then nothing," said Roko, shrugging his shoulders and calming down a little. With the wave of his hand he dismissed this as if none of it concerned him. "What can you do? We have made it this far. There is nowhere further to go, as you can see. Now we are returning. And then back to square one. From the top. Everybody will want to go somewhere, again. Once again we'll take it as far as you can go. What else is there?"

"But all those people, Vladimir, Ivan, the others, and me, at the end of the day you misled us . . ."

"Don't be ridiculous," said Roko. "What kind of Boy Scout logic is that? I did not mislead anyone! Every person finds his or her own way. I was pursuing mine. For a bit there our various paths converged. That is what brought me and all of you together. That is it. That is our glorious community. What do you want of me now? To comfort your downhearted little souls? Everybody can always go back. They are probably already back now, as far as I know. You will go back, too, like all the others."

I had completely lost control of myself and had begun to shriek like a madman. The whole monastery reverberated. The monk looked at me fearfully, wrapped tightly in his habit, hunched over the table. I withdrew from the table deeper into the dark, and from there I railed and cursed as though I was accusing him not only in my name but in the name of all of us. I felt Roko's detachment throw me into a rage. I hated him as I had never hated anyone in my life.

"And what," I roared like a wounded animal, "if there is no return for us, if we cannot go back, if we have nowhere to go back to anymore? Aren't you going to feel at least a little remorse? Shoulder the responsibility?"

"Why?" said Roko. "Each of us shoulders responsibility for ourselves. I am nobody's keeper."

"If you were so smart, so experienced, that you knew there would be nothing at the end, then this entire trip was one big step back and your leadership a hoax!" I shouted. "For you it is all just one more circuit: there isn't even any of the famous spiral! It is nothing to you, but the others, the others risked a great deal more than you did. We haven't nine lives like cats that we can spread out before you like a carpet for your experiments!"

For the others, I knew, there was no longer any real way to get back. They had no way to return, they'd been left out there in the wasteland, lost. For them there could be no starting over, just as there couldn't be for this monk here, at the end of his road, who was staying to die. What for Roko was no more than a brief excursion, for them was the final journey after which there can be no more travel. For us, this adventure had enduring and immutable consequences.

"Cut the histrionics," said Roko. "Can't you see that everybody else pulled out in time but you?"

Roko was sitting calmly at the table, and his eyeglasses gleamed coldly and distantly in the flickering light of the candles, like mirrors. Suddenly it occurred to me that I had never seen his eyes.

I knew that I was fuming in vain, ranting and raving to no purpose and helplessly flailing in the trap I had fallen into. I realized just how futile it was for me to accuse him of betrayal when there never had been anything between the two of us, nor could there have been. No oath, no contract. There never had been a community. We believed and lived with an imaginary, a wished-for, a dreamed-of, community, but why did he live? I didn't know. It didn't matter. His path was predetermined, special, separate, like others.

He would go back, as he had how many times before, mechanical as an ant, blind, shortsighted, possessed, a divine machine, maybe a little transformed so that you might not recognize him as easily, he would set out again for some other destination, with a new set of fellow travelers, never cognizant of what was driving him but helpless to resist, indifferent to the outcome and to disappointment, success and failure, indifferent to others because he was indifferent to himself.

We were each of us finished in our own way. Our fates were not only measured and judged, but even disclosed to us, so we knew what was ahead. Taking pity on Roko, I took pity on myself: I had nothing left but to stay on like this monk, reconciled with the ruins of my world as long as there were any to move on through and as long as I was able.

"I am not going back," I said once more. Now that it was clear that there was no return for me, I calmed down and accepted the inevitable. "There must be some vestige of a path, a gully, a way to take me to the other side," I said, to comfort myself. "Even when there was no way on, our ancestors knew how to build a passageway to save themselves. It may be possible,"

"Maybe," said Roko. "Everybody has the right to try."

"Whatever the case," I said, "I cannot stay here. Thank you for everything. Maybe we will see each other again someday."

"Maybe," said Roko, indifferently. "Though I doubt it."

So we split, Roko and I, and we never saw each other again. I never saw the monk or the monastery either, though I did try to find them later. But there was no going back. I had to move on.

∽

Down a crumbling set of stairs, down, down deeper and deeper into the damp, close darkness. I went down carrying a candle in one hand and leaning against the walls with the other, blindly groping with my toes for each broken step that had been carved into the ground. The candle flickered restlessly, threatening to go out. Was that my hand trembling? Or was it a draft of air blowing through this underground passageway—which would mean that there was hope: would it be possible, then, to make my way to the other end of the passage? The candle was so feeble that its light only made the dark seem all the darker.

For a while I could still see the square shape of the entrance-way behind me. I never gave so much as a thought to turning back. As if the passage were following my movements and not vice versa, it turned suddenly and headed into the depths of the earth, concealing the entrance from view, and cutting me off completely from those threads which had tied me to the outside.

I was suddenly alone. Before and behind was the darkness of the passageway. I felt finally, endlessly alone. There is no darkness more terrible than the darkness of a solitude in which the ember of a single consciousness feebly and timidly lights the way. It seemed to me that my sense of consciousness was even weaker than the candle I was holding. Look at how both of them illuminate a small portion of the world—I thought—a meaningless circle in the dark. An irrational mystic sketch of stones and roots on the walls of the corridor, where moss and white-gray mold were drinking up the moisture. You have to hold to those walls gingerly, just as somebody who cannot swim holds to the shore, because as soon as you strike out, the circle of light does not reach far enough for there to be anything that can give you a sense of orientation in the opaque seascape of darkness, and then you bump into the opposite wall (or is it the same one you were following before?), just as damp and dank, just as pointlessly scribbled with the mysterious geology of Hades, and on you go in an endless zigzag, in a child's game of salvation between the two walls, finding the direction where the earth is leading you, but where you are headed, where it leads you—that much you can't tell.

Under your feet crunch the bones of those who have gone before.

You fill the dark with your own imagination and it is easy to lose your mind. Will I make it to the end? I wondered. Will there be enough of this candle to take me to the exit? The road is so long and the candle short.

> It is very dark down there,
> but why is it so dark down there? . . .

I hummed to myself nonsensically, in a quavering voice, through my teeth, a song that surfaced unexpectedly from the darkness of childhood to support and encourage me in this later and more terrible darkness. I advanced slowly to its rhythm, trembling, patting my hands along the wall, cautiously sidestepping the places where the roof had fallen in, pushing out of my face the damp roots that were dangling here and there from the ceiling of the passageway like the webs of some gigantic spider.

These roots, I thought with longing, they are from trees that are growing up there somewhere, high above me, and they are breathing the free air, vast leafy trees in the wind. Helplessly I fingered them: my terrible desire desperately climbing upward along the roots toward the surface. Roots, you pure heavens!

Onward I trudged along the soft, slimy soil, creeping along the walls of the passageway like some diseased underground polyp, touching with my frightened fingers first the stone, then a crack, then mud, then roots; I advanced step by step along this hollow pipe of earth, and it seemed to me that I was not getting any closer to anything, but rather that I was only getting further away: with each step I went further and further from all that I knew, further from everything that held some sort of meaning for me in the life I was leaving behind. I seemed to be moving further and further away from myself.

> It is very dark down there,
> but why is it so dark down there? . . .

Some sort of creature rushed by me. A bat? A snake? A rat? Suddenly I felt that the dark around me was populated. I knew: my candle couldn't show them in its light, but the animals were here somewhere, an arm's length away, underfoot, before my face. I stopped in the narrow pool of light, not daring to budge an inch further. I was frozen with disgust and fear. As soon as I stopped, the rustling stopped, too. We stood there for a while, the animals and I, trying to understand each other through the dark that enveloped us. Accept me, natives, I begged them as if I were seeking mercy, humbly. Forgive this interloper.

Gradually getting used to the dark and my fellow travelers through it, I thought: this cannot be the very worst place in the world, it cannot be a trap with no way out, it is possible to live here as the animals do. Whatever they can do, I can do, too—and better. Like a true loner, striding again, moving further down the passageway, I almost wished to hear them again—my accompaniment on my isolated path.

I walk patiently onward and hear them in the dark. Then gradually all that rustling, winking, and scampering, the invisible life of the underground, turns into footsteps. My first thought is that those are my own footsteps echoing off the tunnel's curving walls. But then I hear how my steps are joined by the sounds of many invisible feet. I know that I have company. I am no longer alone. I see gleams in the dark—are those eyes, blades, torches, the gleam of armor? An entire silent army marching alongside me without a sound.

They are all around me in the dense darkness that teems with life. I feel I am with them in a mute community. Then, even without seeing them, I begin to recognize them in the dark: these are my ancestors all around. My two grandfathers, who created for me the land and the sea—one a farmer, the other a sailor—my father, maybe, and many others, many dear departed, some of whom are still in fur or animal skins, some in *surka* coats or under a busby, some in armor, among them kings and poets, all my ancestors who passed through this same dark passage at some time in ages past, along the same uncertain route, seeking safety from their enemies, fleeing from conquering armies, the world, themselves.

They entered, one after another, over time, the safeguarding dark, and now, still, they continue on in an endless march, some of them for centuries, like a river of which I was a part. Suddenly, thanks to them, I know many answers: the dead are not dead, closed up on the shelves of tombs; they are coursing underground currents, rich with nutritious juices, quenching earth's thirst. Now I know that this path of mine, this search, has not been pointless. I am not alone. I belong to this river that flows unending, and I am continuing what they have done, continuing their trek, not merely my own private pathway through meaningless time, through the dark underbelly of the world, but also their strivings toward a goal which has still not been given to me to see, but which must, indeed, exist. In me they will come a step closer to that goal, just as I in them have made it as far as I have, to this place. Just as I will reach the goal itself someday in my descendants.

I stepped along with more alacrity and boldness now. You must keep going, do not surrender, do not give up. Your part of the way is short and troubled, but with you goes an underground army. The clanging of invisible swords, the rustling of habits, the sound of a melancholy lute and steps without number filled my darkness. Having given me life you live on in me, I told the grandfathers in the dark. Rest easy, souls of the deceased, your journey goes on.

Now that I was sure that my path was not merely the only path, but also the right one—hadn't my ancestors shown me as much?— I was suddenly filled with a wild, crazed, desperate hope that there would be salvation just as we had been promised, and filled with that hope, while every part of me was trembling with the fever of fulfillment, I rushed along with all my strength (my last ounce of strength, one more superhuman effort) toward the end of the tunnel, along the curving but saving passageway, hoping that behind me I was leaving not only this underground place, but also the life that had brought me to this underground passageway; both the underground passageway and the life in me were becoming an apotheosis as I passed through to the other side, they were blessing, redeeming me.

When I caught sight of the bright light of the exit in front of me after a long time of traveling through the dark, I flung away the candle so that I could get there faster, and, blinded by the light of freedom, I started lurching and staggering, stumbling and bounding toward the opening, trembling with an inner joy, happiness, exultation, as if I had won some great and glorious victory over the dark, over the past, over the world, over myself.

I may have shouted with joy. I may have burst into song with the patriotic, victorious anthems my ancestors used to sing, something like "Freely through the air flies the bird" or "Onward valiant soldiers, marching, marching," or maybe I merely shouted, "Follow me, follow me" or "Forward," or I simply howled like a wolf, which, at such patriotic and great moments, is actually all the same, and the echo, the hundredfold echo, answered me, which sounded to my deafened ear as if my whole underground army were singing with me in a harmonious hymnic choir, marching with me, striding out with me into freedom. The whole underground passage thundered with our heroic song.

Then, abruptly, out I ran. Half blind with the effort, squinting at the light, panting and excited, happier than I had ever been in my life, at first I could not even see where I was. Then, sensing that I was out in the open, I straightened up and looked around.

I stood there for I don't know how long, maybe no more than an instant, but maybe it was for hours, or days. Whole worlds died in me. There was nothing harder to bear than this. Behind me the echo still thundered from the tunnel. Maybe my voice stayed behind me and was living back there with its own special underground life, or maybe those really were the voices of my ancestors. But it was not a song. It was roaring, terrible, cavernous, mechanical laughter. Only ancestors laugh that way. It seemed to me, for a moment, that among them I heard Roko.

Then that died away, too.

I found myself standing in the middle of a vast, gray, rolling stonescape that stretched off as far as the eye could see. The sky was covered with a curtain of clouds and diffuse moonlight lit the countryside in a ghostlike light. There was nothing in the landscape, no houses or vegetation, person or animal—just bare rock and the pale gray moonlight, poisonous like mercury. The sky was lower than it ever had been. I set foot in that world, but I couldn't hear my own footsteps. It was as if I were walking not on rocks, but on mounds of wool, in ankle-deep fog. It was like some ghostly birth on deaf ground. Nothing. Nothing. Nothing.

Where was I? I wondered, wordless, standing in that petrified nothing, feeling that I was lost forever and that of all hopes, of all knowledge, of my entire being, all that was left was the question: where am I? What is happening to me? What's going on with the world?

I stood there and felt as if I were collapsing like some building: the structures were cracking, ceilings falling in, lacy fretwork towers were toppling inside me. I could have borne anything except this ultimate, final disappointment. It seemed to me that not only was one brief excursion over, but my whole life. All that was left for me was to live out my time until my physical end in this gray, mute, opaque world.

Maybe there never was any other world, I said to myself, as if trying to make excuses. Maybe I have been in this wasteland since day one, maybe all of us are in it since day one, maybe it isn't usually given to us to see it as clearly as I see it now. Maybe I never left this place to begin with. Maybe I never set out on any excursion. Maybe this actually is an annunciation, a salvation. Maybe this is that ultimate freedom that my ancestors were all moving toward, and I have made it to the goal.

But then my eyes gradually got used to the light, no matter how weak a light it was; no matter how those eyes were desirous of deception, they pierced the fog of mugginess and the moonlight, and I saw clearly, more and more clearly, how I had arrived at the same world from which I had set out. I saw that I was standing at the heart of the landscape, at the very center of a circle, and I realized that I was nowhere else but precisely in my own place.

What else could I do but accept? After all, what else was left? I bowed my head, and stepping into the landscape, I accepted the stone path under my feet, I accepted the thorny bushes which scratched my bare arms, I accepted the hunger and the thirst and the pain in my blistered feet which would ache until I reached some sort of human shelter, I accepted all that familiar, ordinary, and barren landscape which had surrounded me since we set out on this crusade.

Many of the names in this story I have changed. One of them I had to fabricate entirely: Gradina. I chose it at random from the endless list of neutral place names that fit the town, and that would not mislead you, reader, with their similarity to the name of some other town, suggesting the fragrance and color of their genuine source instead of the fragrance and color of *my* town.

I chose it from the long list of names that I pronounced for myself in a tormented and twisted sequence of my attempts at recalling the original—I lined these names up during sleepless nights, frozen moments, waiting at bus stops, in summer after-dinner siestas, in the long leisure of my failed life. I pronounced them in desperation, as bastards do who try to remember the womb they were born from.

At first I tried with a feverish earnestness, listing the indices of atlases, studying special maps systematically, square millimeter by square millimeter, combing my muddled memory like some sort of dusty attic somebody digs through to find some misplaced family memento before burning the trash.

I struggled and sweated, unable to remember. It would seem sometimes that it was on the tip of my tongue, there, any minute now I'd be able to say it. I'd strain, not daring for a long time to shape it with the cavity of my mouth, fearing the disappointment that would inevitably follow when I heard my voice articulating some strange, meaningless name. The name would approach me from the murky semantic magma like some sort of enchanted beauty that evaporates as soon as you reach for it.

Later, having gotten used to a series of disappointments and defeats in the battle with my own memory, recollection became a habit with me, some sort of spiritual solitaire, a game to pass the time in this empty and meaningless life. I would be sitting somewhere with a glass of wine, at home or in a café, trying to find a name that no longer mattered to me, anyway. But I was left with no other choice. At that point I no longer knew what it was I was trying to remember, and listlessly, out of habit, I would poke through the dusty leaves of memory, for anything, for anything.

These efforts left me drained, with a feeling of ultimate limitations, with a profound experience of futility, incompleteness, like a lifer in prison after frenetic masturbation.

At first I asked people. People listened to me at first, later they just watched me and shook their heads.

"If an expert like Dr. So-and-so has never heard of the place," they would say, "how would we?"

"Somebody has to know," I repeated stubbornly, urgently. "There must be somebody somewhere who knows."

They had heard of Beram, of Oprtalj, of Draguč, of Roč and Vizače, of Foška and Hrastovlje, but that place, *that name*, no one mentioned. There were people who, with a smile, told me of names that were never mentioned anywhere else, so insignificant, places where people had not only never seen frescoes but had seen nothing else, either.

"Oh, I've been there," I'd tell them. I truly had been. I had been anywhere I possibly could go. After a while I got the feeling that I had already been everywhere, not only here, in Istria, but the world over, that I had already seen all that a person could possibly see. But the place I was searching for was missing. Distances, unknown routes, white spots on the map kept enticing me, in vain.

"After all," I would say from time to time, "maybe it was a lost cause right from the start."

I asked around, by now halfheartedly, and people sometimes only laughed, or other times—knowing somewhere deep within them what it is I was after—they would answer against their better judgment. Until all their answers merged into a single, huge NO. No, we don't know where you could find such a place. Where was there any such place, could there be any such place? A library, you say? A monastery? A water fountain with a lion's head? NO.

I stood there the same way I had emerged from the underground passageway—before a mute world.

I sought out the participants from the brief excursion, the people who had set out with Roko and me one silvery, sunny morning in a small, many-colored bus that never made it to where the two of us got, and even the two of us didn't get anywhere. I thought: if they had all had a genuine desire to get there, if only they'd been a little more persistent, had lasted longer, if they had known what was at stake—maybe we all of us together would have made it somewhere, we would have arrived. As it was—I knew—the two of us simply made it a bit further than the others into nowhere.

I looked for them, but I didn't find them. I looked for them the way a man whom everybody has thought has been lost for good turns up from a long imprisonment or emigration and looks for his friends. But my friends had vanished, scattered, disappeared in wars, in pogroms, or simply in life: into the soft, foggy comfort that swallows people whole like quicksand. Or some of them, one day—as witnesses tell it—simply walked off down a tree-lined avenue, or up a blind alley, or along a beach, and never came back. Now I no longer have anyone to turn to. The members of that expedition may have all died off, anyway. Maybe their world really did end with that brief trip.

I even looked for Roko. Of course. I imagined him often in a thousand sharply defined images—there wasn't a camera in the world that could have taken such focused pictures—trying, by reconstructing the links between these pictures, to revive in my memory the entire excursion, and his words, among which, like an unborn child, in the mature thick magma, shimmered always the embryo of *that* word . . . the name . . . the signpost . . .

I pictured him often the way, fervent, exalted, under the pale light of the evening star, he had whispered the name, the name before which all of us stood, barely moving his lips. The moment was so solemn, so brief. I reran it in my memory until it wore out, faded, peeled, until finally my inner eye saw only a spare sketch of the landscape where we'd stood—behind us the bushes, in front of us on the hill something that could no longer be clearly discerned—a landscape that closely resembled the gray stonescape where I ended the brief excursion.

If I had found Roko, he might have told me the name. As it stands, the name is forgotten. And so, sitting with wine, sometimes I think in a moment of clarity: maybe I forgot it out of fear, and maybe that oblivion is the salvation we so longed for. Then I begin again with dry lips going through a rosary of names.

I often think about placing an advertisement in the papers: there is always a shred of hope to cling to. But I know: I no longer have the strength even for that. And yet, don't be angry with me if, after all this talk, after carrying on so, I tell you that tomorrow, chances are tomorrow, I will put an ad in the paper. I will do something.

»»» «««
The Garden of Nightingales

We came to town in late May, or was it early June, I can no longer remember precisely, but the hot spells had already set in and the sea was warm enough for swimming. This was a little town that had been Italian before the war. Afterward many of the Italians opted to go and settle in Italy, leaving behind their vacant houses. In the old part of town the houses stood there spectral, empty, doors and shutters flapping wide, swung by gusts of south wind. For a long time no one could figure out what to do with them.

In the newer part of town there was a housing shortage, and Croats who had moved in from outlying villages had settled there, crowded into rooms and small apartments, several families to a room. Were people still ruled by past prejudices that the older, more elegant town center belonged to the Italians and only the newer neighborhoods to the Croats? Was this ethnic split still lingering in their minds when no more than a dozen Italian families lived in the old part of town? Or was it simply because in the older, more elegant center of town there was no sewerage or plumbing? Anybody's guess. I relished, with an antisocial view on life particular to me, the phantomlike, abandoned sprawl of little streets where large, fat, half-wild cats, and the occasional spectral woman in black, roamed.

I guess everybody finally decided that you can't simply leave the old center of a town to collapse. There was talk of turning the neighborhood into a complex of modern apartments, or into a huge hotel.

The old town had once been, many years before, encircled by walls—before the inhabitants decided to venture beyond the sturdy shelter of stone and overflow into new neighborhoods they had built, out of need or inertia, as densely as they possibly could within those walls. They built up a close, indivisible tangle of houses along narrow streets crisscrossed by arches. Houses spilled over into neighboring houses, spread and squeezed, encroached on the foundations next door and jutted over adjacent roofs, adapted to the available space, which had, over the years, grown more and more cramped. Houses bridged streets with vaulted archways, leaned on each other, tucked into the tiniest nook. And when all the land had been used up, houses sprouted atop other buildings, never touching the ground, interweaving the sky itself with their tall chimneys and undulating roofs. The whole town had fused into a single structure; it was nearly impossible to say where one house ended and the next began. The town had become one inseparable organism.

Understandably, town authorities couldn't make a hotel of it because no one dared broach the question of property ownership, and, furthermore, calculations indicated that even installing the necessary bathtubs and toilets would be more than the town could afford. In a word, when it became clear that the old town center had no economic worth to speak of, they began to insist that its value was historic. But when, despite its value, nothing could be done to save it, the houses were offered to artists for rent—they could make them into summer homes, studios; they could start a colony!

Well, then, throngs of people from all around the country discovered they had talent. Quite a colorful throng of people moved into the old town: perverted maniacs deeply convinced of their artistic calling who toiled fanatically indoors from morning to night while dreaming of shows in Paris, and stolid, potbellied craftspeople from large cities who saw this as a windfall and fantasized a future industry of souvenirs. There were elderly painters who had lost all hope that anyone would ever buy a painting of theirs and value their art, and young adventurers and snobs who thought it fashionable to move in artistic circles. There were people who simply wanted to spend their month of vacation per year more cheaply (they could cook in their own homes, with all their relatives), and nondescript, colorless types who came here for no particular reason, without true desire or motivation, you could see them twenty times a day and still never know what they did, what they were up to, why they were here. And I must not neglect saying that the town was really rather charming in its own way. The sea generously gave it, as it did all the coastal towns, its grace.

Ćuk, Beba, and I arrived in the town to fix up Ćuk's house. Ćuk had leased the place sometime in the early spring, then he went back to Zagreb to sell off a few paintings and scrape up some extra cash, and now he was back to fix up the house, so that his large and motley assortment of friends could spend the whole summer together, partying. Ćuk was, one might say, a painter. What Beba was doing in our company baffles me still today. That afternoon when Ćuk and I were discussing coming down here to fix up the house, Beba had dropped by my place for a friendly visit, one thing led to another, and she became an indispensable member of the society for the repair of Ćuk's house, Ćuk & Co. Otherwise she was, as I recall, a medical student.

Ćuk's house was right on the waterfront, and the city sewage drains stank wretchedly directly under the window when the wind blew from the south. We started our repairs on the house with the discovery that there was excellent wine for sale in a wine cellar about two hundred paces down the street. We bought a broom, two liters of wine, and a soda-water siphon. We got drunk, left Beba sweeping, and went down to the train station to cart back our things, which had come in on the same train.

As far as we were concerned, the house was huge: four rooms on three floors, and a kitchen, cellar, and attic. We demonstrated our enthusiasm for adapting as quickly as possibly to our new Mediterranean surroundings by calling the attic the "*šufit*," eating spaghetti, and singing, in the name of multiculturalism, "Mazzolin di fiori." We figured that cleaning the house from top to bottom would take too much time, so we agreed to sweep no more; it would get filthy again as soon as we started the repairs, so it would be better if we slept in one room until further notice. We blew up air mattresses, tossed our suitcases around, and took dishes from the trunks that had come on the train, banged a few nails into the walls, and established household order. Ćuk did insist on that first day that he would have to negotiate with a few painters and electricians, but that, of course, happened a lot later.

All of us had been living in rented rooms in Zagreb, so we spread out luxuriously, each taking over a room, and the first night passed without incident (later on nothing passed without incident), except that Beba, contrary to obvious fact, insisted that we had given her the worst spot to sleep in and the lumpiest air mattress, proof of our ungentlemanly behavior, and drunkenly she demanded that she move in to sleep with Ćuk, which he categorically rejected.

The next morning Beba told fairy tales about how she hadn't been able to sleep all night because of the rats, which were scampering about and sometimes even ran right over her. Ćuk was mortally offended and claimed that *this sort of house* could have no rats. Out of the question. There were scorpions, of course, but scorpions are clean, and if you let them be they are peace-loving creatures who have never hurt anyone the way Beba hurt him, Ćuk. That is how a very special, very sensitive pride in *our* house was born—the flag of local patriotism was raised—and forgetting all that had seemed important to us in the world just the day before, we gradually moved into the tiny world of sun, sea, and the old, romantically vacant town center, *ours*.

Ćuk quickly acquainted me with countless artistic types who were partying around town and playing at being bohemian. On the lookout for a room painter who would be available for practically nothing to paint the whole inside of the house at the drop of a hat, we stopped in at a few of the more prominent town bars, where Ćuk was greeted like an old buddy. In this fashion, I succumbed to an uninterrupted drunken stupor with painters and housepainters, bringing me to that blessed conciliatory state, a state I always end up in when I am by the sea, where I drink and I haven't a care in the world.

There, as soon as I start talking about the sea, I wax sentimental. The sea for me has always been like a big woman. In cities and other places I would think of the sea the way other people reminisce of their first loves. Even today, wading into the water for me is an experience of the utmost pleasure, as if I am orgasming inside a large and buxom, but also gentle and lovelorn, woman. Maybe that is because the sea has been my home ever since I set out, far too early, into the outside world, where I am now living out my life. And maybe that's why the time always comes when I loathe myself, my own weakness, in the spring, after the city autumn and the city winter, after coats and umbrellas, discourteous people, cold and alien apartments, vacuous and pointless labor, poverty-stricken sorrow on the streets and regal sorrow in bars, I know it is time to go. Maybe I feel this way because the sea is just as grand for everybody.

That year, like so many others, I felt by the sea like a happy lover who has spent the whole night in the arms of a woman who delights and satisfies him. I was cheerful and open, I talked to people, loved my neighbors and the passersby, never once quibbled with waiters in cafés, I was an easygoing, grinning, carefree observer of the sunny place I lived. Forgetting everything, I surrendered to the present.

We ate in a grimy little restaurant where there was always good fish and where we always drank good wine; we wandered lazily around the hot streets and sat in front of cafés on the piazza, our legs outstretched, avoiding the sun. We talked with drunken painters we would meet in the evenings with the half-loaf of bread in their hands they had bought that morning for breakfast. We quibbled with the housepainters so that we could make real Ćuk's ideas of how the house should look inside. There were two of them, and neither of them knew how to speak Croatian properly. Neither of them suffered from an inferiority complex as a result; after all, we didn't know much Italian. One sang opera arias all day long, which grated terribly on Ćuk's nerves. The other talked constantly about how we should buy *come si dice* this, *come si dice* that—brushes, putty, paint. None of it was available. We explained to him in Italian that *questo colore* was not sold in the stores and that it doesn't matter, he can paint with *giallo* whitewash if nothing else works, and he, for his part, did everything the opposite of whatever we told him. We had to move out of the rooms where we were sleeping and move from place to place because of the painting. Whenever we raised the iron bedspring, a deep, weblike trace was visible in the dust and plaster on the floor. The two wine flasks and the heavy, half-gallon bottle for soda water moved with us into each new room, where we'd plant them in the next heap of dusty plaster.

We combed the beaches for pretty girls, sometimes we found them, and we'd roam in couples through the shady woods, which grew everywhere right down to the water's edge. Beba was a bit too jealous now and then because of Ćuk, but then she found some French guy who was in the harbor for a few days on his yacht.

The French fellow was one of those who had learned a great deal more of his geography and history from glasses of wine than he had from books and museums. Ćuk and I tried to explain to him how he ought to base his personal philosophy on that and feel no shame, but I don't know if we really succeeded in this or not. The French fellow was as charming as a Frenchman should be, but Ćuk was particularly pleased that he hadn't an eye for art. Beba told me that his wife was ugly, but you had to take that with a grain of salt.

With girls or without them, we explored the lovely, spacious woods around the town. Both of us were filthy, in smudged blue overalls and grimy blue sailors' shirts, and, carefree, we poked around everywhere, skinny-dipped in remote coves, pulled clothes on over our wet skin, and went right on roaming. In those same clothes we played Italian card games in bars, repaired the stairwell in the house, painted frescoes on the walls of our rooms or in the open hall of the tobacco factory, where a lot of women worked. Beba would critically examine the knees of our pants and the toes of our shoes. For some reason she was certain that the scuffed toes of shoes have never yet deceived the discerning eye.

We were seldom sober and hardly ever slept. We came home after two in the morning and were wakened early by the housepainters when they came to work. Their work, of course, was the purest of fiction, for though they arrived on time in the morning, we never found them in the house during the day whenever any of us stopped in. The whole day long we grinned blissfully behind a foggy curtain of intoxication and sleepiness. The housepainters were our brothers and the whole town was a friend.

We seemed to be living without event.

But two weeks after we came to town, Beba's cousin arrived. He lived a rather reliable life and was, as Beba put it, a bond to her extended family: the favorite of all his aunts, a boy who had gotten good grades at the university, he did not smoke, did not drink, and generally he behaved in a model fashion. It was awkward for Beba to appear in our company in front of him because of the possible denunciations and family scandal that could come of it, so she moved into a hotel, giving as her excuse that the dust and filth in the house were bothering her. Whether she managed to pull the wool over the eyes of her reliable cousin and preserve her saintly halo, I don't know.

The constant buzz of inebriation sapped our strength, we got sick of wine, and affected conversations with artistic types also lost their thrill. The painter-bohemians spoke mostly rubbish, they couldn't hold their drink, they did not know how to dance, they knew none of the local people, and most of them didn't even know how to paint or anything about art. Ćuk and I stuck together most of the time, but soon little tiffs and squabbles erupted; we had no one left to taunt, so we taunted each other. We lay around lazily most of the morning on some empty beach where the occasional painter wearing a black sweater buttoned up to the chin might stride up lugging an easel, or some Slovene woman with two or three children might happen by, or, less frequently, somebody with time on his hands, the sporty type who would suggest a round of cards or Ping-Pong at one of the hotels. The fun of it had been spent. We already knew the painters would go off to the first pine woods and spend the day sleeping on the soft pine-needle cover on the ground, in the shade, taking out and then stowing away their boxes of paints and brushes. The Slovene women were generally older and tubby. Flushed red, they kept to the shade and screeched unbearably from there whenever some scrawny kid started to go down to the water. They were invariably here just for a day or two from Slovenia with their car, and five hundred feet away or so would be the husband, oil stained in his mechanic's overalls, usually lying under the car, which had jostled apart on the bad roads.

The guys with time on their hands began to get on our nerves—professional gigolos after the foreign women, they would spend the entire pre-season in their swimming trunks so that they could be sure to have a deep tan from day one, and put on a show with dyed mustache and bulging biceps. Obviously, a person couldn't hold their trade against them, a man's got to do what he's got to do, but there are times when it is difficult to stomach the features that go along with a particular vocation. It was ridiculous watching them waste their pent-up charm, to no purpose whatsoever, on us. They heaved chunks of stone from their shoulders, not very far but in dashing style. They played cards indifferently and were god-awful at Ping-Pong, but they sported all the gestures of world-class competitors.

It was a breath of fresh air when 180 full-blooded Germans arrived at the lovely pine woods that ran along the beach, a motley array of ages in a motley assemblage of clothing. This was the first largish group of tourists to visit since the Second World War. The colors of their clothing betrayed that they were foreigners. Over the next days green, yellow, and red tents sprouted everywhere around the woods, and then the Germans moved in and fanned out on the beaches in their striped beach robes. That morning several of our gallant young men set forth. One of them appeared unexpectedly with a guitar blithely tossed over his shoulder, although he showed no inclination to play it. Flashing their pearl-white teeth, the gigolos mingled with the crowd of Germans, who were between forty and sixty, and inquired, between romantic sighs, as to the going rate for cameras.

Ćuk got up from the beach with a sneer of disgust, shrugged, and said: "No, this is not Rio de Janeiro."

So we left, lunched in our tavern on grilled mackerel, drank two liters of wine, and decided we would walk, that same afternoon, to

Golden Point. Golden Point was the name of a peninsula about a half-hour's walk out of town, where there was a restaurant with a terrace. It was a favorite spot for dancing: nothing much, but you had a chance there of meeting, aside from the painters and foreigners, some halfway decent people.

Slightly tipsy, we walked along a road that ran along the water's edge. It was hot because the tall cypresses lining the road were too slender, too picturesque. Drunk and overheated, we had to get off this picturesque road and go down over the rocks to the shore to dip in the water. That is where we met them. Where I met Gerta.

There was only one spot along that whole stretch of shoreline where a person could easily swim. This was a small cove surrounded by low-lying smooth, flat stones. Beyond the flat stones rose tall white rocks, the cypresses were behind the rocks, and on the other side of the cypresses ran the hidden road. You couldn't see the cove from the road, but from the cove there was a gorgeous view of the open sea to the setting sun. Everything in the cove was white: the stones, the rocks behind us, and the gravelly sea floor. There were three of them at the cove.

If we had noticed them right off, maybe we wouldn't have gone down, but it was already too late. There were two women and a man. One of the women had on a two-piece bathing suit, which, for basking in the sun, she had rolled up and reduced to its smallest possible size. When she saw that we were coming down, she hastily straightened out her bathing suit and patted her hair, a little groggy from the sun. A moment of awkwardness and hesitation ensued, but then Ćuk started energetically stripping off his clothes with hasty movements, as if he were thinking: we aren't going to let ourselves, here on *our* beach, be bothered by interlopers. I was thinking the same thing.

For a while we gave a free exhibition of swimming strokes, sobered up, got out, shook off the water like dripping dogs, and lay down on the white, hot, flat stones, and the stone and sun embraced us with their warm, intoxicating hands, calmed us, soothed our sharp edges, transformed us into two lazy, satisfied, toasty creatures.

We watched our neighbors for a bit. One of the women was pretty, quite pretty. Or rather: she was pretty compared to her friend or to the general state of affairs in town, but I would not say that she was beautiful in some remarkable way. You have to look at things within a given situation. She had blue eyes, hair that was off-blond, eyeglasses, a slender, agile, tawny body, rather graceful in its movements. She looked as if she were a German woman. An attractive German woman, unlike the other. The other, for instance, was just German.

Ćuk and I, as if by agreement, donned our holiday smiles and immediately became aware of the complexity of the situation. It was obvious that both of our fluids were focused on the prettier one, which would, inevitably, sooner or later, be a source of contention in both camps. Not to speak of the third.

The man who was with the women became fiercely aware of danger and his inferiority complex, and he began to hold forth in earnest. He spoke feverishly, as if he liked listening to himself, and in general he seemed rather pale. During his tirade the women showed profound interest in the less intellectual entertainment at this end of the cove.

"Let's hope they aren't Germans," I said to Ćuk.

"I bet they are," Ćuk said with a broad grin. "Who else could they be?"

And German they were. They pulled on bathing caps and slid into the water, shrieking with pleasure. Ćuk and I rose as if the same spring had sprung us both. I swam after the prettier one. Ćuk stood on the rock as if about to jump in, but at the last moment decided it was too cold and stayed on the shore like a statue, stretching with laziness.

"*Seehund,*" he howled, "*pass auf!*"

The German woman smiled and continued swimming out into the open water.

I plunged sharklike in and out of the water. I even barked once. She thought that was so funny she choked and had to stop swimming, she was laughing so hard. Help came at the very last but best moment. I opened my mouth as if about to gobble her up, just the way every shark is supposed to open its mouth.

Gurgling and choking, she said haltingly in German something that sounded like: "Don't make me laugh, or I'll drown . . . ," and: "We don't call it *Seehund,* it is *Haifish* . . . ," and then: "I'll drown laughing . . ."

I heard it, I heard perfectly well the sound . . . the voice . . . the words. I was startled at how well I'd understood her. After so long. Suddenly I lost the urge to laugh. The situation lost its charm. Suddenly, with a clutch of panic, I was looking at her half-startled, half-amused face and those shortsighted blue eyes, a little red around the edges from the salt.

"Do you speak English?" I asked, holding her as if I were saving her, while I saved myself with touch. It turned out that she did speak English and she spoke it well. That was better. We swam toward the shore, talking.

Her name was Gerta. She would be staying only ten days more. She worked in the international department of the Cologne telephone company and was studying at the same time. I forget what. There are so many things, Gerta, that I have forgotten.

On the shore, we all introduced ourselves. Ćuk saw what was up and switched his focus to the other one, purely out of a sense of collegiality. The other one's name was Else.

"Folk craftsman," Ćuk introduced himself. That explained the smudges of paint on his sailor shirt. "Obviously I am folk. I work with my hands."

He demonstrated on Else, who giggled shyly.

The man who had escorted our German women to the lion's den was utterly and irredeemably a stuffed shirt.

"You must be suffering from a grave internal ailment," Ćuk told him kindly. "A little mountain air would be just the thing."

The paleface was named Robert. I have never yet met a Robert in my short and not very eventful life who had a sense of humor. Maybe in German the jokes are not funny.

Robert explained to us in detail how he had been quite ill two years ago, from pneumonia or something like it, but now he was in fine health, fine health, thanks for asking. Ćuk started to speak, but when he saw that Gerta and Else were whispering and paying no attention, he merely shrugged.

"You understand German," Gerta told me. "I saw you were laughing. Why don't you speak it?"

I didn't answer. Ćuk turned slowly toward us and then said, slowly and evenly, in German: "He fears deformation of his oral cavity. He is, you know, a mouth-harp virtuoso."

No one laughed. It was already late afternoon and the sun, like a vast ruddy ball, was descending toward the sea. Everything had a golden, ruddy glow. Our bodies moved through the shiny, flowing air. The rocks were very white and nicely warm. The sea was calm.

"The sea will be like glass tonight," Ćuk announced to the air. "A great night to go out with the night fishermen."

I lowered my head onto Gerta's thigh, facing the sea. From time to time her head loomed over me. She was better-looking with glasses on. She was very feminine. I was feeling intoxicated by the sun, which was dropping so slowly, with such dignity, golden, horizonward. As if in a sappy movie, a sailboat approached the golden swath between the sun and me, and there it vanished.

We followed the sun with our eyes and were quiet until the golden swath faded. The sea grew gray and the mirror of the glasslike calm reflected all the darker tones: first a mild pink, then gray-blue, then violet and deep blue.

We took one last dip, wordless, and then clambered out onto the shore chattering with the cold, hopping from stone to stone to warm up and dry off. We pulled our clothes onto our still-wet skin. While the women were combing their hair and applying lipstick, Ćuk wandered up and down along the beach, swinging his wet bathing trunks and flipping over stones with his toes. Under one he found a little malachite-green crab and tried to drop it down the front of Else's sundress. Else shrieked, awkwardly hopping back on her bare feet over the sharp rocks. Robert tried to explain to Ćuk that this was not such a great idea since Else might have a nervous shock or something along those lines. Ćuk let go of the crab, which scampered off sideways into the water, and worked to convince Robert that the crab is a harmless little creature, that there are plenty of worse things around here. Like snakes, for instance. Snakes, which come down to the water's edge every evening at precisely this time to drink and are very, very poisonous. Robert showed a high degree of intellectual development and did not completely buy it. But nonetheless, maybe because of that or maybe in general, he hurried his endangered charges.

With a stone I was, meanwhile, prying two limpets off the rock's edge, and offered one of them politely to Gerta. It goes without saying that I ate them both. The limpets were tasty, salty and fresh. Whenever I eat limpets I feel solemn, as if I am taking communion in the temple of some sea god. Limpets, the wafer of the sea. I tried to explain this to Gerta, garbling Croatian and English, but came up against a wall of incomprehension. Gerta then asked me, was I religious? Is one permitted to be religious in your country? Yes, I answered, one is, and I'm a firm believer in the gods of the sea.

We moved slowly along the road toward Golden Point, in the soothing twilight, among the cypresses. With pleasure we walked in the coolness, quietly, watching the edge of the dark grow denser on both sides of the white ribbon of road. It was nice, almost solemn. In solemn darkness like that a person cannot joke around or tease or be silly. In darkness like that people feel closer, press together to shield themselves from alarming thoughts. In darkness like that, the anxiety that lurks in us since birth surfaces, that distrust of all that cannot be held in check, and we seek closeness and people we might despise in the glare of an electric light. We didn't know each other well, so closeness was only possible in silence. Each of us was afraid of saying anything. To keep from damaging the convention of electric light. To keep from being embarrassed. So there wouldn't, as Ćuk put it, be an international misunderstanding. Maybe this is where it all began.

Maybe it had already begun, but none of us knew it yet at the Golden Point Restaurant. The dancing had started by the time we got there. Suddenly confident in the light, we were feeling gay, playful, making noise, squeezing between the tables, twirling our wet bathing suits. The restaurant was actually a spacious covered terrace. The roof stood on large pillars made of coarsely hewn stone.

We sat at a table by the terrace railing, ordered sardines and wine, and looked out at the water. The sea lay before us—a limitless, motionless, mute mass. Looking toward the sea, you could sense it there.

The music was pretty bad, but still within the limits of tolerable. We had fish with lots of lemon and heaps of yellow-green, fresh salad. There were quite a few people on the terrace, many among them the recent arrivals from Germany. Between two dances we heard a group of young men singing with quavering voices but ample goodwill. They must have been singing while the music played, but now that it was quiet their voices suddenly rang out, confused and helpless to harmonize. It wasn't the cacophony of drunken singers, but rather the self-consciousness of people acutely aware that they are suddenly the focus of attention, that had disturbed the order of people unused to singing and disturbances.

They sang something that sounded like this:

> *Čivabdžidži, čivabdžidži*
> *Das haben wir alle gern*
> *Das alle Leute fressen hier*
> *Die Damen und die Herren.*

I may not have remembered the words precisely, but what they sang was along those lines, to the melody of "Tampico, Tampico." The third time they repeated the melody, somebody asked them to stop, and they did, and fell silent almost apologetically.

Robert kept insisting that we converse. He inquired about the system of higher education in Yugoslavia and how much was an average salary, and that he had heard how guns for underwater fishing sold well here. No, he had never gone in for fishing himself, he didn't even know how to dive, but he had brought the gun so he could learn, and he was considering selling it if he didn't learn or ran out of cash. He kept asking things and had a lot to drink. We advised him not to because we were well-meaning souls and looked after our own, but we kept on filling his glass whenever it emptied to brighten the mood. Robert was full of pride to be talking with natives and he looked around confidently. The Germans at the nearby tables watched with envy this man who had established contact with the locals so swiftly. Such acquaintance had great advantages: the natives provided free information on where you could buy the best and cheapest wine, they could direct you to the least expensive accommodations, the best food, and local points of interest. Though Robert needed none of it. When you took a closer look at him, you had to wonder what this man would do, for example, with better wine.

Robert got pretty drunk off the first liter, and aside from that it was clear that he was no good at dancing, or at least not so good that anyone could ever want to dance with him, though that was fine with me. Ćuk, certainly, demonstrated a certain scorn for characters as unreliable as Robert, because he, then, had to dance with Else. When we came back to the table after the first dance, I noticed that Ćuk was drinking heavily to help him bear the situation.

Gerta and I danced really nicely together. She was one of those born dancers who puts heart and soul into every step and never tires. She might not do in *Romeo and Juliet,* but her complete surrender to the dance gave her movements a kind of grace, and I had the impression that in my arms I was holding a living, full-blooded being, full of strength, élan, rhythm. That means a lot when you're dancing. In her surrender, she lost all sense of constraint, all concern, effortlessly she freed herself from the earth, she freed me, too, setting us apart from the other dancers, from thinking, from the world, even from the music itself. Separate from everything we could blossom like flowers, offering one another all we had to give, we could free our bodies, aware only of each other, asexual and yet shameless, dancing to the rules yet unbridled and fancy-free, grinning and talking nonsense yet primally honest and close. Dancing like that you feel as if you are creating something in sync with your partner, yet there is nothing quite so treacherous. You trick yourself into feeling as if you are at play, but in fact you are living in the most primeval way. Off you go thinking you are dancing decently, when in fact you are utterly and shamelessly exposing yourself.

The sax player was pretty good, unlike the others; the sax had a nice hoarse, guttural tone, and it turned this fresh outdoor terrace by the sea into a smoke-filled city dance hall full of sweat, exhaustion, strangers who go to big-city parties. The dance affected Gerta like opium. She was happy the way only good dancers can be happy. She made me happy. We spoke only a few words in the breaks, waiting for the next dance out on the floor. We woke from each dance stunned, thrilled, tired, tipsy, as if we were coming from another world in which there were different rules, different relations between people, where there was no past, no future. Where you couldn't make a mistake.

But things invariably unfold to our detriment. When we came back to the table we were confronted by an awkward scene. Robert was red in the face, very drunk. He stood, weaving, on his feet, holding the chair, doing what he could, mumbling, to interrupt the torrent of words with which a fat man from the next table was inundating him. The fat man was also flushed, but in a healthy, bourgeois sort of way: with the kind of flush you get only after your third bottle of wine. The fat man was a family man on his summer vacation with his wife and children, and who more than anything loved a round of cards on the beach and a drop of healthy home-brewed wine after dinner, all in the immediate circle of his family.

"You snot-nosed pig," he shouted at Robert. "Keep your hands to yourself or touch your own Kraut women, your own kind. Stay clear of my wife! Where did you go to school, you pea-brain! They go around thinking that all they need is a little foreign currency, they can pinch any woman's ass they want . . . You Kraut pig."

Robert tittered foolishly. He hadn't, of course, understood a single word and kept grinning like a buffoon, swaying like a mast in a walnut-shell boat. This completely enraged the fat man. He lunged over, knocking down the chairs before him, and struck Robert with all his strength.

"You can't just waltz in here and . . . to us . . . Goddamn you . . . ," hissed the fat man, blindly swinging at Robert among the chairs, flailing drunkenly in the air. Robert still didn't understand a thing. He tried to shield his face with his arms, stuttering drunkenly, and kept tripping among the knocked-over chairs. Ćuk leaped to his feet and in two strides reached the fat man behind his back. He grabbed him by the hand, just at the moment when the fat man was readying to deliver his final, murderous blow.

"Stop!" shouted Ćuk. "Can't you see he is drunk . . . the man is drunk . . . let him go, damn you . . . stop!"

"I'll get you, too, I'll get you, too," the fat man puffed with fury, grabbing Ćuk by the throat. "So they're paying you, are they? Is that true? Q-u-i-s-l-i-n-g, turncoat, hit man, servant to the occupying forces! You are whoring with German women! Down with traitors to the people!"

Ćuk stepped aside, and then, clearly infuriated, forgetting the reason for the fight, quickly and adeptly turned, firmly took hold of the fat man's arm, and the man, with a grimace of pain, followed him. The fat man lunged toward the chair overturned at his feet, tripped, and tumbled groundward, headfirst. He straightened up slowly, brokenly, with curses, brushing the dust from his suit with a bloodied hand. He left bloody smears on the suit, and it all looked far more terrible than it really was. Ćuk stood, arms akimbo, before the man and, threatening, said very softly: "Don't do that again, because next time, believe me . . ."

Some women screamed. The onlookers were mostly on the fat man's side. One man behind me said: "Look at him, who is he standing up for?" "Typical," said a woman. "Where are the police? Where are the waiters? Look . . . ," they exclaimed with alarm.

A woman came over to the fat man and took firm hold of him so that he wouldn't lunge at Ćuk again. The fat man tried to wrench free, but not too earnestly. Gerta and I stood near the scene, but in a somewhat sheltered position. "Get out of here, Ćuk," I said. Ćuk merely nodded, grabbed Robert by the hand, and made his way to the exit. Else went with them, shaking her head as if to say: didn't I tell you?

I never learned what exactly had happened. Ćuk had seen nothing because he was dancing with Else, and he arrived at the scene of the incident only seconds before I did. Robert didn't want to talk about it the next day, and he avoided us until the end of his brief and unhappy summer vacation. He clearly felt that either he had done something wrong or that we had.

But the precise course of events is a thing of history. For contemporaries the consequences are what is interesting. Gerta and I sat stiffly at the table, not speaking and not moving, not looking around. We, too, felt guilty. We felt the enmity of the surroundings, the repressed scorn, the hostile shoulders. With an expressionless face the waiter straightened the chairs around our table. Three empty chairs stood before us like accusations. The man at the next table over talked constantly, breathing heavily, and appealed to the support of the crowd: "I'll tell them a thing or two . . . they can't just come here and . . ."

The whole terrace was subdued, heads bowed toward other heads, lips moved swiftly, and people glanced over at our table from time to time. All the eyes glared accusation. Somebody at an adjacent table spit. It all had to do with me, an enemy of his people, a traitor.

"The bill," I said to the waiter. He didn't blink.

"What did you say to him?" asked Gerta.

"I want the bill."

Gerta put her hand on my arm.

"We don't need to go yet, do we? This was none of our business, was it? I like it so much here."

She smiled, watching me, confused, expecting kindness, friendship, the continuation of our closeness. But at that moment I no longer could remember that it had been pleasant dancing, I no longer saw the charm and sweetness of her smile, nor did I feel the femininity with which she tried to erase the atmosphere of blood, dust, enmity, raw excitement. I looked at her, blind with unjust accusations, blind with old hatred, blind with fear that the world repeats itself, deeply convinced that she would not understand and that she was smiling simply because she felt like smiling, that she liked everything because she saw nothing.

"You like it?" I said. "Maybe you think this is amusing? What do you care? You, of course, cannot see what it was that was speaking and cursing from that man who attacked your pitiful Robert. Do you think that a dozen years is enough time to forget? You don't know, none of us knows, what Robert actually did to that man. Do you imagine that the man likes it, that I like it, that anyone likes it that you are here? We put up with it. That's all. Put up with it! With these kids who are singing here in a language we learned too well. We had the opportunity to learn it. And here they are, singing in my face. Next thing they'll start singing 'Lili Marlene.' They are drinking and eating and sitting here by the sea, you understand, and who can guarantee that one of them wasn't here ten years ago, eating and drinking and singing along the road, marching, what do you say to that?"

"Those were soldiers, the army," said Gerta softly.

"Yes, you are right, the army, your army. With guns and bombs. Like any army. But that army was here, see? And who can be sure that the man over there who is eating grilled *ćevapčići* didn't heave a bomb at this man's father? Five years of that army and ten years of remembering. And now here they are, singing, getting drunk, molesting women, and we are supposed to feel guilty because of them, because of some asshole named Robert. These people look at me as if all that was only yesterday, see? Our famed hospitality conceals fifteen years of darkness of the worst memories, inkblots on the brain from ink they never showed you in grade school. Even today, when I see a German I restrain myself. I have to restrain myself when I look at you."

"I was only ten years old when the war ended," Gerta said very softly, suddenly, in German. And that woke me up. Not what she said (oh, I've heard that before), but the way she said it: so quiet, no emphasis, no pathos, no anger, a little sad, sympathizing with my outburst, prepared to continue listening to my preaching, my insults, my hatred, prepared to suffer for the sins of others, maybe for me, maybe in general. And suddenly I felt tired from so much talk, from so much wrath, I felt empty and drained, as if everything I had said was useless and pointless.

We tried to dance again, but we were exhausted and strained by so much irreparable misfortune, by so much unnecessary pain, so instead we simply stood there on the dance floor, holding each other, our heads touching, and people looked at us, interpreting our shame of the past as shame of the present, and soon we had to go, both of us unhappy, distanced by the fight, incapable of bridging this sudden, yet so ancient, chill. We left like a beaten army, not knowing what to think and what to feel, blaming one another because of the defeat, tripping up in our souls over one another's movements and every word, whether spoken or not. We felt, however, compassion for each other, but sensing the compassion we despised each other all the more.

We sat among ten cheery, singing, tipsy people returning to town on the shuttle ferry. Not saying a word, we pressed into a corner, looking at no one, shielding one another from the cold night wind and tiny, sharp particles of sea dust. The boat motored quickly, but it was not quick enough for us: we could hardly wait to finish this anguished trip, to stop feeling like living accusations for one another, and we wanted deep in our souls for something to happen that would prevent us from parting, since we were not capable of avoiding it ourselves.

It may have been around midnight when we landed at the harbor dock. The town was completely empty, and the people who got off the motorboat vanished quickly into the winding streets. We stood there for a bit on the dock staring into the darkness.

"Surely you must go home," said Gerta into the dark.

But I didn't want to.

"I'll see you back," I said.

We walked by the locked-up cafés on the square, where chairs with their legs in the air were lying on the tables, lit by feeble streetlamps. Everything was horribly empty. The steps echoed among the tall old walls. A fresh breeze blew and rustled the phantomlike fronds of palm trees, which stood out in front of the restaurants in green pots. We said nothing until we reached the camp.

The camp was completely dark. You could see that these were elderly, stolid working people, though Germans, who had come on their vacations. The white gravel gleamed on the beach in front of the camp, and you could hear the soft plash of steady waves.

"Say something," said Gerta.

"What should I say? I don't know . . . what to feel. I'm empty somehow . . . and I have no will for anything. I have no will for anything at all. I don't feel like going home."

"Stay," said Gerta simply.

So I kissed her and stayed that night in the cozy little green tent where there were two narrow cots, because Gerta's friend had suddenly taken ill that morning and had to go back to Germany, to the hospital, where chances were she'd spend the rest of her vacation, because the illness was serious, and they hadn't placed anyone else in Gerta's tent, maybe as a precaution, a warm, cozy tent under pine trees right on the beach, where the sea murmured and where I taught Gerta to say the word "cricket"—"*cvrčak*," and where when she said "*cvrčak*" it sounded like the sweetest music. So I did stay there that night as if I were never going back, forever cherishing the words and movements and smells, only to lose them all except the listening, to forget them all except for the longing to keep them from oblivion.

When I woke in the morning, Gerta was gone from the neighboring cot. I felt broken and empty, my mouth was dry. I smoked a cigarette in bed, waiting.

Gerta arrived, fresh from a swim, her hair wet, smiling in a striped bathrobe. She kissed me very cozily and said, "Master, your breakfast awaits."

I got dressed and went out in front of the tent. In the golden, restless, sun-speckled shade of a large pine, in front of our tent, stood a little garden table with two chairs and breakfast all set out. Gerta played the hostess and tried to outguess my every move. We drank dark golden, fragrant tea. Around us, in front of the other tents, many German families were sitting at similar tables, having breakfast. Actually, it must have been quite early. The men were sitting and reading the paper, and women were cleaning up. The shouts and splashing of children could be heard from the beach. The atmosphere was all in all pretty domestic.

"What will they say, what do you think?" I asked Gerta, pointing with my thumb behind my back to the familial idyll in the woods.

"They can say what they like," Gerta said brightly. "What do we care?"

"I'm not going to Cologne," I said, shrugging my shoulders.

"Who knows?" Gerta inquired of her tea.

I smiled.

"At least not anytime soon," I said.

She was hurt.

Abruptly she put away the breakfast things, in and out of the tent. I sat there, smoking, and stared at the shiny, morning sea. I felt rather lightheaded, but much better than when I'd first woken up; Gerta's anger soon abated and she kissed me on the neck.

"Be good and sit still. I must return the dishes to the hotel."

She went off carrying the dishes, but after a dozen steps she turned, grinned happily, came back, and, putting the dishes on the table, sat in my lap.

"I don't know," she said, smiling through tears, "it's as if I am afraid to go. I am afraid I won't find you here if I go. I am afraid that none of this did happen, or maybe it never will happen again."

I merely smiled emptily into her face, mocking her sentimentality to myself, and mocking myself as well, because I felt unworthy of her.

"I would like you always to be here, at this table, that whenever I come, I can be sure to find you."

I didn't know what to tell her.

"But I won't think of that. I promise you I will no longer think of that at all. I will not allow anything to ruin this short time we have. I promise."

I sat, empty and unworthy. What can a person say to that? She is promising that she won't think about how she is here for only ten days and that after that it will all be over and that there is no force on earth that can change things. She is promising and she expects me to help her, to give her strength to forget all but the present, to forget how impossible it is to live forever the way we are living now, cut off from our worlds, alone and happy on garden chairs by the shining blessing of the sea. She promises because she knows full well, just as I know, just as everybody knows in this kingdom by the sea, that our envious winged kin will come, that they will separate us by kilometers, days, oblivion. This is as certain as the purest mathematics.

Gerta took away the dishes, skipping cheerfully, whistling some German children's tune. I watched after her for a few minutes. In the place where the path running along the seashore vanished from sight, Gerta ran into an acquaintance and talked gaily. The two of them laughed, greeted each other, and parted ways.

Three Germans between the ages of twenty and thirty passed our tent, carrying first-class fishing gear. I have always wanted to have gear like that. But by now it was around ten o'clock or ten-thirty, and they certainly weren't going to catch any fish. But I didn't have the slightest inclination to laugh at them. They wouldn't catch the fish, I didn't have the gear; such is justice.

Children were playing on the beach right beneath where I was sitting. There were a dozen of them, some in the water, some up on the rocks. I noticed the loudest one. He had an underwater mask and a short gun for underwater fishing, but without ammunition. The gun was obviously broken, but the boy proudly displayed it to the others. The boy was a true little German, hair the color of corn silk and freckled, obviously arrogant, and ruder with his playmates than children of his age usually are. He was playing war by threatening the others with his rusty gun and shooting at everything that moved.

One, who was quite a lot smaller than he, pointed his finger at him and howled, "Boooom!" The boy with corn-colored hair dismissed this scornfully with the flick of his hand and said something I couldn't hear. Then he slowly turned his underwater gun toward the boy and hissed, "Kssshhhhh!" But I was no longer listening . . .

I listened to heavy, dull rumbling from a distance, which shook the ground beneath my feet. It lasted all that night and all morning, and on until three o'clock in the afternoon, and we stood high up on the hill outside of town, in front of our house, and watched the town gleaming with the brightness of the day. And then above us, out from behind the hills, for the last time the English, partisan airplanes attacked and the city filled with dark mushrooms of smoke, the crack of explosions, tongues of flames, plumes of water that the bombs sent spurting from the river, around which the town abruptly and fearfully gathered like a frenzied herd. The dull thudding approached quickly and became distinct explosions; among them we heard the high drone and staccato rattle of automatic weapons and guns. The smoke rose high and suddenly turned the bright, sunny day into a threatening rain of ash and dark clouds.

Down on the fields around town, little figures wearing green uniforms were running, falling to the ground, getting up and running again, in no discernible order. Along the road that passed along the foot of our hill moved columns of German automobiles, trucks, motorcycles, wagons, tanks, moving vans laden with furniture. The fighter planes stopped strafing the town after a while. They retreated behind the hill, and coming out one by one, they flew very low, right over the road, gunning and dropping bombs, which hit the panic on the road, where we could hear the whinnying of horses and the uneven noise of the buzz of motors. And then the town guns turned on us and fired very low, and one of the antiaircraft shells exploded right near the poplar growing by our house, for the planes were flying right at the level of our eyes and the gun barrels, quite low. The poplar was suddenly left ragged, shaved, and the broken branches dangled dead from the bare trunk, swinging.

"We have to get down to the bomb shelter, quick," they said. We raced as fast as we could behind the house to the shelter, but before we got there two more shells exploded near us. One of them hit the vintner's hut in the vineyard beneath us and blasted it to pieces. But we saw that only later, after we stared into the darkness for ages in the shelter, which shook from the explosions and where fine dust filtered down from the ceiling into our hair and eyes. Silence reigned for a long time in the shelter, and all of us waited anxiously for something to happen. But nothing did, except that we listened to the constant thudding of the guns, machine guns, and the screeching thunder of airplane motors when they pulled out of a dive.

After a while somebody ventured out to look and see what was going on outside. Later it was my turn. I went into the house and looked out a broken window. In front of the house, broken in bits and pieces, lay parts of our wicker garden furniture; it was there we usually ate dinner and watched twilight thicken over the town and the shining undulations of the river. Guns were still being shot, but less frequently, and nearer by. I noticed down in the vineyards some people who were hastily clambering up the hills. They stopped from time to time, sheltered by a tree or a ditch, and shot. Suddenly a tall pillar of smoke, dirt, vineyard posts, and vines erupted from our vineyard in front of the house. And then another one, a little closer. Those were mortar shells. One of the men who was running bent over suddenly straightened up, flung his arms into the air, stood tall for a few seconds as if he wanted to touch the sky and pick a ripe cloud ruddy from the setting sun, spun in place, and fell on his side among the vines, moving no more. Others ran faster toward the house. Down there, along a road winding among the vineyards that farmers had used to transport their barrels of wine every fall, came German armored vehicles, firing from large-caliber machine guns. One of the bullets came through the window, which I, crouching, was looking through with one eye, and hit the wall behind me. There it made a large hole, which I later inspected carefully. On the combat vehicles I could clearly see a cross framed in white.

I figured it would be too dangerous to stay in the house, so I turned to go back to the cellar. As I was going, I saw I was no longer by myself. In another room two men were mounting a machine gun on a windowsill, hurried and troubled. One of them had blood dripping down his forehead. Both were grimy, their expressions severe and pained. I looked at them from the door without going into the room. They started shooting and a mortar hit the windowsill. I fell to the ground, my eyes full of plaster. Something thumped me on the shoulder and my arm went limp, but at the time it didn't bother me. I got up and looked around the room. The dust from the explosion was settling, clearing the air. The machine gun was gone. The window was gone, and one of the men was gone. A large, jagged hole yawned where the window had been and through it I saw the city and the river. That is how I remember the exact shape of the hole and how much of the view it held.

The other man was lying by the door, at my feet. I looked at him, with total calm. The man was dead. He had bulging, still eyes, and one of his arms lay on his chest, or, rather, on what used to be his chest. On a filthy mess of blood and plaster, rags and bones. I remembered this image with full precision, though I wasn't thinking I'd remember it, though I wasn't even thinking I had seen it at all. But now, as time passes, I know that I did see, that I've been seeing it better and better, that I will never forget it. Then I simply turned as if I hadn't seen anything and went out of the house, meaning to go back to the shelter, and at the door of the house I met two more men, hurrying. One of them turned toward the front door of our house. I greeted him with total calm, leaning on the door frame like a real host, as if it were completely natural for me to be standing there then, and natural for him to ask me, like a man in a hurry: "Where are the other two?" and natural for me to think about it, not very long, look at my left arm, which blood was dripping down, and say, with total calm, as if it were obvious in and of itself: "They are dead. A mortar hit." And natural for him to turn at those words and leave, first with ordinary steps and then running toward the woods from the house, not turning to look back, vanishing into the branches like a ghost.

I went back to the shelter without a word. In the dark we heard armored cars going along the road by the house firing their guns, and then the door to the shelter flew open, gaping in the light gray sky, drawing our faces like a magnet, and a German soldier stood in the doorway with no helmet on, holding a machine gun, outlined in black against the sky. "Out," he barked. No one budged. We all watched how he plucked the grenade off his belt, holding it in his hand like a fancy apple, and yelled "Out!" a second time, more brusque and edgy, and out we went, one by one, squinting in the light, looking into the barrel of the machine gun, which squatted on the ground on spindly legs like some sort of gray-green bug at our feet.

Aside from the man who had opened the door, there were two more Germans in front of us: they were standing behind the machine gun.

They were out of breath and looking restlessly around, but their faces were strange and blank and I do not remember them. My arm was still bleeding and I felt weak, as if I might fall, but I didn't want to fall, and I clenched my teeth, holding myself upright only by effort of will not to look weak and so that the others wouldn't see I was hurt. A group of three or four Germans ran by the house waving their machine guns. One among them, an officer, held only a revolver. He ran over to us and, waving his revolver, shouted something in German that could not be understood. Our Germans abruptly began hurrying and hoisted the machine gun. The officer waited impatiently. A couple of them ran toward the woods, while the third lifted the machine gun and propped it against his lower arm. A moment before he began to shoot I fell toward the ground waiting for me kindly, I began to fall deep into sleep, and my eyes closed while I was still falling, which lasted a long time, giving me the time to fall asleep in the soft air before I hit the ground. I only saw how the machine gun spat fire furiously, jerking left-right and forward-back, and how others were falling around me, faster than I was, surer than me, and more eternal.

That is how my mother died, my older brother, an old retired judge who had given me a carved chess set for my most recent birthday, the wife of the vintner who had joined the partisans two years before and died in Bosnia, the son of our neighbor whom I used to play with, and a little girl who had come to stay with us from the city that morning to get away from possible air raids. The vintner's wife lived that whole night, groaning on the ground, slowly growing cold as the morning dew fell. I tried to move her, but then I fainted again. When I came to it was daybreak, and I brought her a glass of water which she no longer needed. That was how I learned that, though I was twelve years old, I was still very little and helpless. Later, grown, but still helpless.

I sat before the gleaming, sun-polished sea, on another garden chair, after so many years, alone, but inhabited by shades, like some gloomy medieval castle. I sat there and watched the children of my shadows, unable to move, appalled at the innocence in their eyes when they passed one by one near me, the corn-haired one last, seeing in me only some strange man sitting in the sun and shivering as if he were cold. I was shivering out of fear of myself, I didn't dare turn so that I wouldn't see the peaceful older people as they sat and read papers, paying no heed to the darkness and explosions all around them, they didn't hear the staccato of machine guns, they didn't notice the smoke and dust everywhere, but instead lived in the sunny, warm world of today. I concentrated on the blinding glare of the smooth sea surface to keep myself from turning.

I scarcely noticed when Gerta got back. She came over and hugged me with her long, warm arms, and I flinched convulsively as if something had singed me, as if two heavy smothering wreaths had enfolded me, the kind they lay on coffins for the dead, and I leaped up suddenly from the chair and shoved Gerta back, and turned, freezing in place. Gerta stood in a grotesque position, her arms half-raised the way I had shoved her away, her eyes mirroring astonishment. She looked at me, frightened as a bird, not understanding, afraid to move for fear she'd make the next mistake, that she'd commit the same, unknown transgression, which she had no sense of the cause or effect of.

"Forgive me," I said. "I was lost in thought and you startled me." I sank suddenly and wanted to say something nice to her, as nice as if I were speaking to myself. But I didn't know the words. "Forgive me," I said. "I didn't mean to."

Her tension visibly relaxed. But she still didn't believe me and kept looking at me suspiciously, the way a mother looks at a child whom she senses is sick.

"You really scared me!" she said.

I hugged her tightly, pulling her close, trying to show her in movements that it was over, that she needn't know any of it, that she shouldn't fear corpses, guns, the dark, me. She hugged me and soothed me as if she understood it all. But it didn't matter whether she understood or not.

"Let's go for a swim," I said, suddenly calm, and we went down to the beach where the benevolent sea readily took us in.

There, that is how I fell in love with Gerta and was happy that she was in love with me, though even that no longer mattered the most. We didn't part that whole day, or the next, or even the entire next week. I forgot all about Ćuk, Beba, the rest of town, repairing the house, I even forgot about our imminent parting. I'd run into Ćuk now and then on a street or on the beach, and he would wink at me, knowingly, as if to say: "Way to go!" Only at lunch would she and I think of the moment of parting, approaching imperceptibly but implacably, when the waiter gave us a receipt with the date, or in those night hours between dark and morning when we talked long, sleepily, about nothing in particular, loving each other without touching, from afar, each of us on his own cot.

I forgot the town, but the town did not forget me. The time came when I had to go out among people. The day was Saturday and a group of the Germans was going home, so Gerta said that she was obliged, socially, to join their farewell dinner.

"Since I haven't been with them once this whole week, which they will certainly hold against me, at least I ought to see them off."

So we agreed that I would come back late in the evening when the party was over at the hotel. I felt very strange without her, as if I were embarking on some new, interesting adventure, and my sortie into town was exciting, as if I were returning to someplace I hadn't been for years.

I stopped in at the barbershop, where they greeted me like an old friend who was coming back from a long trip, who was expected to produce travel yarns, what had happened and what had not; they were expecting shared laughter, after the return of the errant son. The barber winked mischievously, while lathering me up.

"Well, well, then . . . I see you have gotten into the . . . tourist . . . biz? . . . And so you should. You have lost a little weight, but no harm in that. Before the war it used to be the Czechs who fell into our hands, heh, heh, and some of them were damned pretty . . . now it is these German ladies. A gold mine, I tell you, what a gold mine, paradise for our boys. I say let them have their fun, let them! I saw yours . . . not bad, not bad at all. Ah, good lord, a man cannot be too picky, after all. Do you want a little trim around the edges while I'm at it?"

The barber addressed me cozily, with a profound grasp of my problems. How could they be different from everything else he had experienced so many times before? If I were to have told him, for example, that it was not what he was thinking, he would have chuckled familiarly and said: "Love, that's right, love, why not! You know, people are always saying that, a little of this and that, and then when they travel back home, it all evaporates . . . whish . . . love or no love, it all comes down to the same thing in the end. The boys have to have their fun, and the girls, too, you can be sure of that, heh, heh, that's the way it goes these days: we have to earn a little, too. You buy some, you sell some. That is tourism, my friend."

And who can guarantee that he, in the final reckoning, isn't right?

Like many others, the barber pronounced the word "tourist" with a certain scorn, generous, but scornful nonetheless, the way a man would talk of a useful but, of course, dumb dairy cow. To sit here year after year watching, over and over again, those pale, and a little later painfully red, sunburned women who were being naughty and childish, to watch silly city people on their pale, scrawny legs behaving irrationally with food, drink, swimming and sunbathing, to watch the ugly, worn-down elderly people who came from the whole world to spend their pensions or savings in this town, to watch how these foreigners fell for the amorous advances and business deals our boys put to them; no, it wasn't easy to sustain a high opinion of foreigners. Sure, the foreigner was useful, and hats off to the things he had or sold, but the foreigner himself? Please, keep that nonsense to yourself, the foreigner is a tourist! He comes here, eats himself silly, takes a shit, and leaves! Heh, and we, you know, we have to live here after he goes.

It is entirely natural that the barber assumed I was one of those boys, one of the predators strolling the beaches all day; one of those calculating partygoers who is always out to strike a deal, for a woman or a good camera, it made no difference, and he figured he had spent a pleasant summer if he took some naive fool for everything he had; that is perfectly understandable, no matter how angry it made me. He spoke with full approval of what I was doing, the way an older, more experienced man talks to a boy who is behaving precisely the way he behaved twenty years before. And I repeat, who knows? He may be right.

I paid and went out to eat, and there I bumped into Ćuk. Ćuk, as you might imagine, was already drunk. Some supposed painter was sitting with him at the table, in a black shirt buttoned up to the neck. His name was Rade, and aside from painting he worked as a middleman, buying and selling. He was, so to speak, the local pawnshop.

"Have you got anything?" he asked bluntly.

I didn't understand him right off the bat.

"A radio, watch, jeans, air mattress. Ask around, you are at the source. And other things, too, I'm sure you can figure it out . . . anything that will sell." He leered, nervously tweaking at the buttons on his shirt. "Let your brother in on the action."

So he, too, knew I was living with a German woman. He was doing his job and for him there were no problems. Rade said, "If anything turns up, I'll be here," and he went over to one of the neighboring tables, to some other people, where again he leaned over confidentially, plucking at his buttons, his jaws moving rapidly. I drank a glass of wine and glanced over at Ćuk.

Ćuk looked at me, leaning back in his chair, his head back, his eyes half shut, saying nothing. Suddenly I felt guilty for some reason.

"So, how are you living at the house?" I asked uncertainly.

"Living," said Ćuk. "Beba came back."

"I really should stop by and have a look," I said.

Ćuk didn't answer. He looked at me as if he weren't seeing me but something deep inside me, something strangely foreign. Maybe it only seemed that way, maybe Ćuk was simply drunk and looking the way drunk people look. I felt guilty somehow that I had forgotten our house and him, my friend, with whom I would live when all the others left and to whom I would surely return, just as a river flows to the sea. I felt guilty as if facing the member of some tribe I had abandoned. I felt guilty facing the priest of our unwritten faith in the armor of isolation and self-sufficiency, and me the sinning novice who has just received his robes. I felt like a traitor.

"How is Else?" I asked.

"Don't ask," said Ćuk wearily and slowly got up from the table, holding the table's edge to keep from toppling. "We are going to play billiards."

We went over to the café across the street, just as we had often done before all this happened. But nothing was as it had been before, though we were greeted by just as gleeful shouts, the loud smacking of billiard balls, the curses and boisterous kibitzing of the onlookers. A dozen people were standing around the table sipping spritzers or holding cues, which they had smeared with blue chalk. They were all intent on the game and conversed lightly, bantering words across the table through the tobacco smoke, like the much lighter and less important billiard balls.

Looking into this room where nothing had changed, I stopped at the door, where the evening when I was last here a week ago, or a year ago, or ten years ago, was still in progress. I stopped because I had suddenly seen the uniformity, the stagnation, and I wanted to tell all these people that nothing like this had happened before, that this was an apparition, that things were changing. I wanted to tell them that a certain quantity of time had passed, regardless of the same billiard balls, regardless of the repeated words, and that the last ten years had erased in us something that we were still pointlessly rewarming, that we still only imagined that we felt. I stood there helpless, feeling in myself the sly passage of time that was vanishing for good. But there were no words, then or anytime afterward, to explain this to somebody.

Somehow I was proud of the fact that I had managed in a short time to rise above the insularity of the café, above claustrophobic national feeling, and I was hurt, I was sorry that all these people, that moment, could not rise with me to the same height, the same freedom, to look at themselves, at the time behind them, precisely and objectively. But I understood, looking at the endless mathematical intersection of the billiard balls, that my pride was vain and empty: the truth was that they were not able to rise up, maybe they preferred not to, because their experience ran deeper and more ancient than mine, for every such rising would cost them dearly, and because maybe even I would not be able to stay above things when this had passed, just as I had not been able to before. It may well be that even now I was not, indeed, above anything, but merely performing for myself in a vain and selfish role, rife with bad dreams and an unresolved past, just as they were.

I stood by Ćuk, watching the billiards. Ćuk was reeling, drunk.

"No, don't go straight: rebound off the edge . . ." Ćuk was sticking his tongue out with effort, as if he himself were playing. Tensely he followed the shot. The billiard ball rolled over to his fingers on the edge, bounced off spinning around its axis, and missed, dropping slowly down the empty, spacious green table.

"Ah, it's gone, way off," they shouted. The player nervously smeared the cue with more blue chalk, wiping his fingers on his pants.

"Ten dinars down the drain," somebody said.

"Up for a game?" asked a dwarflike nameless man who spent all day here and clearly made his living at billiards.

I shook my head.

"So stingy," the man said. "What's ten dinars to you?"

"If you are low on cash, borrow some from the lady with the cute ass, why don't you," said somebody from the crowd.

"She ought to be paying for it," said the dwarf.

"Don't let yourself be fleeced," they said behind his back. "For a German woman she's not half bad."

Ćuk giggled drunkenly, swaying, studying the billiards game.

"This guy knows what he's doing," one from the group added, rubbing thumb and forefinger together. "Money, money!"

"He didn't go after her, she nabbed him. He is so much in love he can't see straight. Do you intend to change your name?" the dwarflike man asked.

"I'll change the features on your face," I said softly.

The little man continued spinning the billiard balls around the table. He chortled, "Sounds like this man's serious, gentlemen, what did I say, she has him begging for mercy."

"If you so much as open your mouth one more time I will beat the living daylights out of you," I said to him.

Movement suddenly froze in the entire group and a hush fell on the room. All at once the little man was alone in front of me, his legs akimbo, swiveling around uncertainly. There was a fight in the air.

He still hadn't caught on. It was incredible to him that what he had said could spark a fight. It had all been so ordinary and normal.

We were making small talk about the usual things, the way we always do, a little fun, what is everybody so agitated about? Some German lady? He did not want to fight about some German lady who was messing around with one of the guys the way hundreds of other German women had, and we all know why, and we all know why those things are done, so what is the point of fighting? Hey, a little teasing never hurt anyone. We joke around, we shoot a game of billiards, we have a drink, we leave, each goes his own way, do what you like, it is none of my business, but don't be a baby, we all know what you are up to, don't we?

I spun around and walked without a word toward the door and out, without turning to look back, seething inside with helpless rage, now knowing I would stay helpless to the end. I felt stiff, frozen inside, as if some very tangled but healing process had been halted in me, and as if all the material that had been engaged in that process was left unprocessed, raw, forever, in me, as if in some warehouse of useless, rusty, but stealthy and ominous weapons.

The farewell dinner on the hotel terrace was not yet over and I went back to the tent, lay dressed on the cot, and waited. I waited a long time, a long time. I smoked in the darkness and listened to the pines rustling overhead. I was still stiff and did not dare to release my muscles for fear that I might completely fall apart. I clenched my teeth so I wouldn't show myself that I was hurt, and that I was waiting mutely inside for all this to pass so that I could drift as soon as possible into sleep, to return to the everyday life of the sun and sea. I plunged my fingernails into my palms, digging them in with all my strength. To deal myself the final blow.

I was at the end of the second cigarette when Gerta came in. She did not see me until she had clicked on the lamp. "Here you are!" she shouted delighted, threw herself onto the bed, and hugged me.

"I was so afraid you would not come back." She began to take off her clothes calmly, with no self-consciousness, carefully removing her nylons so as not to rip them with her fingernails. "I had a bit too much to drink. You know, I've gotten so used to you these last few days that it was really rather odd . . . you see. We haven't been apart at all and this was the first time. I thought you might not come back."

I lay there motionless, wordless, and stared into the darkness outside the tent. You could hear how the sea was lightly lapping the beach.

"I got a telegram," I said.

She dropped the piece of clothing she had just been stowing away and halted as if frozen. The clothes dropped onto the edge of the bed, hesitated for a bit on the very edge, and then slid slowly to the floor.

"A telegram?" she asked.

"I have to return to my job immediately. I am traveling tonight."

She didn't respond. She bustled about in the dark tidying things around the tent, not approaching me. She put on the striped beach robe, went out, and after a bit she came back in and sat down heavily on the bed.

"When will you be leaving?" she asked me, wearily.

"Soon," I said.

Very soon, as soon as possible, if I don't want to stay I'd better go soon, while I still have the strength, while there is still cruelty in me, immediately, while I have the reason to do what I know I must do. Gerta, forgive me.

I have to leave, because otherwise you and I might believe that such a thing is possible, such a thing which could never happen. I have to leave, because if I were to stop believing in the teachings, in the power, in the message of the past, I would be lost, I would be left with nothing to stand on. I must go, so that you and I do not lose our countries, which are always stronger than you are and I am. I have to leave, because otherwise I might think that there really is true forgiveness and true forgetting. I must leave, because I will never be able to bear the inevitable moment of parting which our envious winged kin command us to. Forgive me, Gerta. I saw something in you, something larger than you, and forgive me that most of all. Forgive me now in a way that, if this were to go on, you would never be able to forgive me later. For in you and in me there is nothing left of who we are, and we must be subject to more powerful forces, which are always right. Which would never forgive us ever, because they have no capacity to forgive.

I arrived in front of the house around two in the morning. Turning my pockets inside out produced the key. I was startled that I still remembered I had it somewhere. The lock squeaked, as if no one had opened it for a while.

I climbed the wooden stairs, which echoed dully. The door to one of the rooms opened and Ćuk appeared, staring tensely into the darkness to see who was coming in so late.

"Oh, it's you," he said with relief when I approached the door. I stopped on the stair. Ćuk yawned, scratched his head, and turned toward the lit inside of the room. "The mosquitoes have been eating me alive," he said. "I should light one of those tablets."

"There sure are a mess of mosquitoes," I said. "There weren't as many when we first got here."

Ćuk looked me over slowly and carefully.

"Would you like something to drink?" he asked as if he were worried.

"No. Time to go to bed."

"Wait. I'll give you a bug tablet." He went into his room and brought me a box of the tablets. "Light one."

I went on up the stairs, slowly and deliberately. Here I turn left, into the room. Ćuk shouted from below: "Light two, in the ashtray. That'll get rid of them . . ."

I should light two, not one. That will get rid of them. I came into the room and opened the window wide. The cool night air wafted over me, good for sleeping. For a quick, deep sleep.

I lay down without taking off my clothes. I groped for cigarettes on the bedside table, but couldn't find any. The effort drenched me in sweat. There were no cigarettes. There was no peace of mind. My shirt stuck to my sweaty, hot back. It seemed to me, in the darkness, that my eyes would never close again. They seemed to be getting bigger and bigger, so big that all you could see was the whites. I tried to stop them from growing, but I was no longer master of my muscles. Or of anything else for that matter. I was supposed to light two tablets in the ashtray. KOK smoke tablets to get rid of mosquitoes. One began to hum the beginning of the night battle tentatively, nearing me in irregular circles. I followed it in the dark, guessing by the sound as it faltered and as it finally resolved to attack. I lay still, concentrating on feeling the place where the mosquito would land. I raised my right hand slowly, and when the mosquito perched on my temple, I struck it carefully and precisely. I should get up and light those tablets. That will get rid of them for sure. I didn't have the oomph to budge. I repeated, in my cold sweat: that will get rid of them for sure, that will get rid of them for sure, every single last one of them.

Traitors

I had meant that the story I will tell would be a story about Pierre. But if the events and people in my memory related to Pierre's fate seduce me and I end up writing more about all of us, that will be because I am trying to be accurate. I am trying to reproduce literally every detail of the story so that we can be objective and our subjectivity does not lure us into believing all manner of explanations after the fact. I fear that the simplicity of this story springs far more from the simplification of an imperfect memory than from the simplicity and logic of the events themselves. The past seems pretty pure and simple to me. The present is so tangled and tricky that you can't believe anything anymore.

I cannot, therefore, promise you the truth. Although the story started, in a manner of speaking, with me, I was, all in all, only an observer. I can relate to you in detail only what I saw. The real events are hidden deep in the people who lived them. And just as we cannot participate in those events, we cannot ask those people to explain them to us. Some of them are no longer with us. I do not mean they are dead. They are gone. We are forced, as others are for their needs, to write history.

There are no sources that might inform us precisely who Pierre's parents were, but I imagine that his father was a miner, one of those who emigrated during a time of crisis, or, rather, a man confused and weak who never, even in a completely new environment, knew how to shake off the past. All his life he never mastered the language of the country where he worked, and he lisped bilingually to the woman he married, a peasant woman from the French countryside, just as he lisped bilingually to the son she bore him on the first floor of a house in sooty, standardized workers' housing. When the father was killed, buried somewhere in a mine shaft, or lost in a traffic accident, or succumbing to tuberculosis—slowly, far from his son, in some sanatorium for miners—the wife chose to flee from the claustrophobic, grimy isolated mining town and return to the sunny vineyards, to her land. Or maybe she died, sooty with nostalgia. Or it was the work of a bomb, German or American, everybody bombed those mines. And maybe the son after that was appropriated by some Board for the Care of War Orphans, certainly an international committee. The son explained to them bilingually that he was fourteen, that he had two pairs of shoes, a name. Until his eighteenth birthday the international committee exchanged lengthy correspondence with a number of subcommittees re: under number such and such, moving him several times from orphanage to orphanage, where he would commence his schooling yet another time, and finally they shipped him to a distant relation in Zagreb, whose reputation in the eyes of her neighbors was thereby significantly elevated. And so, maybe, that is how it came to be that Pierre, at the age of twenty, took his secondary school exams privately in broken Croatian and got work as a car mechanic at a service station, where he also lived in a narrow, concrete-block room, with no friends.

All this demonstrates how limited the imagination is and how it tends to seek well-trod routes. Nothing can be fabricated, everything has already happened. Pierre's fate may have been different than what I've described, but this one fits him as if it had been tailor-made. It is, so to speak, logical. We needn't fear that the parts that are fabricated and different than Pierre's real fate might influence the further course of events or the objectivity of our judgment: the very fact that this story can, on the basis of known facts, be told in many and varied (though every bit as familiar) ways shows just how irrelevant that is.

If we set aside interpretations, guesswork, and fancy, we are left with bare facts, which I shall not distort at any cost. Pierre was rather small and runtlike. He had a funny little head with big ears and glasses that were larger still. Behind the thick lenses blinked his frightened, gray-green eyes, watery and timid. And that was how he moved, too: nervously and timidly, holding his hands out in front of him as if at any moment he might bump into something. His hands were skinny, long-fingered, cautious—he touched things as if they were hot. He dressed in haphazard, sacklike clothing, but his shoes were unbelievably polished, very noticeable, all the more so for his ducklike, awkward waddle. He spoke brokenly, frequently repeating segments of sentences; he made mistakes with accents and prepositions. He never could properly pronounce the letter "r"; the best he could do was try: Piehrrrr.

Despite all this he was always smiling; he scoffed at his own failings with good humor, joining in with others, even exaggerating his faults, to spark laughter. He accepted derision as a compliment, harsh jokes as a special honor. At the burst of laughter he, too, would laugh, staring anxiously around, peering into the faces of others as if to insure himself against some invisible danger, or maybe merely seeking confirmation that they were indeed laughing at *him*, at his self-effacement, not at some other person or thing but at him, Pierre. He was surrounded by people, their laughter, and therefore—he existed. All that he could share with those around him was a mocking grin of half-scornful acceptance: Pierre knew the value of that precious commodity. He wanted a place, he wanted to be somewhere and have others accept him as one of theirs. He knew that this price was greater than all he had paid until then. He was ready to pay:

only it was hard to say what currency one pays with. Not everybody's sacrifices are accepted. Maybe no one is actually able to pay
that price. Maybe it is just one of those things. Or maybe the endless sacrifice of a runty shortsighted auto mechanic was only one
form of paying everybody's price.

It all would have been easy if he had had a friend. But he didn't.
No one took him seriously enough to be his friend. He wanted a
friend more than anything in the world. He worked hard to earn
one, and created newer and harsher jokes on his own account,
encouraged by general derision. People gladly invited him everywhere—to parties, dances, summer vacations. Maybe they didn't
invite him, but he did show up everywhere anyway, and always
went home from wherever he was alone. To the concrete-block
room where he would study all night to the point of exhaustion
to avoid thoughts, or to avoid something which in his scrawny
head resembled thoughts.

He wanted a girlfriend and he worked hard to find one. But
girls did not take him seriously; they did not consider him manly.
Girls behaved freely in front of him, without affectation, as if he,
too, were a girl. They felt no embarrassment in his company and
did not take him seriously. He would head home alone after
socializing with girls, walking down Petrinjska Street to the train
station, and find women who were looking for a little extra money
for their train ticket. Out of principle he never went to prosti-
tutes. He would sit until morning in Adria-Bar or the train-sta-
tion restaurant, and in his broken Croatian he would talk to
whores who hadn't found a client, baring his heart to them, welcoming their confidences in exchange for his. And then he'd go
back to the concrete-block room alone, with a bottle of cognac,
disgusted with himself, his face a grimace.

That was why Beba and I were startled when we ran into him
on the terrace of the Golden Point. I couldn't say precisely

whether the surprise was good or bad. In this town on the sea we were cut off in a special, separate world; we had lost our sense of the past and future, of responsibilities, of the people we were attached to. Catching sight of Pierre so suddenly was as if everything had surfaced at once (the city, streets, pavement, grime, nagging worries, illness, politics), here, in the final haven. I felt as if I were an Indian watching helplessly as they laid railway tracks through my last hunting grounds. As to how Beba felt, I couldn't say. She was grinning.

"Hey, there's Pierre!" she said while we danced.

Pierre was dancing pretty far away from us, in the semi-dark, in a corner of the covered terrace. I couldn't see whom he was dancing with because the woman kept dancing with her back turned toward us. Here, I'm thinking, this is the place where I have a chance to say that even now, as I write this, I still feel that same flash of guilt, the same qualm I always felt whenever I ran into Pierre (guilt in the name of all of us) and which I felt then as well, on that carefree terrace.

I was always the most prickly member of our gang of friends, and I behaved particularly badly toward Pierre. His comedy routines aggravated me, his unending fake smile, his slimy ingratiating manner, the imposition of friendship which I did not want in the least grated on me. I tolerated him in company and went along laughing with the others, but I always felt disgust mixed with scorn and pity. His self-humiliation filled me with a profound sense of shame, as if it were my own. Whenever I found myself alone with him, I never knew what to talk about and what to say. Sometimes it almost seemed as if this put me in a greater fix than it did him. It irked me even more because I felt so superior. Sometimes in situations when I was witness to his humiliation or awkward scenes with women, I felt sorry for him. He was sweet, in his own way. But I had my own friends and my own worries. To accept his friendship would mean to accept his torment. That would be too much, brother, I have plenty of worries of my own.

Beba and I both knew Pierre from before. I found space between the heads of the dancers and waved. His thick glasses flashed opaquely and cheerfully from the distance.

We went back to our table to bring the news. Ćuk was sitting there, half drunk as usual. The skipper of the ferry that would take us back into town was grim, drunk, and sarcastic, as usual. An ugly girl who was sitting next to him and hanging on his arm gazed at him amorously. She was obviously enormously impressed by the fact that he was paying her no attention at all. He, of course, was somebody who never paid attention to anyone. He drove the ferry line staring into the distances where he would never voyage, and he drank staring into his glass. He was looking into his glass.

"Pierre is here," I announced.

"On this very terrace?" asked Ćuk, listlessly.

"Small world," said the ugly girl. We all looked at her as if she had said something shocking. "Isn't it small? Don't they say that?"

"Too small," said the driver, startled that she was there at all.

Ćuk grimly toyed with crumbs on the tabletop and said, "Just what you need. At least Beba won't have to console you anymore."

"Jackass," I said angrily.

"Cool it," said Beba.

"Tell me, Beba, sincerely, has he bared his heart to you?"

"Jackass," I said, and sat down.

"Did he suffer terribly? Did you take pains to console him?"

"Shut up," said Beba. "You're drunk."

"I will. What matters is that Pierre is here. Surrounded by whiners I can be happy. I need nothing more in life."

Pierre came over to the table, bumbling and nearsighted as ever. Behind him came the girl with whom he had been dancing.

"Hello there, boys," said Pierre, peering nervously from face to face. He turned vaguely toward the girl behind him. "Do you know Vehhra?"

"Of course we know Vera," said Ćuk without even raising his eyes.

We did, indeed, know Vera. I half rose to greet her. She was just as beautiful as ever. Even more, maybe. A slender, blond girl with fabulous legs. She had long blond hair in a ponytail. Pale, blond, fantastically smooth skin. A blue blouse and a very wide, bell-shaped, slightly darker blue skirt. I don't know many streets where heads wouldn't turn, as if on a string, when she walked by. She had a sneer around the lips and nose as if something smelled distasteful. That is the kind of beauty she was. That is, so to speak, a sneer of class. You know what I mean: I know everybody is looking at me, but I don't care. Or maybe: how dare you stand there, can't you see that I am slated for somebody better than you?

"Everybody who is anybody knows Vera," said Ćuk to his darling crumbs.

"Pierre, how did you get here, Pierre?" I asked him.

"A train. Choo-choo-choo. Too-tooooo."

Then he flung himself among the tables in search for chairs for Vera and for himself. Meanwhile, Vera stood like a statue by our table, from which the emanating smells were apparently most distasteful. She stood like an insulted dignitary. Pierre clumsily arranged the chair for Vera, clearly terribly concerned that she be comfortably seated.

"Hunt down a pillow, why don't you," said the driver.

Vera smiled for the first time only when Pierre sat down. She smiled straight at Pierre.

"This is a great terrace," he said, returning the smile.

"It is," said Vera heroically.

It was clear that she was confused (the way insulted beauties are confused) and that she felt awkward being seen by all of us with Pierre, just as it was obvious as well that Pierre was thrilled to be seen by all of us with Vera. But, clearly, he is not the only one of us who would have been thrilled, or she the only one who would have felt awkward: it was all pretty easy to figure out.

Less easy to figure out was how this had happened at all. I noticed a change in Pierre: he was beaming. Not just in a good mood, not just cheerful, but beaming. As if filled with a deep inner glow. He was still a one-man comedy act who entertained the company at his own expense, but the comedy act seemed more sincere, less bitter, without that anxious peering into the faces of others, without all the restless fidgeting about where he might flee. As if he were, for the sake of argument, a man in love. Like some pauper who has found himself suddenly surrounded with unexpected riches and doesn't know what to reach for first, and where to start enjoying himself.

I found Vera's frame of mind equally perplexing. She seemed like a girl unhappily in love. Certainly what was happening did not leave her indifferent. She was forcing herself to maintain a cheerful facade and smiled as seductively as usual, though now at Pierre (instead of at me), but it was a front, maybe a little shaky, checking our faces as if trying to judge what we thought of it all. I looked over at Ćuk. Ćuk was investigating the color of the wine, holding the bottle up to look through it at the light. Nothing, I said to myself, nothing. She has forgotten that we don't think.

But Beba's reaction was worrisome. At first for a while she assessed Vera's good looks with curiosity and admiration, and then she whispered, "Catch this number! Have you seen her legs? This touches the male part of my character. She has got to be as stupid as they come."

"No," I said, "just too beautiful."

"Whatever can she see in Pierre? I could swear that something is going on between the two of them. Isn't there? And look at him! He is strutting around as if he caught God by the beard. Isn't that

the same Vera you used to date? At the university? I remember—
you kept it a secret, as if you were ashamed, you know?"

"I was not ashamed," I laughed.

"I know. You are a sucker for stupid women. Stupidity is your
blood group. You even used to like me—before, I mean—because
you thought I was a featherbrain."

"Who says I don't still like you?"

"But whatever does that dish see in Pierre? Whatever has gotten into her? Somehow I can smell that this is no game, that this
is, you know, serious."

That was when Beba began to study Pierre.

She studied him for several days the way that only Beba knew
how to study somebody, the way a hawk stares before it plum-
mets lightning-fast onto its victim from above. She studied him
until a day when we all went out for a walk in the afternoon,
all four of us, and when it turned out that Beba and Pierre
took a path along the water's edge, covered by the murmuring
of the pine trees, almost embracing, while Vera and I stopped
in at Golden Point and sat on the high stools at the bar, drinking double cognacs, sentimentally admiring our good looks in
the mirror, among the bottles. She, of course, had something
to admire.

The troubles started when we ordered our second round of
double cognacs, and when the weak lights in the restaurant flickered on. From the terrace you could hear music and the clinking
of dinnerware. I poured a little of my cognac on the bar and stubbornly sketched sad, soggy figures on the smooth, Formica surface with my finger.

"Let's get drunk," said Vera.

"Yes, let's," I said. "We are drunk already, anyway."

"I'm going back to Zagreb tomorrow."

I looked her over carefully, and then I sketched on the bar the face of somebody who drowned ages ago. I said, "You only got here a couple of days ago."

She looked to me as if she were about to burst into tears, but then I remembered that Vera never cries.

"Is it action you are after?" I asked. "*Alte Liebe* and that sort of thing? . . ."

She chuckled, in a way that suits a true beauty: "I have had quite enough of that for the time being. Time for a break."

I ordered yet another round of double cognacs as consolation for the losers. By the time we drank them down, I was drunk.

"Do you want me to tell you a little secret?" Vera said.

"In the name of bygone love, I will keep my silence like the grave. I swear that I will be as silent as a fish. I am, after all, the fish king."

Vera listened to me carefully and would have listened more, just as I could have gone on talking drunkenly if I hadn't noticed that she was listening far too carefully.

"I am going to have a baby," she said after a pause.

"Forgive me," I said and traced a fish on the bar.

Instead of the ermine robes of a fish king, confessional robes slowly draped my shoulders. I shouldered my duties: to take the confessions of others, to rule incognito over my unwilling subjects.

"With Pierre?" I asked hoarsely.

"Yes," said Vera. "I'm in my second month."

"What will you do?" I inquired.

"Nothing. I'll have the baby. I will have a chubby baby."

"So it is serious."

"What is serious?"

"This business with Pierre. I had figured it couldn't be."

"Nothing is serious if you mean whether I mean to marry him. I will not get married."

"Now or never?"

"Never. I don't love him. It means nothing and I won't get married. But I actually think I should probably get an abortion. Though I would like to have a chubby baby, like the one I mentioned earlier while you listened benevolently. Maybe I will after all."

"That's fine if it is all up to you."

"It's not. But it would be great."

"How did you come to get involved with Pierre in the first place?"

"I don't know. It happened. He was so miserable and everybody made fun of him. He was terrified of me. You know how fearful he was of me? He feared me so much that he didn't even dare to talk to me before. I liked that—and, besides, he was in love with me. Differently, at least at first. In awe. Then it turns out that nothing is different. Or maybe that it is too different. Whatever, I don't know. I tried to love him, because no one else did and because I knew he loved me as he'd love any other girl, and I wanted to teach him to tell me from the rest. He was afraid at first, and then he wanted me to be his mother. He couldn't tell me from the rest. He couldn't even tell me from his mother. I had to comfort him a lot. That was nice. After a while it wasn't so nice. He kept crying. What goes around comes around. He probably cried because I don't. In company he would put himself in awkward situations, he even wanted me to join in his antics. To make fun of myself. He got moodier and moodier and was angry whenever I spoke to anyone. Then we stopped going out. Then he would get hurt when I told him he was a big ape, a comedian, a crybaby, and that what he needed was a nurse, not a girlfriend. Then we came here. And now it is over."

"Does he know?"

"No. I haven't told him. You can't tell something like that to a person like him. He would go berserk. He wouldn't be able to sleep, worrying about what will come of it all. He would scream at me as if it was all my fault."

"Maybe you should tell him anyway."

"Why? What does he have to do with this baby? It is mine. I made it, it just so happens I made it with him. I was the one who was careless, not he. He isn't capable of looking after anyone. Why talk to him? It is over now, anyway."

"Has he lost his interest in you?"

"How do I know? I don't care. He doesn't say anything, as if everything is fine, and he and I both know that nothing is fine. I see that he is circling around Beba, but he doesn't mention a single word about her. As if she isn't even there. As if everything is fine and dandy. I guess I wasn't a good enough mother for him. He is looking for a better mother so he can whimper in her lap, so he can tell her all about how he is so alone and how no one likes him and how everybody laughs at him . . . They should. They shouldn't like him. He should be put out of his misery. The half-wit."

"Maybe he just hasn't figured it out. Maybe it all happened too quickly for him to figure it out," I said unconvincingly to the woman in front of me.

"He has understood all he is capable of understanding. He can't go any further. He will never be able to go any further. He cannot love anyone. He was on his own too long. He would simply disappear if he were to love somebody. He'd melt away into his love. He exists only in his need to love somebody. If you take that away, you have taken all he has. What could justify that? I mean, what could justify him to himself? How could he explain to himself all that joker business, the make-believe, the fear, the cruelty, the selfishness? You tell me that, Mr. Wiseguy. It is easy to be generous in somebody else's shoes. It is easy to understand from here and say: it isn't the poor kid's fault. I don't care whether he is wrong or not. For me he's wrong. Just as I am wrong, for me. It is all their fault, if you understand me, all their fault."

Vera downed her cognac to the last dregs and banged her glass on the bar.

"Two more," she said wildly, "because it is all their fault."

The waitress looked at us suspiciously.

"It's all his fault," Vera told her, pointing at me. And I felt, again, as if she must be right.

I saw Vera to the hotel, where we learned that Pierre had not gotten back yet. The same thing happened the next night, and so it went on day after day. Vera kept getting more unhappy, and I was getting guiltier. I began avoiding them, so the walks continued as a threesome: Vera, Beba, and Pierre. I tried talking to Beba, but she did not want to hear me. She was angry and overwrought. Vera kept announcing she was about to depart, but she never did. I escorted her often to the hotel, where we'd ask for Pierre. She cried in the stairwell on her way up the stairs, alone and beautiful, to her room. I comforted her as much as I could, but I couldn't ease the insult to her pride and I couldn't lighten the burden of misfortune. Now she wanted (maybe) for me to love her (now) and let her see it, but I could not. I was far too guilty and I didn't want to load onto my back yet another sin: compassion. I comforted her in the hotel stairwell, before the eyes of the sleepy night porter who winked at me behind her back. I would go back home thinking about all of them, but especially about Beba, who was like a sister to me.

And so it was that I came home once, opened the door, and suddenly felt as if I was awfully tired. I saw before me the narrow, steep, wooden staircase, and I knew I would not be able to climb up. The sea has drunk me to the dregs, I thought. Ćuk squinted down from the landing, took a look at me, and figured it out.

"Do you want some wine?" he asked, grabbing a bottle from somewhere.

"Sure," I said and sat on the threshold.

Ćuk brought the bottle and a glass, and sat down beside me. We drank chilled home-brewed wine, which was fairly foaming in the glass. We sat on the threshold looking into the darkness of the long, twisting street. A cat glided silently by our feet.

"Beba's not back yet?" I asked.

"Nope," said Ćuk curtly, after a pause. (Only the slightest tinge of something peeved, even disgruntled maybe, in his voice.) I looked at the ember on his cigarette. We heard, in the silence, a bell.

"We have to save Beba," he said suddenly, "from stupidity."

I took a breath, about to shoot from the hip, say something cynical, make a joke (as always), but I stopped. I waited. I felt that Ćuk was struggling with how to say what he wanted. I struggled with his struggle.

"We both have known Beba for a while," he said. "This has never happened to her yet. I think that she is making a mistake. I don't remember that she has ever made a mistake—not like that, you know what I'm trying to say. To make a mistake."

"To err is natural, said the rooster, leaping off the duck," I said to my half-empty glass. To that chilled consoler which never errs.

"Sure," said Ćuk.

"Come on, don't be a child," I said. "Why get angry just like that?"

"I am already at half-mast," said Ćuk. He flicked the butt way across the street. The butt made an elegant arc of light and landed like a firefly on the wall across the street. "The thing is we have to save her. Everything depends on it. You and I depend on it."

"Begin at the beginning," I said.

"There is no beginning. Everything is middle. It is only about us. Get serious for just a minute and tell me: what good are we without Beba?"

"What do you mean, we?"

"What are we worth without any one of us? What good are we without you, and, I hope, without me? Pieces of an . . . an idea. Of course, no one has come up with the idea yet, formulated it, but it's there. I wasn't aware of it for ages, but it is there. You know that it is there and that it . . . obliges. You've felt its yoke. But she hasn't yet. Beba, I mean. She is female. She is glad to be here with us, but she doesn't know what it means to be with us. She has no idea how privileged she is. She has no idea how much privilege she gives us."

"Forgive her, oh Lord," I said.

"Maybe it is better if she doesn't know. Cheaper. But she is one of our kind and we have to save her, not for her sake, see, not for her sake, but for ours. You couldn't escape, she can't either; no one can. There is nowhere to go. It isn't just that some hollow idea is going to evaporate, some sense of togetherness; it is we who are going to evaporate. You will pop like a soap bubble."

"I thought I did," I said.

"So you did. Absolutely right. You popped. A soap bubble. Me, too. And Beba doesn't exist if you think about it—what do we know about who she is? We are here, *we* exist, we are contained in all of us, in each of us. You and me and Beba and others. We determine what each of us is individually. You can't have it any other way. She may not be aware of that and that is why in her case the clearest beginnings of betrayal are so visible. She, who was the center, will be the first to ditch us, in the name of something that doesn't even exist."

"Each of us is a little bit the traitor," I said, conciliatory.

"Sure, betrayal is part of our credo. We are together precisely because each of us is a little bit the traitor. But to betray the betrayal means to be a true traitor. To be truly faithful to something, outside of us, genuinely to rely on something, that is betrayal. It means to be weak, to let yourself be bought."

"I know," I said.

"You know. That is why I am telling you, because you get it. Beba we have to save. For her own good."

We thought about it for a while.

"I feel sick," I said.

"From the wine?" asked Ćuk, as if relieved by the change of subject.

"No," I said, "not from the wine."

We sat there looking out into the darkness, we, like medicine men of our little tribe with the burden of responsibility on our shoulders. In the cool night air soaked in the smell of wet fishing nets, which fishermen, somewhere on the invisible piers, were moving from their boats to the shore, empty. We sat feeling sick because of the need to be cruel. We were like tyrants who send subjects to death in order to preserve the meaning of tyranny and the meaning of subject. We were salvaging fallow land in which only we knew how to live, destroying the sprouts of infectious weeds. We sat like a couple of nocturnal, sage, motionless owls.

We heard footsteps on the street. A man trudged by us slowly, carrying a fish spear, mumbling something like a greeting.

"She still hasn't gotten back," Ćuk said.

"She'll come," I said. It couldn't be any other way. It didn't dare be any other way. I was hoping that we wouldn't have to undertake anything; that our shared life, which we cared so much about, would flow on of its own accord.

"Each of us is a little bit the traitor," said Ćuk, as if we hadn't stopped talking, "because each of us from the start has been nourishing an ambition which is the germ of our ruin. We know we cannot fulfill the ambition. We pretend it doesn't matter to us anyway. We try not to think about it. And that is good. We sidestep the ambition itself, and that is best of all."

Suspicious, I shrugged. I knew these theories; one has to find one's happiness in sacrifice! Wealth in poverty! The world in a nutshell!

"You tried to wing off on a tangent. Not because you wanted to, because you are no longer in a state where you can want, you have run from it for too long, you know the danger too well—not because you wanted to, but because you had to. It happened. It came your way. But you know you cannot move mountains. Beba hasn't figured that out yet. She is in the grip of a danger she doesn't even see. She is capable of destroying herself, and us, in a snap. She has the ambition. She thinks she can."

"She always has been an ambitious girl," I said.

"That is what bothers me. She has gotten the greatest ambition of all into her head. She wants to live a full, free life, or something like that. Not only does she want to break away from us, separate herself from us. She'd like to create something. She'd like to sacrifice herself for something, save somebody, at the very least. She'd like to love, you might say, in a healing, salvatory kind of way. She'd like to have something we haven't got, which would be hers alone; she'd like to be proud of herself: I've succeeded where the others haven't!"

"I can see why she would," I said.

"You can?" said Ćuk belligerently. "It is only vanity that leads to chaos. She had her place and her role among us. Doesn't she have to be the way we are . . . crippled?"

"Maybe she already is. What do we know?"

"If she is, then she knows it. Then there is no danger. Then she will do her duty to the end. I mean, she is not only her own person, she is the girl for all of us. It is her duty to be the center of the community, of our idea, to be what we'll believe in, what we count on."

"In a word, not to be herself."

"Better for her if she isn't herself. But I am not saying this for her sake, I don't care much about her personally. You know that."

"I know," I said, though I didn't.

"We have to save her so that we can salvage our hearth and home—in her we save ourselves. We save a world we have managed, I don't know how, to create. A world without unhappiness and without happiness, for it is a world where happiness and unhappiness are the same. A world of cards, but for us the only world we've got."

"Beba will be back," I said, all at once absolutely certain she would. Don't worry: everybody comes back. Beba, too, would be back.

I knew that there were other people seeing to it. I thought a little about Beba and Pierre and I knew that others were looking after us so well that we didn't have to lift a finger. And I felt much better that we didn't have to. I sighed with relief because I knew I wouldn't have to tyrannize anyone. Other people were working for me just as they had worked against me. The *for* and the *against* were the same, like everything else in the world built of cards, which we, I don't know how, had not created ourselves at all. Other tyrants chased us into this corral and would see to it that we didn't wander. Other tyrants who are for us and against us, for Beba and against Beba, for poor Ćuk, community priest, and against poor Ćuk, member of that same community.

"Beba will be back," I said to Ćuk.

"I know," Ćuk said. "I just spouted a whole heap of nonsense."

It was easier for us, and now the old sorrow, which there had been enough of without all of this, descended upon us like the great shadow of the street. We sat there, silent, staring aimlessly into the darkness.

"It would be smart to find a third for cards," I said to Ćuk, resigned.

∽

And so it was that we played cards and drank, went fishing, danced on the terrace, watched how the calm was replaced by southerly gusts, how mackerel and bluefish and sardines began moving into the waters, how the figs ripened, and how a new, cloudy white wine began to appear in the little wine cellars. Beba, Vera, and Pierre took long walks, the three of them, talking late into the night, getting drunk, cutting themselves off from us, that small, unhappy, special world of three people for whom everybody else was superfluous. Vera had red eyes every morning from insomnia and crying; Pierre got edgier, gloomier, he avoided us when we asked him things, and he'd seek our sympathy and our confidence when he couldn't stand it anymore. Once there was a fistfight between him and Ćuk, and after that (as always) Pierre and I spent a whole night walking along the waterfront—a cold wind was blowing, which chilled us to the bone—so that he could unburden his heart to me: how sorry he was that he had had a fight with Ćuk, but that he couldn't do things any other way, that everybody was set against him, and that now when he needed it most of all, no one respected him, and they liked him even less because he was a foreigner and hadn't gotten his university degree and because he didn't know the language well, and how he had always been alone and that I was his only friend (which was a lie), and that only I understood him (a lie), and he nearly burst out crying talking about how he really loved Beba and not Vera at all, and that he couldn't figure out how to get rid of Vera, who was pestering him and plaguing him with her jealousy (which was the most brazen of lies), and that Ćuk was on her, Vera's, side, and that he, Pierre, hated him. He was in bad trouble and he no longer had even enough money to stay on in this town and pay for drinks for two women, and could I lend him a little cash, and could I put in a good word for him with Beba, and could I talk Vera into leaving as soon as possible, and it can well be imagined that I did none of these things, because I had had it, and I went to bed and left him, insulted, on the waterfront, where he was nearly ripping out clumps of his hair in fury at himself.

Beba, too, became edgier and less tolerant. In the morning she would get up ready and angry, like a person who hadn't really slept at all but rather had agonized on the bed hardly able to wait for morning. She wouldn't respond to our questions, she wouldn't make us tea with rum the way she used to, but she'd go out to meet with Pierre and Vera, and she'd be nowhere to be found until late at night, when she would come in ever so quietly, so as not to wake us, only because she wanted to avoid our questions and our looks. Sometimes we'd see her swimming, or in a bar, or dancing in the evening, but never alone. Always in the company of Vera and Pierre, and you could see that they were constantly discussing something, debating, gesturing, almost always serious, Vera with her eyes red, Pierre bewildered and edgy, Beba angry and sharp.

And then one day Vera left. I saw her to her seat in the train car; we talked about the baby and about her parents, who would faint when they heard, since it was already too late for an abortion. When the train departed, both of us sighed with relief. Vera stood at the window of her car waving to me as if she were bidding farewell forever. But she wasn't. I was just a person who happened to be standing on the platform.

Vera left, but the feeling of guilt did not. We all kept feeling ashamed of something, and we all kept playing cards and drinking, expecting something to happen. But, of course, nothing did. Beba kept being angry, frantic; Pierre kept edgily trying to cheer her up, he hovered around her, but you could see that these were the gestures of a man in misery who was doing all he could to hold on to what was left. I was sorry for Beba that she was tormenting herself so, but I couldn't help her. No one could do anything. I was especially sorry for Beba when all of us went together to see off Pierre, who finally had to go back to Zagreb.

Ćuk and I stood by Beba like two guardian angels, maliciously watching Pierre, bungling and disheveled, as he stood by the window of his train car. We didn't say a word, but rather grinned vengefully, feeling our victory and savoring our superiority, again, as it once had been. Our faces said that all was as it had been before, that nothing had changed, that the scales had returned to their natural equilibrium after a temporary disturbance due to our negligence. Pierre, an outsider and a clown, was standing by the window of his car (a circus car), which was taking him back to his true place. And we, the only chosen ones, the only kin in the world of cards, were standing on a platform where plenty more trains would arrive and plenty more trains would depart. Beba was biting her lip, feeling our presence, afraid that we were blaming her, still not knowing that there was nothing we could blame her for. Nothing at all.

His face, bewildered and nearsighted, peered from the window until the train had pulled far away from the station, but he never raised a hand in farewell. It was late fall, and Pierre seemed to be the only person leaving on that train. There was no one on the platform but us and the engineer. The engineer went into his office, slamming the door, and the three of us were left alone, people suddenly happy again, full of cheer, looking forward to adventure.

"So, it's off for a drink, then, is it?" said Ćuk, rubbing his hands together as if he had just negotiated some great deal.

We were starting out well. I swiveled to look once more at the empty platform.

"He's not your brother," said Beba, not knowing what I was looking at.

That night it started raining, the first of the long autumnal rains, which finally convinced us to leave. We were alone again and drunk at Golden Point, among the last of the lingering guests, who were as indifferent and strange to us as we were to them. Summer had ended in fall, just as every year, every single year, ends no matter how it seems at one time or another. We were among the indifferent natives, confirming in them our own isolation.

Beba got nastily drunk. I noticed that she no longer minded how much she was drinking. She drank down her drinks in a particular, drunken way, draining them to the last drop, and had fits of some sort of forced, hysterical laughter. Other people could see that all was not right with Beba.

I told Beba she should go out onto the terrace a bit, collect her wits, cool off.

She swung abruptly around at me, red in the face, ugly and disheveled, and screamed, furious: "Is that what you're thinking? . . . That I'm drunk? . . . Does it bother you? Maybe I'm embarrassing you? Flush the toilet, mind your own business."

I looked vaguely around the hall. People were laughing drunkenly and derisively. I lightly touched Beba's elbow and said softly: "You goose. You are as drunk as a cork. Come on, I'll go out with you."

"Flush that toilet!" Beba howled, backing off from me, yanking the tablecloth with her, and the glasses on the tablecloth. The glasses overturned, and a smudge of moisture spread quickly across the white of the cloth. Beba was holding her glass, half full. "What's wrong? You are trailing me around like some bloodhound. Are you my father, is that it?"

I said nothing, stood there, and looked at her. She quieted down, stood where she'd been standing, drank down her drink, and calmly concluded: "Flush the toilet." Then she laughed hysterically, good-natured and a little befuddled, and added, looking me straight in the eyes, coquettishly: "Pour me another one, be a pal."

I filled her glass, and carrying it, she followed me out onto the covered terrace surrounded by a forest of driving rain, where she leaned against the white stone wall, bowing her head and closing her eyes as if she were asleep, and where her glass dropped from her hand, hit the rocks somewhere way down below at the dark foundation of the terrace, shattering with a smash, like a lightbulb. Beba wasn't sleeping, she was crying. She wept silently, convulsed with repressed sobs, leaning against the wall, turned toward the dark mass of the sea, clouds, and rain, hiding from me, and then she burst out crying aloud, holding nothing back, wailing from the depths. She leaned on my shoulder. I hugged her, feeling how her tears were drenching my shirt.

"I am drunk, you can see how drunk I am," she sobbed into the curve between my chin and my collarbone. "It is disgusting to see a woman drunk like this."

I couldn't laugh. I saw how a light was moving out over the water pretty far away, maybe a boat, in the sheet of rain.

"I wanted to get dead drunk, drunker than . . . I've ever been. You know what I mean . . . let it all go to hell," she said in a voice full of deep, drunken grief.

I was silent. I knew.

"I've been feeling guilty," she said simply.

"Why?" I asked and I couldn't help laughing. Words like that simply didn't sit right with her. They weren't her vocabulary. That was not the language of a good old tough cookie from Zagreb. Feeling guilty?

"Haven't you ever felt pangs of guilt? When you worm your way in and then make a mess of everything . . . When you elbow yourself in somewhere where you don't fit, and afterward you feel ashamed. You do something wrong to other people only because you are a . . . selfish beast."

I patted her lightly on the back, as if soothing a horse. She sank into a trance: she moved away from me, pulled out of my arms, and, all tearful, disheveled, stared out into the darkness, as if that irreparable mistake of hers was out there somewhere.

"And what's worst, you can't ever . . . you can't ever forget it or fix it . . . it is going to stay in my permanent possession . . . Like some disaster of a prom dress: the prom is over, you came out looking awful, and you cannot throw the dress away."

She calmed down a little, smiled through her tears, and looked at me.

"Sorry to foist all this on you. These are my things . . . you needn't listen at all . . . we know each other so little after all, just the dances, the parties, you know . . . we hardly ever talk, really."

"There isn't much to talk about. Really."

"I know. There isn't. But now I can't keep it in anymore. When we can't keep it in anymore, that's when we talk. Whom can I talk to if not you? Who will listen to me?"

I would listen to you, of course I would. Who else would listen, you good old Zagreb tough cookie with guilt pangs! I'd listen to you as if I were the last confessor in a world from which all the confession-takers had disappeared, along with everybody who came to them to confess. There are probably lesser things one could talk about. I was overwhelmed by a huge sympathy for this woman who had only me to be with, and for myself who was only with her.

"Is it a sin to want a little happiness? A little love? Is it a sin to look for something we have all forgotten already: something maybe romantic, maybe sentimental . . . Is it something we are only supposed to see in other people? Experience only at the expense of others, over their dead bodies?"

I laughed.

"Who is the dead body here? Vera? Pierre?"

"I don't know who the dead bodies are. Maybe he is. Maybe all of us are dead bodies. Something has been killed, and it is my fault. I was selfishly trying to be a part of their love, not just to share it but to wreck it, to replace Vera. I wanted their love because I had none of my own. I never did have . . . and I won't ever. I am a little bit in love with all of you . . . we went everywhere together, and even now . . . but that's not what I mean . . . that is something kind of collective in a way . . . we love each other, but not quite . . . it's on the surface, I guess."

"We help each other survive," I said.

"We just need each other, that's all . . . the whole crowd, to drink, mess around, to keep ourselves going, pass the time . . . but they were different . . . you could see it. And I saw it, that they were different, they loved each other from inside . . . yes, from inside, with their souls, and they were apart from me, from you, from all of us, from everything . . . Vera and Pierre, doesn't that sound just like Bonnie and Clyde, or Romeo and Juliet?"

"No," I said shortly.

"It does to me. They didn't need anyone else. They were complete by themselves. They soared. As if they didn't belong to us . . . to our crowd or to the world . . . as if they didn't even need it . . . As if they belonged to one another. We always wanted to belong to one another that same way . . ."

"To a point," I said, a little hurt, I can't say just why.

"They didn't have that point. That is real belonging. They were one. They didn't want me. OK, so maybe I am foolish and superficial, maybe I am vulgar and have no feelings at first glance, maybe everything is just a joke with me . . . but I have to belong, in the end, somewhere . . . not to you, that is to us, but somewhere just like that, deeply, forever . . . I wanted their relationship to glow in me, too, I wanted to drink from the same source of that love . . . I didn't want anything bad, did I? I wanted them to take me into their secret fold, I didn't want them to slam the doors of paradise in my face."

"And I was thinking it was all just about Pierre," I said softly.

"I don't know. He is so ugly and pitiful. All of his charm is in the fact that nobody loves him, that he is alone in the world. But I know that Vera found in him . . . something secret and precious we

hadn't noticed . . . Doesn't it bother you sometimes that we are all
so superficial . . . we never see anything . . . deeper . . . but she
did, she dug something out of him, something new, untainted,
something special that we haven't got . . . You see, I wanted to find
in him, scrawny and half blind as he was, what she found . . . She
was proof to me that it was in him somewhere . . . you just had to
look for it . . . I wanted this to be our thing . . . I wasn't shutting
Vera out (or maybe I was later on) . . . our thing and no one else's,
something that no one had ever discovered before us, something
that none of us contained by ourselves, but that only existed in that
shared discovery. Something that we had somehow forgotten to
look for. No, it wasn't love, or at least it wasn't only love; it seems
to me that it was something more, something further beyond reach
. . . like looking for coziness and warmth that is hidden in entirely
different things and not where we usually look for them . . . That
is different, much deeper, and more serious than what we probably
always figured we wanted: to be separate, to stick together on the
basis of those few values a person can still believe in, and we pro-
claimed everything that wasn't ours invalid! . . . I felt like a novice
who has just taken his vows and is beginning to grasp the gravity
of his oath. I saw through the meaning of our isolation, which was
pointless because there isn't . . . anything of what you can find . . .
maybe in Pierre . . . Our isolation is pointless because it is only by
consent, not by blood . . . We've forgotten things, we've neglected
soul, gut, blood, *seriousness*. We no longer trust our own blood,
because it has betrayed so many before us . . . We were convinced
that that didn't exist, that it is naive, crude, even evil . . . we tried
to talk ourselves into that with drinking and cavorting, transient
romances and quick changes, superficial jokes . . . Things worked
that didn't last too long . . . things worked where we didn't have
to take too profound a stand . . . things worked that didn't require
that we solve problems, that we think ahead . . . everything worked

best that didn't matter. We didn't talk, we drank together . . . we judged precisely who was an ambitious pain in the neck or an incompetent bungler, a moralist or a saint, an informer or a spy, and who belongs to us . . . that is why we cut Pierre out . . . and Vera . . . and now you will leave me behind, too . . . because you have to, because that agreement of ours binds you like a chivalric oath, and it seems to me that there is something that is worth more than that agreement, more than our nonchalance, than our pitiful standing apart . . . Is there something more special about us than about other people? I know what you are thinking. All of us figure this out, and then we come back . . . I know that you think I got carried away and fell head over heels . . . I know you resent all these wise words, it is a disgrace to think too much, it is a disgrace to be carried away with anything. It is all passé. It is a disgrace to betray your old friends and that is all that matters . . . That is why I said I have a guilty conscience, because I have a double guilty conscience: because of them and because of you. But I will give you the right to lord it over me, just the way you always have, just as I lorded it over you when you came back to us more cowed than ever. Maybe you are right: we are repeating the same proven error over and over again . . . I didn't get them to accept me; instead, I destroyed what it was that they had. As if I am poison, as if I brought the destruction with me. This is an nasty power: to destroy. It is horrible to feel it in yourself. They let me feel it to the hilt. They did not let me in, there was no place there for me, only for them . . . and then it occurred to me that we haven't got what it takes . . . there never will be a place like that for us . . . it hit me pretty hard . . . that no one will let me in."

"They had nowhere to let you in to," I said in the rain. "Even if they'd wanted to."

"I smashed everything they had. I was so sad because of Pierre, because of Vera, whom I never understood, because of you, whom

I betrayed, because of something which maybe isn't even there, because of the fact that what matters most is either out of reach or smashed, because there are no Romeos and no Juliets, because I am drunk, because I've hurt your feelings, because I'm breaking everything I touch, because I am selfish and because I would like something more than what everybody else has . . . or maybe everybody wants the same thing, but they are not crazy enough to let it show. And I am so drunk that I go right on smashing things, because what is left but to smash things to the finish, until nothing else is left, to kill everything in me, which I shouldn't even have because it is some sort of rudimentary remnant or something. Because, there, I have been trying, I have been trying with all my strength as I have never tried before, and I didn't think I could ever want anything so badly, I have been trying and I only managed to smash something that already existed, something that maybe had been put together with just as much anguish by somebody else."

"You didn't," I said. "There was nothing there to smash."

And so it was that we had a good talk, wiped away the tears, quieted down for a while out on the terrace, away from all the others, waiting for the rain to stop. The rain did stop soon, and the terrace got chilly and breezy. Shivering from the chill, half embraced, consoling one another, we saw that the rain had stopped, but we knew that later it would start again, tomorrow, the day after, in an uninterrupted series of days, and that it was time to leave.

We knew we had to recuperate. That we would always be returning from the illusion that we had been somewhere. We knew, finally, that summer was over.

»»» 《《《

The Third Team

Beyond who knows which turn in the road glistened, suddenly, down below us, the vast silver-gray sea. I rifled through my pockets for my dark glasses because it stung my eyes. A man wearily moved over to the side of the road to let us pass. He was completely black against the backdrop of the sun and the sea. Our car wove a bit, as if deciding whether to run him over or to continue descending down the hairpin curves, the brakes screeched, the car swerved uncertainly and then continued more slowly down the road.

"Feels like one of the tires blew," said the driver. He spun the wheel to compensate for the way the car was careening to the side. "We've got to pull over."

We pulled over by dusty locust trees, inspected the flat front left tire, looked out at the sea among the locust trees. The heat and stench of gasoline hit us from the motor. Ćuk, who was lying on the backseat, woke up and peered out the window, rumpled and drowsy.

"Do you have a spare?" I asked.

The driver was crouching by the tire and pretending to think about what he should be doing about it. But it was too hot for thinking.

"Nope," he said. "Who would give me a spare?"

"Who gave you the car?" I said mechanically. "Are you a driver or are you not?" (We had been quibbling like that all day.)

"What's it to you?" he answered unperturbed. "I am a driver as much as you are."

"He is the captain of the *Titanic* in retirement," said Ćuk. He had come out onto the road in his socks, and, dancing on his toes, he checked the lines holding the paintings on the roof rack. He studied the tire expertly and spat: "What kind of a driver are you? Whoever heard of somebody going on a trip with no spare?"

"What kind of a painter are you!" the driver spat on the same spot and stood his ground, ready to quarrel. "If we are short a tire, we are short a tire."

A person is quick to quarrel out in the sun, with the choking stench of the motor, with a flat, overheated tire. Particularly if he has been quarreling all day anyway. I could see why the man was furious that he had to drive us to Rijeka. Ćuk had asked the county administrator, a devotee of the arts, to give us a car and anyone reliable he had around to drive it. They would never have let us take the car ourselves, since we were considered unreliable. We were given a man who ran a motorboat for tourist cruises, who was expected to spend his two free days driving Ćuk, Ćuk's paintings, and me, to Ćuk's art show in Rijeka.

"Be a comrade and take them down to Rijeka," the administrator had said.

"He never does much of anything anyway," Ćuk said, relieving us of the burden of sympathy, "except for goosing German women. Tourism is going to be the undoing of our hardworking people."

"A flying f . . . !" said the driver. "We must demand an investigation of how the city government is spending its money."

So now the tire was flat. The man we had barely missed hitting a few minutes before approached the car and interrupted the fight. He, too, crouched down by the tire.

"How far is it to the nearest town?" I asked him.

"To Raša?" said the man. "Pretty close. Five or six kilometers."

"Why don't you walk into Raša and borrow some sort of tire?" I suggested to the driver.

"Damned if I do!"

He got into the car in a fury, slammed the door, and, muttering into his whiskers, gunned the motor and took off so fast that Ćuk and I barely managed to scramble back into our seats. The man leaped to the side in terror, and then he cursed, enveloped in the cloud of smoke that remained behind us.

"You will really destroy the tire now," said Ćuk maliciously, "and you'll wreck the rims."

"Is this your car?" asked the driver, turning. "Is this yours?"

We arrived in Raša on three wheels. With a screech we turned off the main road, and, lurching like a drunken boat, we cruised into the front yard of the town, which was called Raša and had a main square indistinguishable from somebody's big front yard. We got out of the car into a cloud of dust and looked at the wheel. In no time a small gathering of men had assembled who were appraising our wheel. Most of them were drivers of the buses and trucks that passed through here: Raša was halfway between Rijeka and Pula. The entire town square–front yard was packed with buses, trucks, and passengers. All of them watched us with pity. The front left wheel looked like a tin lard can that had been tied to a fast train and dragged on train tracks a long way.

"So this is Raša," I said, turning to the square.

In the focus of general attention, I waited uncomfortably for our driver to finish a string of curses that seemed too loud for the occasion. Ćuk peeked out the window, waved to the audience, and, opening the door, began to put his shoes on shamelessly slowly. I started searching the walls of the houses lining the square, as if seeking a way out of a cage. At the foot of the square was a church of an odd geometric shape: the apse resembled a hangar. Around the church I noticed quite a few people wearing dark suits and white shirts. On their heads they wore low, dark hats.

I wiped sweat away. A gray-brown stripe was smeared on my handkerchief. I felt the dust between my teeth and on the collar of my shirt; dust also covered our unfortunate automobile.

"We are going to have a drink," Ćuk explained to the driver, "and you see to it that we get there today."

"Have some lunch while you're at it," said the driver, and when we had gotten further off through the crowd he shouted after us even louder: "I don't care when we get there! Have dinner, too."

It seemed wise, what with all the audience, to leave that last comment without a response, so I dragged groggy Ćuk toward a little tavern with a dusty, stunted grapevine trellis in front of the door.

We went into the pleasant cool inside, talked for a while with the cute waitress, and then began systematically drinking cognac. After the third round I went out to take a look at how the repair of our car was progressing. The square was empty and looked now like one of de Chirico's paintings. There wasn't a single shadow on the square. Where have all those people gone? I wondered for a moment. The hot noon sat in the dust like a big, swollen arm. Our car was nowhere to be seen.

I squinted for a while toward the red-hot cauldron of the square, and then I went back in for another round of cognacs.

"What sort of people are we?" asked Ćuk rhetorically, sitting bolt upright, a shot of cognac in hand.

"What sort?" I asked indifferently as I took my seat.

"For the first time in our lives we have arrived in a town called Raša, where there are mines and things. No to mention miners. A town we have never seen before. And instead of going out to appreciate the cultural and historical wonders, going down a mine shaft, getting to know the lives of our miners, or simply strolling through this town we have not yet seen, instead of all that, here we sit in a tavern that is identical to thousands of other taverns where we have been before, and we drink cognac. At the very least we should be drinking some local vintage."

"There you are very wrong," I said. "There are huge differences between one tavern and another."

All during our conversation people in dark suits with dark, low hats perched high on their heads were passing through the tavern. They came up to the bar and drank. They always had the same drinks: beer, wine, brandy; and then again: beer, wine, brandy. They rarely took a seat at a table; most of them drank standing, leaning their large, calloused hands on the bar.

"We might have some lunch," I said to Ćuk. "Who knows when he'll be back."

"We are out of touch with the lives of normal people," said Ćuk. "I propose that from today, from this moment, we choose a new direction. We have cocooned ourselves, we have lost our roots. I propose that we start living in harmony with the broader national masses. We must go to the people. We must come down to earth. But first, of course, let's have lunch."

For lunch we had either roast veal or veal stew and we drank either a liter or two liters of wine in the cool of that empty little bar at the end of the world, just off the main highway along which noisy life in transit was passing by. Strange, serious men in solemn suits, several sizes smaller than what they needed, walked by our table paying no attention to us, ordering always the same drinks with dignity, raising their glasses with calloused, calm hands always in the same way. The bar was just like thousands of other bars like this, every last one of which is situated at the end of the world. And it seemed as if we were not actually traveling through this town, nor that we were there for the first time, but that we had been sitting in the same tavern day after day for years and having for lunch mediocre veal stew with slightly better wine.

All of our travels are only a search for one more tavern like this, which will inevitably await us at the end of every stage.

"We are getting old, Ćuk," I said to him after lunch. "It is high time we found wives. If for nothing else, then for the quality of food."

"For some of us it would be for a second time. I have tried that already, thank you very much," said Ćuk.

"OK, so it doesn't have to be marriage. Why not settling down, a home, a steady job? We are two homeless bums too old for the road. We keep wandering from tavern to tavern, here and there we sell off a painting, we have enough for a little wine, and then off we go again on a trip, glad to be going, although actually we are sick of it. And each time we are delighted as if we expect every trip will finally settle something, something they will serve us up at the end instead of the veal stew, and the two of us will sigh with heartfelt relief."

We drank a glass of wine in silence and then Ćuk said: "It's not that we're wandering, we are running away . . . Check, please."

The tavern was empty, and the cute waitress was changing the green-checkered tablecloths and shaking out the ashtrays. We were alone in the cool of the tavern: the waitress, Ćuk, and I. Ćuk had always been an expert at cute waitresses and those things, so I strolled over to the door while he was paying the bill in his inimitable fashion. Standing, leaning against the door frame, I heard how the waitress was laughing loudly, while Ćuk's monotonous, soft, confidential mumbling filled the pauses between the resonant cadences of her voice. In front of me lay the empty square filled with thick, heavy sunlight. The baking heat rose from the square, and I felt limp. I wanted some empty, fresh hotel room, in which I would quickly fall asleep with the Venetian blinds down. I didn't have the strength to cross the square, let alone venture any further.

I went back in. Ćuk and the waitress were standing at the bar, drinking cognac.

"I really have to stop," she giggled. "We're not supposed to drink with the guests. Imagine if somebody were to see me!"

"I have just resolved to stay in Raša forever," said Ćuk, turning to greet me, "until the end of my days. This is a gorgeous place, a place in which a person really could make a home and live with people."

The waitress thought there was something funny in that.

"Where is the car-repair place?" I asked. "Our driver still isn't back yet."

"Who cares!" shouted Ćuk, as sweeping as a count. "What do we need drivers and others like them for? We are the drivers of our own destinies. Against all flags and reasons, I have decided that we will become miners. Miners! Miners get to the bottom of things!" He was gesturing widely, invoking the sky to bear witness. Then he went back to the bar and drained his cognac. "We won't be digging up coal, we will bury ourselves on the spot. If there is a spot. In Raša, I mean."

"You don't know?" I asked the waitress.

"A car-repair place? I don't know," she said, huffy. "Ask one of the drivers out there in front."

"There is no one out there in front," I said. "I was wondering where all those people who were milling around this morning went. Was it a wedding or something?"

"Today they are holding the miners' games, competitions, for prizes," said the waitress. "Everybody's gone off to the soccer match."

"Off we go to the soccer match," said Ćuk, eager, forgetting the waitress. "The two of us will be the third team on the field. An independent team without its own goal."

"Straight, and then left," said the waitress tersely. She went behind the bar and began energetically rinsing out the cognac glasses under the faucet. She was already tired of us. How could we not be tired of each other, stuck together as we were for good?

We went across the hot square and into the shade of several dark buildings, in front of which there were rows of dusty oleanders in flowerpots. The blossoms of the oleander were wilted and a dark, lipstick-red color. On the wide steps of a building sat a tired, listless man, picking at a dark cluster of grapes. He looked at us, then lowered his eyes and went on with his slow eating. I felt as if we knew each other. But it was completely out of the question that I could know somebody in this part of the world, so I shrugged off the thought. Though it was definitely odd that somebody was perched like that on steps eating overripe grapes in an empty town.

We came out on meadows near the town where the festivities were being held. The meadows were crammed between dark, high, unforested hills, and people were crammed into the meadows. A solemn black-and-white crowd that moved, met, and parted with holiday solemnity, greeted acquaintances with broad smiles specially set out for the occasion. Stiff and restrained, unaccustomed to white shirts and holiday courtesy, they enthused awkwardly about the adroit, colorful, mobile soccer uniforms that dashed about on the dust of the trampled meadows. The waitress had been wrong—not everybody was at the soccer match. With white chalk the meadows had been sectioned off into temporary playing fields for handball and basketball, and there were improvised racing tracks for runners.

People circled around everywhere, none of them overly enthusiastic or too cold, but solemn in their belief that this was a festivity that should not be ruined by too great an exhilaration at the other team's defeat or too great a disappointment at one's own.

They felt somewhat freer the nearer they got to the playing fields, where, in a clearing surrounded by stones, there were five or six lambs turning on a spit, ruddy and greasy, young lambs like ripening fruit. A fat man, his sleeves rolled up, wearing a colorless, greasy apron, turned the spits; his slight, small wife in a black cotton dress was basting the ruddy corpses over the fire with mutton tallow, while on another outdoor table slapped together of rough-hewn boards lay carved portions getting cold, which the fat man was serving, swiftly wrapping each one up in newspaper, dropping the money into the deep pocket of his greasy apron. The heavy smell of tallow hung in the air like a curtain.

That smell, the fire, the spit, the lamb (ah, and those raucous games), all of it reminded me of the old days of Turkish rule. Impaled on a stake. Tallow and circumcision. Flesh and blood. Spits and scimitars. I glanced around the hills thinking I might catch sight of the cavalry, lances, turbans with the crescent moon. Or other insignia. These festivities were so modest, so besieged by belligerent hills, that any moment you'd expect the enemy. It didn't matter what banners they'd be bearing. An enemy who would swiftly crush this idyll of prosperity and peacetime leisure. The proximity of the enemy was a warning to me: friend, keep both eyes open wide! Do you see how these people are having fun as if they are taking communion—how they do not waste games or time, how they are judiciously soaking in these cherished moments? Don't you see how they are strolling from the playing fields to the shooting gallery, where they solemnly shoot several bullets from an air gun, linger there a moment longer, and then approach, with dignity, the tracks and here they pick a blossom of brief oblivion? And then abruptly they spin around and with panic in their widespread eyes search the ring of stony hillsides, sigh with relief, and continue watching the soccer players or drinking wine or shooting from those harmless air guns. I liked the solemnity and alertness of these people—I recognized them. I recognized their cautious amusements, I also recognized their fear of the same enemy I feared. That is how you know you share a country, belong to the same nation.

Ćuk and I each drank a glass of red wine without talking about anything. Then, in the slanted afternoon sunlight, cheerful in the calm, dignified manner of our surroundings, a little solemn, we felt how inside of us, from within, one of those profoundly happy, total drunken states was welling, the kind of state that was as rare as happy sobriety. Grinning cheerfully and showing one another details of the scene, wandering about among the people, even a little human ourselves, we started to drink the hearty homemade red wine, which was the only thing that could convince us we might stay here forever. In Raša, maybe, but with our feet on solid ground. We paid for some of our drinks, and other people offered us theirs, taking us in as if we were one of their own. Their wine seemed even finer, even more natural! I had had so little of it in my lifetime! You cannot, after all, drink a lot of wine like this!

Following an elderly man with a jug who was the most generous in serving us (courting the newcomers, just in case), we joined a boisterous crowd of people who were elbowing each other in a circle around a white pole stuck in the ground. The pole was tall, straight, and thick, more or less resembling a telegraph pole. But unlike a telegraph pole it had been cut down only recently, a freshly lumbered log, its bark stripped, smooth and slippery-moist, partly from sap dripping from the tree's veins and partly from the lard with which it had been greased. At the top of the pole there was a round, wooden platform, and on it, tied to the middle, shivered a little, still scrawny, piglet, decorated with a silly red ribbon. The piglet was fidgeting nervously and moving; every so often one of its legs would slip over the edge of the abyss, and with desperate squeals and clambering it would secure more solid footing, until it found its way back to the very center of the platform, where, shivering with horror, it didn't dare budge. Its dying squeals excited a certain malicious energy among the onlookers. It seemed to me that the entire upright pole was shaking from the shivers of the little pig.

No matter how cruel it may be, a game is a game, and after it sweeps you up, it invariably loses all real meaning. Only the rules remain. As long as those rules are kept, there is no other reality beside the reality of the game itself. In no time I had forgotten about the pig with the grotesque red decoration perched atop the absurd pole. I focused everything on the efforts of a man in black pants and a vest, white shirt and short socks, who was trying to inch up to the top of the pole. The man had climbed only a meter or two up from the ground, his movements were full of convulsed hunger, his expression contorted by a rigidly indifferent grin: who cares if I don't climb to the top—he showed everybody with that grin—all that matters is that we are having fun. And truly: everybody seemed at first glance to be having a splendid time. The kibitzers were encouraging the climber with pantomime, repeating his movements, clapping, urging him on, aping even his grin. But behind the carefree air of the climber's smile I felt, as they all did, his desperate desire to make it. I found myself longing for him to reach the top, as if all sorts of things were riding on it. And I knew that none of us was genuinely enjoying himself, and, what's more, we were all drawn together by a force stronger than we were, an irresistible draw to the top.

"What is this?" asked Ćuk of an old man carrying a large plastic wine jug. "Miners sick of going down, so they go up?"

"This is a game," said the old man helpfully. "Whoever makes it to the top gets the pig. We hold it every year. Take a crack at your luck, why don't you."

"Thanks a million," said Ćuk, accepting the jug along the way. "I've already resolved the question of my luck."

"It is a traditional miner's game," some wisecracker piped up unsolicited in the tone of a badly written newspaper article. "Last year lightning struck the pole the day before the festivities."

"Luckily the day is clear as a bell," Ćuk told him. "Otherwise the chances for luck would be barely minimal."

The climber had now made it more than halfway up the pole. He was obviously wearing down; his movements had slowed. He slid limply on the pole like a squashed frog. Pretty soon the slipping in place became slipping toward the ground, first slowly and then so quickly that it was nearly falling.

"Aaaaaahh!" everybody aired their disappointment in a single voice as he touched ground with his foot. The man continued chuckling a cheerful dismissal of his failure, wiping his skinned knee, looking disorientedly for his shoes, as if after this excursion into the sky he wasn't doing too well on earth.

But, as one could have predicted, his fall was not such a big deal. The next anonymous climber took his place at the foot of the pole, spitting into his hands, shaking out his legs, assembling the mask of his face.

"Has anyone ever made it to the top of this contraption?" Ćuk asked the old man.

"Oh, of course they have! Somebody always comes along," said the old man fatalistically.

"Aaaaaah!" the mob greeted the fall of the second climber, derisive and disappointed.

"How many have tried so far?" they asked. "Six of them? Seven?"

"Our boys aren't what they used to be," said the wisecracker with a feigned sigh.

"Nothing is," said Ćuk.

"Somebody will turn up," said the old man. "You be patient."

I stood there and watched them fall, one by one. My body began to fidget and I didn't dare let myself finish my thoughts. Something I had long since forgotten wriggled out of the gloom like a pale, underground fish. A fluttering I hadn't felt inside me for ages shook the nerves of my whole frame. A paralysis, not deadening, rather readying for attack, stirred my weary, neglected limbs. I suddenly felt an irresistible surge of defiance, a bubbling of strength. Defiance and strength that were wasting away, unused. Rebellion and hatred, rage and decisiveness, veins and blood woven of memory and of dreaming, of what we are not, of what we could be, of what we never will be. Somebody had to be found, I thought, somebody would turn up, we cannot all of us, always, without exception, through time and change, without meaning, without defiance, be nothing but victims.

The crowd wanted some action.

"I used to be pretty fair at climbing," I said to Ćuk, watching the helpless fall of the last climber.

"You aren't thinking of climbing, are you?" asked Ćuk, derisively.

I knew what everybody was doing wrong. I knew how it could be avoided.

"I can make it to the top," I said, "as long as I can keep from slipping."

"You're nuts," said Ćuk. "The wine has gone to your head."

"Let him try," said the old codger. "What can he lose?"

"If you are in need of a pig," explained Ćuk, "I still have some money left over, I can buy you one exactly like it in town. Don't be an idiot! You are probably going to go and lose that crazy head of yours. Listen . . ."

"What do you say, should I give it a shot?" I asked him calmly, as if he hadn't said a word.

"What is there to lose?" said the old codger.

Ćuk looked at me for a moment, then at the pole, then at me again.

"I bet five liters of wine you won't make it even halfway."

"You're on," I said.

The people around us started egging me on. It appeared there were no other candidates in the offing but me. I was preordained to be the one who turns up.

"Come on! Come on!"

"Where is this stranger from?" they asked.

"Somewhere else," the wisecracker said, as if my proximity afforded him the privilege of inside information.

"Let's get on with it! How much longer are we going to have to wait?"

I felt an tinge of malice in the voices around me. Some guy from away who will entertain us for a while with his lack of gumption and his naïveté. But I had known voices like those for a while and they didn't throw me. I always heard them and I knew that I'd be hearing them as long as I lived.

I mused for a while on what I would like more as a prize: the piglet, the wine, or to conquer the pole itself, old age, the label of outsider? I opted for the five liters of wine and winked at Ćuk. I stripped to the waist and handed him my clothes for safekeeping. Then I took off my shoes and socks and walked over to the pole. The dust under my bare feet was soft and warm. Without clothes I suddenly felt strangely light and insignificant on the warm earth. I was no longer so sure I'd make it to the top.

But then I went to work. I rubbed my hands and feet in the dust, rubbed the pole with dust as high up as I could reach, and then I filled one of the pockets of my pants with dust. It was good, gray stone dust, which never makes mud, but which would adhere nicely to greased wood and sweaty palms. I felt, more than I heard, how people were laughing.

I jumped up onto the pole, grasping it with my feet like a gymnast: with the instep of my left foot and the sole of my right. I didn't slip. I rested here for a bit, and then, rubbing the dust in as I went, I changed my grip so that I was holding the wood between the two soles of my feet, and slowly I began to climb. First hands, then feet; then hands, then feet. Then I stopped again, switched my foothold, and rested. The dust filled my eyes, my mouth. Then I moved my hands up, drew up my legs, hands, then legs, then rested, then climbed again.

I turned to look beneath me: the earth was far below, a round, paltry ball spinning on the point of the tall, slender pole. Around me I felt the dangerous wind of the heights—I felt a slight movement, as if the pole were swaying. It was a mild inner rocking like on a large ship—and the first signs of nausea began to get to me. I stopped looking down. The trunk is a lot thinner up here, I thought, the second half will be much easier.

I heard from below the clamor of garbled calls, but suddenly I understood, so far away from them that I didn't care what they said. We were alone, the two of us: the pole and I. And there was no more reason to pretend to one another that we were anything but what we were.

What sort of a tree are you? I asked. An Istrian oak? They skinned your bark and left you a bare skeleton? Maybe not; maybe instead you are a skeleton from my past, and this encounter of ours is merely a page from memory, a wan reflection, a worn-out repetition.

And suddenly, with chilling clarity, I remembered the story of the oak tree. That, too, was an oak, but it was a Pannonian, not an Istrian, oak. I was only an arm's length from the top.

The first time I climbed that oak I still didn't know anything. I climbed up to the first fork in the branches, where many had climbed before me and after me, and then I gave up, placing no special importance on climbing further, and down I went. Maybe that was my big mistake: I should never have even tried.

I came down and told my friends how I had seen from the branches that Vlaj's herd of horses was out to pasture beyond Black Hill. The herd belonged to this invisible, nearly legendary man whom they called Vlaj; there were a whole lot of riding horses. The pastures were fenced in, but we knew ways of getting through. They guarded the horses, but we knew how to steal an occasional ride on one. It was a kind of proud, risky game against the horses and the keepers.

I told them the horses were back. They were excited and ready to go, but they were even more excited about the oak tree. You are a newcomer, *they told me, you don't know. The oak is enchanted, accursed, dangerous. No one can climb it. Plenty have tried. One by one, their names are remembered like names from fairy tales. One by one they were sacrificed like ancient warriors to the dragon and they fell to the foot of the oak. As if death dangled suspended like a ripe acorn in the gloomy, dark crown of the black oak. Ever ripening, awaiting new harvesters. You should never have climbed even to that first fork in the branches. There used to be Turks around here. When their time came, they took all the rings and jewels they had stolen and stored them in a chest, carved out a hole for it at the highest fork of branches, and placed the chest there, never to come back for it later on. Now everybody is dead and gone, even they. You should never have gone up there. Other climbers, better than you, have been killed.*

That was when I first saw the oak tree. I had looked at it with ordinary eyes, the way I always do, but this time I truly saw it. The oak. Tall and black on the chalky horizon, like a finger raised in admonition. A dark tower, a friend only to the clouds, ill-tempered and inaccessible. Alive in some independent, lone way. And my small childish heart chilled at so much coldness, such indifference. Could it be that the oak cared so little for me? I, who had thought until then that I was the better of the two of us, ached for equality. But he kept on standing there motionless, silent, upright in the silvery-colorless sky, and looked at me without noticing me at all, as if I were a caterpillar. Me? I wondered. A Lilliputian with a soul?

I was scared, sure, but then again I was a newcomer. *Here, as everywhere. A person without roots, without prejudices, without prenatal fears. A newcomer to this world. I was scared, but fear didn't chasten; rather, it challenged me. I looked once more at the oak and felt small and nameless, an unnoticeable yet fierce opponent. And I told the tree: you are proud because you are ignorant, a local scarecrow. But it was too large to heed my words. It was too large and too superior: it did not even sense the breath of the whisper with which avalanches start.*

My days were filled with images of the oak on the horizon, my personal nemesis, while the oak didn't have the vaguest idea that this was so. I circled around it, eyeing it, never coming too close so that I wouldn't give myself away. Now and then I would dismiss it, trying to free myself, to forget this secret embittered struggle, but then I'd come back, bide my time, wait for the right moment.

Day after day I felt a bitter taste in my mouth because of it, I slept restlessly, ate too hastily, kept turning toward the window. I got to know the oak in the most varied of moods: at six o'clock in the morning, restless and fluttery, when youthful vigor would course through its aged veins and it would shake the diamond earrings of dew from its sharp-toothed leaves. In the heavy afternoon, when it was all stiff, silently bearing the heat, but proudly calm and self-aware, with the knowledge that noon was passing, the heat was passing, time and life were passing, yet the oak remained. In the vampired dusk, when it would be disheveled by the evening breeze, rustling like some sort of huge hen before sleeping, waving its branches about, and finally settling them in quietly for the night. It did all these things with brazen simplicity, uninhibited like a hundred-year-old man who no longer finds anything distasteful about urinating in public places: no one can do anything to him anymore! The tree did all this like a tyrant who can allow himself what he pleases before his subjects while losing none of his dignity in the process. If you only knew, people, how I hated it for its thoughtless and shameless nakedness.

Carefully I nurtured this hatred, for I had to beat the tree. I sustained the hatred even when our mystic little enmity was encroached upon by the larger hostilities all around us. The war had swept over us several times that year, back and forth, back and forth, leaving only me and the oak unscathed. We stayed standing where we had been, waiting for one another. It was, it seemed, the only thing worth waiting for.

Since those were times when all values had been destroyed, when no one waits for anything anymore, I decided to settle my score with the oak before the things that were larger than both of us settled matters with the tree and with me. Ah, how petty that satisfaction of extra hatred seemed! The hatred was all I had left, the only thing I was capable of satisfying. All else had long since eluded my grasp, including, in the end, my life on the sidelines.

Maybe the mistake lies here: that I embarked on such a large, such an exalted task out of petty, personal motives. (But, of course, I was still young then, I didn't know whom I was out to destroy.) I was certain I would succeed, but instinctively I was calculating that it is better not to tell anyone what I meant to do. After all, people might understand chance failure as a final proof—and at that time I thought that I would always be able to muster in myself enough strength to climb, if need be, that same oak tree for the rest of my life, to prove to the world that it could be done.

I set out toward the oak at a time that was not morning, or afternoon, or evening. It was time to approach the tree. A sort of colorless haze filled the semi-dark of the hour. An hour of frozen windlessness, stilled grasses. An hour without people, without animals, without a past or a future. I walked without thought straight to the oak, expecting no respite, no resolution. I steeled myself for a climb that would last forever.

It would be wrong to call what I was feeling fear. It was rather a feeling that something fateful was happening.

I climbed to the first fork in the tree branches easily. I looked up. Above me the vast mosaic of the treetop covered the sky, inaccessible, tall, carved like the ceiling vault of a cathedral. I entered under the dome of the treetop as if entering a motionless and coldly solemn temple. I took the coil of rope with a metal hook on its end off my shoulder and tossed it further up. I missed the next fork several times and had to recoil the rope patiently, retrieving it from down below. That irritated me a little and I shivered, all sweaty. Then I threw the hook again, almost slipping off with the strength of the swing. I hugged a rough-barked branch convulsively. Then I calmed down and kept climbing. Now the branches were thinner and you couldn't see the ground anymore. The ground or the sky. I was halfway between the ground and the sky. Only leaves, leaf to leaf around me. It was a marvelous and alien world of still leaves. Whenever I stood on one of the smaller branches, it would shake, alarming me with the sudden rustle of leaves. Who knows what sort of forgotten creatures might dwell in this leafy desert?

So it was that I climbed all the way to the last, large three-way fork. I thought about how, here, I break out into the light of the free sky and how the ordinary, cold, earthly, human winds cool me, which, at this height, must be blowing. I thought that it was good that I was there. That by doing this I was resolving, if not everything, at least a great deal.

For the first time I turned to survey the landscape. The four corners of the great, wide world. It was not morning, or daytime, or dusk. The earth was shadowy, dark green and gloomy, like a large, flat wheel, and the horizon shone murkily in the uniform and monotonous light on all sides. At the edge of the wheel there rose dark pillars of smoke. Larger ones, then smaller ones, then larger, then smaller, in some sort of order. The smoke rose slowly upward and flowered at the top, mushroomlike. There it hung, as if somebody had painted it with a paintbrush. But I was taller than the tallest smoke cloud, I was on the top of the world.

This must have been what it looked like when the Turks passed through here, I thought masterfully, victoriously. Smoke, smoke on all sides, smoking ruins, the semi-darkness, not morning, not noon, not evening. There was nowhere to escape to but the top of the world, where you could be above everything else. But the top is merciless in its hostility. It knocked down those who fled, one after another, reserved through time and the generations directly and exclusively for me. Here, oak, I have come to claim my own. We have come to claim our own at the end of a long series of nameless seekers.

I sat in the fork as if in a heavenly armchair, seeking the treasure that was mine by rights. But all around me the oak's bark was ancient and virginal. Nowhere were there any niches, drawers, chests. In the next fork over a bird had its nest. Maybe it was some very remarkable bird, maybe nothing but a crow, probably neither. An empty nest at the top of the world. Maybe the bird had been shot down somewhere out over the smoking fields. Even birds can no longer be refugees. I had come up with, it seemed, an accomplishment that was worth something—I congratulated myself. I had run away and come back bearing news, justifying thereby the valuable sacrifices of my ancestors. I was excited imagining how I would inform them that there was no treasure chest, a truth so meaningful in its authenticity that it was worth dying for. There is no treasure, no bird, no death from the oak tree. Only a solitary oak at the top of the world, surrounded by smoke, smoldering ruins, fires of danger, a morning of horror, noon of terror, night of death. Smoke, smoke, smoke, and more smoke all along God's great horizon.

All this was work I had done. To mark my accomplishment, I took out my pocketknife, and sitting in the hazy wind, which brought the stench of fire, the sticky moisture of death, grinning, half happy, half bloody, scratched, scraped, marked, I cut a round, large, juicy, yellow brand for all time into the great slanted branch.

And then I went down, swinging on the branches, down to the dark green ground, bidding farewell to the leafy world of peace above me. I patted the oak on its aging trunk and set out to be among people, where I live to this day.

I told my friends that I had finally climbed to the top of the oak. There was no treasure.

We went out to the field around the oak so that I could show them the white wound I had cut precisely so that everybody could see it. Like, for instance, a marker on a hiking trail. They looked and they did not believe me.

"His father and his mother were killed," they said to each other. "He has lost his mind. Or he is imagining. Or lying."

"But that spot! Look at the white mark on the highest fork! Isn't that proof? Listen, there is no treasure, no danger, no curse . . ."

They shook their heads, listening while I spoke of the smoke on the horizon. They looked like a heap of slobbering, bald old codgers.

"That spot was probably cut by a piece of antiaircraft shrapnel," one of them said, end of discussion.

Furthermore, the war was close at hand and we did not have the time to deal with such things for long. We thought for a while about whether to run or to stay where we were and wait for the army to arrive. Some decided this way, others that way. I was for running. I had no parents, I was not from these parts; nothing was holding me here. That evening, as I rolled my few possessions up in a bundle, I thought: did I really climb that oak? Was I truly up there? Did I carve that brand? Who knows? I can't really remember clearly. And maybe it doesn't matter so much after all. I'd better get out of here.

I came back a long time later. There was no more oak, or carving, nothing was left. The oak had first been hit by lightning, the crown had burned, and then bombs finished it off.

They say that many more people died around it. And it stopped mattering to me whether I'd climbed to its top or had fallen. All of it was past.

My hand faltered on the edge of the horizontal platform. The piglet caught sight of me and squealed straight into my face, expecting help from me, maybe, or maybe smelling danger. I held on to the edge of the board—it was sturdy enough to hold me—and here I stopped. From below you could hear calls of encouragement.

"Another centimeter!" howled one voice that resounded above the general uproar.

Another centimeter, I'd make it to the top, and then what? I'd start falling? Fall to the ground? I looked over at the pig and felt sorry for it and for myself because of all that was to come. Many had tried: many had climbed and many had fallen—what was their reward? The victor and the vanquished in an empty string of years in which there was no victory or defeat, no ascent or fall, in the selfsame gray sequence, containing only memory of equal successes and failures, a presentiment of one and the same finale. I knew full well how much more dangerous and serious my fall would be from the very top; I knew how much more crushing the remorse would be. I was sorry for both sides in the fight, regardless of the outcome. The combatants are condemned in advance—a skeleton of a tree and a skeleton of a man—a gnawed white skeleton up which another skeleton shins to reach the sky, the reward for every skeleton. And finally, what that sky was reduced to—a pitiful little suckling pig atop a pole somewhere in the middle of nowhere!

"Another centimeter!" howled that same voice from below. But I knew the voice very well, and the blindness and the impotence and the rage in that voice. No, the accomplishment which I would strive for I would make not only for, but against, myself. For that voice husky with passion and impotence. What sort of tidings would I bring? Who would believe me?

I started to descend, slowly. Slowly and heavily, downhearted, as if bidding farewell to somebody who had died. I descended not through the pull of gravity, but at the very heart of a struggle between two merciless forces. One was still shoving me upward, not letting me relinquish the fight and give up, while the other was calmly and convincingly drawing me earthward, certain that in the end I would have to obey. I went down slowly, leaving parts of me behind along the tall pole. More and more tired, longing to touch the ground and vanish as soon as possible from my own sight. The skeleton slid down the skeleton heading earthward— the fate of every skeleton.

My descent was shrouded in funereal silence. The people didn't know what to make of it: had I lost my strength at the last moment, or had I been duping them all along? Had I seen an apparition at the top that had frightened me, or had I intentionally, cruelly, betrayed and shortchanged them? It seemed to me that no one below me was budging, all were frozen with surprise or insult. But when I got down there was so much of everything on my wretched back already that I didn't care what they thought, what they had to say to me.

A hellish clamor rose toward my face, which I turned away, shaking my muscles loose. They were all shouting something and offering interpretations, but I understood none of it. Around me there was an empty ring like around an ailing sheep.

I wiped away the sweat and shook the dust from my pockets, standing among people who dared not touch me. I knew that they were right: I was tainted with a disease for which there was no cure. Ćuk came over to me, one of the tainted to another, and handed me my clothes and shoes.

"You won those five liters of wine fair and square," he said to console me.

We moved out through the crowd, pushing our way. I felt terribly tired. Around me people were debating noisily whether I could have finished the climb or not. They were paying no attention to the fact that I could hear every word they said. For them I no longer existed. The old codger with the demijohn looked at me and wagged his head. I wondered for a moment what that head-wagging meant, but he was too old for me to figure it out. Old people wag their heads like that: you never know what they have in mind.

A little further on the car was waiting for us. The driver looked at me with curiosity, but, fortunately, he refrained from comment.

I sat on the back bumper, pulling on my shoes. The quick shadow of the mountain fell across all of us, a sudden twilight.

And as I'd expected, once we'd settled into the car, after the necessary interval of silence passed, Ćuk offered me some wine to drink, which he had pulled out from under the seat, and he said, gently: "We are out of our league with this stuff. People our age have homes, families, a cozy corner; we shouldn't be out cavorting all over the place like monkeys."

"I made it," I said succinctly.

"You only missed by this much," said Ćuk, with only a trace of malice.

"I could have climbed up that last centimeter," I said.

"Maybe," said Ćuk, "but you didn't. Therein lies the difference: old people haven't got what it takes for that final push."

"I could have climbed," I said again, "but I decided not to. I wasn't in the mood."

"I wasn't in the mood, either, but I wasn't the one who took on the climb in the first place."

"And I don't give a shit what you think about it, either," I said, and I really didn't. Because even if I had made it to the top, no one would have believed me. Even Ćuk didn't believe me. And it wasn't a question of whether you'd make it to the top or not, but whether they'd believe you. No one believed anyone anymore. This was only one more proof that even though you can do it, a person can do something, you will never be believed.

On the other hand, maybe it is just about how older people haven't got what it takes for that final push.

The driver flicked on the headlights, and we, angry at each other, sat deep in the dark of the backseat, staring in silence as the light fled before us, always in front, like a terrified rabbit. We raced along the high road between the hills and the sea. The landscape around us was uniformly gray and melancholy, the hill and the sea, the sky and the road.

"I feel sick to my stomach," I said after ten minutes.

"Let's stop for a minute and have a drink," Ćuk proposed nonchalantly.

We got out on some twilit curve where the driver managed to pull the car off the narrow road onto the even narrower shoulder. Ćuk handed me one of the bottles, and he took the other himself. I climbed cautiously down the stony slope toward the sea, weaving my way among the thorny blackberry bushes. We drank slowly, climbed slowly down. At first the slope descended steadily, and then it leveled off, only to drop, at the end, straight to the sea. Here we sat, sipping the wine and looking out at the sea. The Rijeka lighthouses were flashing in the distance, a neon string all the way to Point Kantrida, a multitude of tiny windows in the warm ball of darkness.

Ćuk was humming an old tune, sotto voce, poignantly. He was singing the only way he knew how: as if by chance, loosely but nice—not too loud, not too warmed up, right in tune.

"It would be good to jump from here," he said after a pause, spitting from the cliff down into the depths, swinging his legs over the large expanse of sea, "and see what happens."

"Rubbish," I said, glumly. "We are too old for that sort of thing."

Ćuk was suddenly overcome by a bout of spryness, and he began to pace up and down over the stones, flailing his arms about theatrically. Far down below on the twilit sea some large fish sliced a swell on the oily surface, and then leaped, gleaming like a mirror.

"That, my friends, was a whale, an ordinary whale of a domestic variety," announced Ćuk as if he were master of ceremonies on stage, "one of the last of its kind on the Adriatic shore. The rest have succumbed to a massive incursion of barbaric fish people with a different social order."

"Fish people or people fishing?"

"Go fish," said fish-drunk Ćuk.

"All fish bite the tails of other fish," I said. "All of them, in the end, succumb."

"There is no poetry in you, even when you are sober, and especially when you are drunk as a fish," Ćuk said. "You can have an inclination, but the only inclination you have is for pig. *Per aspera ad* pig. But let's say for the sake of argument that what we saw out on the sea there was a pig. It was a sea pig, straight out of Herodotus. It heard me singing so sweetly. Or was it some other kind of creature?"

"You are a sea pig," I said and lobbed the empty bottle out to sea.

"You are ignorant," said Ćuk with dignity. "It was a sea pig that saved Arion on its back. In my version they throw Arion into the sea because of his alliance with the dark forces, after which he swims up on a pig. Or maybe they threw him in just for the sake of throwing him in. They were expelling him as an undesirable element. Because he sang too nicely. They threw him off a cliff exactly like this one."

"Thank goodness you don't write history," I told him.

"Regrettably, I do not. But at least I participate in its making. Here you go, now I will sing out loud in the face of the darkest of destinies, and I will tell all. Or won't I? Do you think I shouldn't? Oh, all right, I won't sing, I won't make history, but really I'd like to."

He said this stretching out his arms in feigned longing. I stared into the dark sea before us, into the dark history behind us.

"You wouldn't like it really," I said yawning, "you'd find it boring. And besides, who would allow you to anyway?"

"OK, OK, I won't. But the problem lies in the fact: what do I, actually, want? Explain to me, damn it, what it is that I really want? I wanted to jump off this cliff, but you heroically saved my life—why would I want that if I don't want anything? What a paradox, eh?"

"Do you make history only by dying?" I asked him.

"Things are getting a little too serious around here for my taste," said Ćuk.

"As if we want to make history!" I said, uncommonly serious for where we were. "All you and I want is a drop or two of purely unhistorical life."

"Of course," said Ćuk. Though I couldn't figure out whether he was serious or mocking me. "There always has been too much history, too little life. As if it is a constant state of war."

"I have this feeling I'm going to sober up quick," I said after a brief contemplation on the value of being serious. "It would be better if we climbed up to the car and had a drink of something, if there is anything left."

"There is," said Ćuk conversationally, "but we are not going to feel like coming back down here."

"So what?" I asked. "Are you sorry?"

We went uphill through the bushes, toward the road suddenly, as if we were in a big hurry. Stones trickled down and rolled underfoot. Ćuk cursed under his breath, he tripped on the tendril-like branches of the blackberry bushes. I wanted to whisper to him in a muffled hiss that he should hurry, but I bit back the words. Some danger seemed to be lurking. It was pointless, and too dangerous, to speak, I thought.

I stopped to catch my breath, waiting for Ćuk, who was getting himself unstuck from brambles a few steps down the slope from me. The only sound I could hear was his panting and the rustling of the bush he was walking through. As if all the existing sound were focused around him. A sacrilegious ball of sound that echoed shamelessly far. In this solemn, unliving, majestic stillness, the two of us were vulgarly, shamelessly alive, agile, brazen. It was as if we had polluted the landscape.

I looked back at the seascape. The water was leaden gray, all smooth, but shining and full of an inner trembling tension, like a vast drop of mercury. Nowhere on the horizon was there light, but the sea shone like a jewel in the darkness. As if some miraculous, cold, diffuse light were filling it all the way to the bottom. The sea radiated this fluorescent light, delineating the odd outlines of an island that floated like a dead granite whale in a basin of mercury, glowing on the dead and motionless brambles of blackberry and rose hips, on two or three contorted branches of the pine trees in front of me. When Ćuk came closer to me, his face in that light was bluish-yellow, like a face from the underworld. I looked at my hands—they looked clenched and shriveled, they stayed hanging motionless in the space where I had raised them. Where am I? I wondered. Why am I here? What's this chill that came over me?' Ćuk had reached me and, peering at me from above, halted.

"What's up?" he asked, panting, propping himself up with his hands.

"Something is happening to us, Ćuk," I said, appalled by my own quavering voice, staring as if enchanted at the cruel mercury mirror, now covered by a metallic sheen of violet. "Something horrible is happening, Ćuk. Something completely out of our hands."

"You only just now figured that out," said Ćuk.

"No, Ćuk, this minute, here and now, we are in terrible danger," I screamed. "I feel as if something is squeezing my heart. I haven't heard this voice in my ears for ages," I tried to convince him. "I haven't been this loud for ages, Ćuk, something is waiting for us, they are lying in wait for us, and we are nowhere again, in the brambles, snared, unprepared, helpless." Panic squeezed me like a steel hand.

Ćuk suddenly put a finger to his lips and hissed. He turned around cautiously, slowly, listening. He was tense, bent over, all a single nerve. There was nothing to hear, nothing moved.

"Now we are done for," I whispered, feeling the final horror, ready to weep for helplessness. I knew 100 percent that we were done for.

"Don't shit me!" hissed Ćuk, listening to voices that weren't there. But he knew as well as I did that it meant nothing: when you don't hear them, that is when they are the most ominous. The sea was covered with a dark blue velvet color, deceptively gentle and soft. I moved my hand and touched some jagged leaf, sharp and cold, like a sheet of some icy alloy. As if singed, I flinched. Suddenly it erupted into my consciousness that everything here was dead, metallic and frozen like this leaf—there was no salvation. We were done for, everything in the end shows its true face.

But Ćuk, Ćuk the fearless, feeling me flinch, ran like an arrow. He ran desperately like a rabbit that has understood for the first time that it has just spent its entire life until that point in a land of rabbit traps. He ran hopelessly like that experienced rabbit which has known for ages that there is no other land than the land of rabbit traps, it knew that it ought to be feinting and weaving to avoid the wheels and traps, but it runs straight as an arrow, nonetheless, to a single destination. Ćuk sprinted mindlessly, spry as a deer, unexpectedly fast.

When I pulled myself together, Ćuk was already a dozen paces off. I saw how his broad, living back in the dark was disappearing among the branches of the blackberry brambles. I raced with all my strength after him, not feeling the scratches, tripping on the rocks, falling and getting up with the same explosion of muscles, panting with poisoned lungs, breathing poison air, until my mouth was filled with bitter spit. "Don't leave me, Ćuk," I whispered, thinking I was shrieking. Don't leave me now, I thought. We will do this together, we'll do this together. But he kept running without listening, not wanting to hear my mute cry. "So, that's the way it is, you bastard," I said, wheezing, "you won't get away from me. If I am going under, you are done for, too." I felt how foam sprayed from my mouth.

I was nearly blind with strain and practically smashed into Ćuk when he stopped. Ćuk looked at me, nonplussed.

"I don't know where we are," he said, trying to pierce the dark with his eyes. We were standing, shoulder to shoulder, in the dark. I turned to orient myself in terms of where the sea was, but its light had faded. It wasn't there anymore, there was no way of telling where it was. We were surrounded by total, impenetrable darkness. I felt more than saw that Ćuk was standing next to me. We turned around helplessly but didn't dare start moving in any one direction, because each direction was an equally hopeless guessing game.

"It looks as if we're lost," I said, gasping for breath.

"So it does," said Ćuk a little more steadily, "but the road can't be too far off now."

"Really," I said. "How far did we run? Didn't we cross the road?"

"We would have seen the car," explained Ćuk. "Even if the driver fell asleep, he would have left the parking lights on. And besides, there is always some traffic along this road. It can't be far now."

That steadied us a little. We stopped feeling the horrible panic. The road couldn't be far now. But the darkness that now surrounded us was the same darkness that had surrounded us since the beginning of time. A darkness with no phantoms, no secrets, apparitions, or creatures—uninhabited, a precise darkness from which we had been stealing life for generations now, and in the end we stole it. The corpse of darkness. We learned that this darkness was nowhere except in the corpse of our very own eyes, inside of us. A darkness that was not dark, an absence of light. Why should we be the ones to give it back the life we'd stolen from it?

We slowly started moving uphill, steadied and sure of ourselves. Nothing could be very far anymore. And the direction—

did the direction really matter so much? Whichever way we turned, we had to come out somewhere—this land was criss-crossed with roads, rivers, railway lines, sooner or later we would come across the direction we were looking for, sooner or later we would recognize a line that would guide us to our destination. Again we stopped talking, each thinking our own thoughts. It is superfluous and dangerous to talk about these things. This had shown, as always, that it is for the best to keep silent, clench the teeth, and walk on.

On all sides we were surrounded by a wall of dead darkness, but we knew full well that even if we were at the gateway to hell itself, that hell could be no worse than the one we carried inside ourselves.

We walked for a few minutes, or hours, that way, not thinking about anything. We weren't the least bit surprised when we spotted a little light in the distance—a glowing point we had been anticipating. It shone quite suddenly, born out of nothing, but to us it was entirely logical, we had expected it. That was the natural, logical destination of our walking. We were prepared to swear that we had always known that we were headed for the glow, that its light had determined our choice of direction from the start. The glowing light came closer. A precisely defined pre-sentiment filled us, which wasn't pleasant or unpleasant. The glowing light meant the final arrival of light. It was sufficient that we await it prepared. That would be the end of our suffering. Ćuk and I, both before the glowing light and before all that was coming with the light, grinned happily as we walked toward it.

And when the light did arrive, it was so bright that our pupils, accustomed to the dark, were blinded forever.

"We will," said Ćuk later, "get used to the dark and to one another. It will seem to us that we were never even given the chance to see."

The White-Haired Pavlićes

The village where I was living was a big village on a plain, just like all the other villages on the plain, spread out, monotonous, and backward. The plain around the village was uniform and eternal like the village itself, the river was completely ordinary, always the same, serene, the hills on the horizon were dark. You couldn't see over the hills, as if nothing was over there beyond those hills, nothing worth mentioning, which is why I don't, because no one mentioned it while I was living in the village. No one in the village ever talked about anything beyond the village, they rarely spoke of anything. The village was like a world unto itself. The world consisted of houses, the river, and the hills, but only from our side. The hills on the other side contained nothing that concerned us and they did not belong to the world of my village. As far as I could tell, there wasn't anything at all on the other side of those hills. No one could predict what they could not see, what would come to us later from over there. The other side was merely where the sun and the darkness lived, and in the evening a bluish haze would rise from there, as if something were cooking.

Wolves belonged on that other side, wolves that people talked about but no one had ever seen. The wolves howled at night, but there was only talk about that howling, no one had ever really heard it. Still, the wolves still did exist and did howl and I was scared of them, just because of knowing that. Or who knows, maybe it was because I was little. I was little ever since I could remember. Wolves howled mournfully as if they were calling to somebody, but I think I was the only person in the village who heard them and I didn't tell anyone about it because they would think I'm crazy. I thought that the wolves were calling me, luring me to them, to the other side of the hills, and I sort of wanted to respond, but I was scared so I didn't. I wanted to tell Dad to go tell the wolves not to call me anymore, to leave me alone, to chase them away. But I didn't say anything to Dad because I knew that Dad wouldn't. Dad usually had to mow one of our two meadows the next day, or plow a field, or harness horses to the sleigh.

Dad always had to be doing something, and when he finished, he had no more time for me because he was going off to the walnut tree or to the tavern where there were other men so they could talk. The men who lived in the village were a lot like my Dad. One of them was lame Griška. The others had special names, too, but I don't remember them. I remember Griška because they called him that. He was like my Dad, too. He had a meadow and a field and a vineyard, too, and on the same days as my Dad he would be mowing or plowing or pruning, but he was lame and so I could tell him apart from the others. Lame Griška was a part of my village, just the way our cow was, or our horse. You could talk about lame Griška, and people did, every day, the way they talked about the cow, and for me they are somehow the same, now when I remember them, but it was easier for me to talk about Griška than about the cow, though I liked the cow more. Our cow always looked as if she were crying, especially when I went off to her after I'd been beaten. I thought that she was crying with me or for me. But I never dared say so, and even now I don't exactly know why I'm not scared to be talking about it, in case they might think I'm crazy. No one will think I'm crazy if I talk about lame Griška— and besides, he used to shave people and pull their teeth. He pulled my mother's tooth out . . . this big. I was with her: I looked at that tooth for a long time, then at Mama. The tooth did not look as if it belonged to Mama. Since then I have known what a tooth is.

There were other people in the village, too, but I forgot all of them a long time ago because they all looked alike, like the houses, like the stables. The whole village looked as if only one person lived in it. Everybody wore the same kind of shirts, the same kind of vests, the same kind of pants. I've forgotten them as if they never were there at all. Sometimes it seems to me as if they really weren't. I wouldn't want it to look as if I am boasting that I was so smart when I was only so high, but I was already thinking that way even then, I mean, that they never were there at all, that they were like shadows, like haze coming up off the ground. A person could hold a tooth in his hand because the tooth was real. You couldn't get ahold of people, stop them, they merged with the village, with the plain, with the plantings. I couldn't tell that to Mama. I knew what Mama would say: anyone can hold a tooth in his hand.

I think it is because I never told a lot of things to Mama that I never told them to anybody. Now, from afar, they all seem somehow the same, and Mama does, too. I'd go off into the fields where our corn was planted and I'd wander around the rows and hide among the tall sharp stalks, which were ripening. I'd sit there in the corn, among the rows, and talk out loud. At first it seemed stupid to me and I was nearly ashamed, but afterward it went all right. In the cornfield I saw a lot of things which I otherwise wouldn't have seen anywhere. The corn ears ripened slowly before my eyes: first they were milk white, soft under my fingernail, then they'd yellow, harden, grow; they'd knock me on the hips and shoulders while I passed among the stalks. Sometimes I pulled off an ear, stripped off the soft, colorful silk from the top, and arranged a mustache for myself, and then I'd stroke it, naked and smooth, with my hands. The corn silk squiggled in my hands like fish. I began to love those large, serious cornstalks. I loved to be among them. I knew each one individually, by the number of ears it had and by the way it stood. I called them by names as if they were good friends. The cornstalks were like a house to me. Sometimes I tried to sleep in it, under interwoven stalks, as if I were in a real house, but there were too many ants. The ants climbed up onto my closed eyelids, crept into my mouth. Tendrils of the melon vines were intertwined on the ground, and among them hopped little green lizards and black grasshoppers. I tried with all my strength not to squirm, and I let the corn leaves, which the wind swayed, touch my face and let the melon vines hug my feet as if I had grown into the ground, let the grasshoppers hop across my shoes, let the ants crawl around my skin. All that was nice, because it was mine. So that is how I figured out what was nice: it was like ants, only from the inside. My little world enclosed me like a lambskin coat. I felt great because I wasn't in the village but in my own little house, which belonged to no one but me. The village was like some other, big world where I didn't fit. I was little, I needed a little world that fit me and I had it. Living in it, I grew. The cornstalks got smaller with each new year.

The loneliness started bothering me more. I wanted somebody to be there with me. There was a girl in the village whose face I liked. I can't remember any longer what her name was or how she looked. I told her once that she should come with me to the cornfield, that nowhere was it like the way it was among my cornstalks, that I would show her all manner of wonders that I was hiding there, but when I told her all that, it sounded completely ordinary, just like when all the other boys invited girls to go into cornfields with them. She came with me only to the edge of the field, and there she hesitated for a long time and squinted at the tall rustling cornstalks, which were swaying ungraciously in the dark. None of the miracles I had promised her were visible. She said that she wasn't going any further. She said that she simply was not going to go any further, and then, when she was leaving, she told me that a lot of boys bigger than me had invited her, too. I was glad that she thought I was a big boy, but that was poor consolation. I went off into the field, but it wasn't the way it had been there before.

I kept going off into the cornfield, but the golden light that had shone through the leaves, through the combed silken mustache, seemed slowly to be dying. When it got dark, the whisper of the cornstalks was hostile, and in that hard, metal rustling I could detect more defiance, even threat. I got more scared, and dared less to look around, and more and more I felt alone. I wanted to bring in somebody else, even if it meant using force. There was one boy from the neighborhood whom I was stronger than and could beat up whenever I wanted to. All I needed was to have him there next to me so that I could tell him something when I felt like it, now when I could no longer converse with the cornstalks. But halfway there he got scared and ran away, because he was even more afraid of the dark than I was. Maybe he was thinking that I wanted to beat him up. But I didn't want to beat him up, honest.

I never said anything to the other boys because they kept wanting something that I didn't want: games I didn't like, things I didn't know. Using pocketknives they carved stripes on canes and shaped bowls, saltcellars, spoons. "All you do is wander around," Mama said to me. If I had said something, they would have said that I was crazy, they would have made fun of me. Maybe they would crown me their white king, the way they did with humpback Raša. Even Raša's father stood in the doorway of his house and laughed when they crowned his son white king. "Serves him right," he said, "the cripple." Raša had a crooked back and a runny nose and stuttered, and that was why he was always white king. I always got chills whenever they crowned him white king. Whenever I thought about how I might be in his place, I wanted to cry out with horror. But I was sly, I hid my fear the way I hid everything else. And aside from that, everybody knew I was best in the whole village at throwing stones; no one would crown me white king as long as they were all scared that I could bash them in the head with a stone from where I was hiding. I knew how to smash a bowl of yogurt from three houses away. So no one wanted me for white king. No one wanted me for anything, ever.

I went off into the cornfield and felt that even this place wasn't mine anymore. I bit my nails and knew that I had to do something, but I didn't know what. I couldn't get out of my little world, and I couldn't save it. I felt as if it were slowly falling apart, and when the cornstalks ripened once again and people harvested them and cut them down, my little house would be destroyed forever, barren stubble where nothing would ever grow again. My little world was gone for good. It was gone for ages, and then it seemed to me as if I'd never had it at all. I couldn't even imagine it anymore.

I grew so much that in the end they told me I would have to work. I worked at whatever they told me to do and I did everything badly. They told me I was good for nothing. They told me to look to the others. I didn't get mad, I already knew I wasn't like the others; I was angry at myself because, when the cornstalks grew up again, I no longer knew how to live in the corn. I had forgotten some skill I had known as a child. Sometimes I went out there, but nothing was the same anymore. I'd put on the corn-silk mustache and try to make it be the same. But it was silly wearing the mustache, it was silly sitting out there alone in the corn.

The only thing I still enjoyed was mowing. At the crack of dawn, before the sun had dried the dew, I'd mow our meadows with my father, and again I'd see wonders. All the mowers could see them, but for me they were wonders. Mowing, I would happen upon smooth, shiny, violet moles that had been accidently sliced by the scythe. I collected them after the mower passed and arranged them one next to another on the ground and stared long at the heap of dead moles with their smooth, shiny fur, alive moments before in the tall grass, now in the mown world. The sight said something to me, but I wasn't sure just what. I got worn out with the strain of understanding. Then I had had it with moles and mowing and I wanted to go off into the willow grove by the river and fall asleep somewhere in the shade under a willow tree, on my spread-out coat, while the river was softly murmuring, but I didn't dare go because of Father, because we had to finish the mowing. You always had to be doing something. I looked at my father: Father stared at the sun and cursed a little.

The next day we mowed and the day after that we mowed. The grass was always the same and it fell at equal intervals like the eddies of some restless, green river. In the evening, when we went back to the village, I would ride on top of the hay wagon, which was full of damp hay, while my father softly cursed the horses. I lay on my back on the hay, and the sky over my head was open like a box that there is nothing inside of: the sky was empty and the whole plain up to the horizon was empty; nevertheless, I felt closed up as if shut inside the box. I almost started crying out of some nameless sorrow. But I didn't talk to anyone about that. One evening I wanted to die. That was a long time ago, the days passed, winter came, and during winter I forgot to want.

I don't know how many years passed until the moment when I discovered that the entire village was not equal and that all people were not the same (except for the lame man and the hunchback). At the upper end of the village, pretty far from the last houses, lived the Pavlićes, who were different because they all had white hair. They were not white-haired like old people. Their hair was simply so blond that from a distance it seemed whitest of white. When I first saw them close up, I noticed that their hair was really yellow-ish and silken like the silk on an ear of young corn. But everybody called them "white-haired." There were six of them, the sons, and all six lived in the same house with their father at the upper end of the village. The house was like all the other houses in the village, just larger, but it was further off from the other houses and it seemed different. A little later all the Pavlićes died off (a while after I met them). I saw them only for a brief while and then they all died off, one after another. There was a lot of talk about it. There was talk about them before, too, but no one knew anything for certain, so everybody thought up whatever they wanted, and the Pavlićes couldn't defend themselves because they didn't visit with anyone in the village. I remembered a lot of those stories: they said that they were fairy princes because they lived without women, they said they were Germans because they were always working at something, they said that at night they wandered around the plains like sinful souls and caught frogs, snails, and snakes, and later sent them off by train to the devil's very own dinner table. They said that whenever they took a fancy to a girl, she would fall into their hands like a ripe pear, and that it was wise to lock up all the women in the house when they were around. They said that no one knew how many of them there were because they looked as alike as peas in a pod, so you couldn't do anything to stop them if something were to happen. Only later, when they died off, we counted them: one, two, three, four, five, six. So there were six sons, in identical black open coffins, one after another, and behind the coffin of the very last walked old Pavao all alone, upright, white-haired, defiant, wordless, following them soon enough himself with no one left to escort the coffin. When he died, the house stood empty and no one dared to come near it, let alone go inside.

While I listened to all the stories about the Pavlićes, I knew that they couldn't be true, I knew that the people who told the stories didn't believe that everything was true, I knew only that they were not liked. No one seemed to know precisely why, but everybody spoke of the Pavlićes with hatred. I had no idea why they hated them, but I know now. They hated them just because they were different. I asked the village boys why they hated them and they answered me that they weren't like us, that they weren't ours. I didn't know what "ours" meant, I couldn't imagine why on earth we should have to be "theirs," I didn't know how you could become somebody's. Once one of the Pavlićes got into a fight, they told me, with one of ours (theirs, I thought, but I didn't say so, for I wasn't sure whether I was "ours" or not), and when the others of ours (theirs, I thought) jumped on the Pavlić with knives, the other Pavlićes stepped in and took on our guys with their fists, but they didn't touch the guy who was fighting with the Pavlić over some girl. Even that didn't help him, though he was the strongest kid in the village; he was beaten just the same. There was something fishy about it. After that, no one messed with the Pavlićes, time passed and it was forgotten, everybody got used to living with them as if they weren't there. No one talked about them anymore.

I don't know what it was that drew me to learn something more about the Pavlićes, but whenever I asked somebody about them they would shrug or change the subject. As if anybody would be more interesting than the Pavlićes. But all the stories they told me I heard over and over again, and everybody in the village knew them all. I wanted to hear a story nobody knew. I decided to go visit the white-haired Pavlićes and find out for myself what they were like.

I slipped out of the house at dinnertime, because I didn't want anyone seeing me when I went to see the Pavlićes. When it is dinnertime then people have dinner and everybody in the village has dinner, engrossed in their plates. If anyone were to see me, I felt as if they would be catching me red-handed in some vile act. I was terribly excited, my hands shook. I crept up to their house and stayed right by the fence. There were nettles growing among the weeds along the fence, which stung me all over, but I didn't dare make a sound, for fear they might find me out. Still, I didn't want to leave until I'd seen the white-haired Pavlićes. It was a warm evening and the white-haired Pavlićes were eating dinner under a tree in their yard at a long wooden table. I could watch them quietly, invisible from my hiding place behind the fence. They dined, talked, and laughed. Old Pavao sat at the head of the table, cut bread and passed it around, and said something I couldn't hear. They all laughed. His laughter was the nicest, his face radiant, and I felt kind of warm around my heart while I watched him. He was such a different man than my father was. My father never laughed at the table: he'd slurp his soup, hunched over, and stare at his plate. I was spellbound: I almost didn't dare to breathe and stared at them without blinking, and I kept wanting to giggle. It seemed funny how they were sitting there calm as you please, dining congenially, as if there were nothing in the world but this yard, this table under the tree lit by kerosene lamps, and their glowing faces, where all six of them were sitting, three and three down each side of the table, and old Pavao was seated at the head, handing out bread and laughter as if they weren't besieged by the great globe of darkness that encompassed the entire plain, as if they weren't shut out from the world by hatred that didn't even seem to touch them, but rather, like the dark, came only up to this fence and no further, to this bubble of light in which their white heads bobbed like playful lanterns. It was pretty funny that it was as if the whole world were against them, and they didn't care at all. It was funny the way they thought even now that no one was watching them, and I was hidden behind the fence watching them. I watched them, and then all at once I was ashamed because they didn't know that I was there and they didn't know that I was watching them. It was as if I were watching somebody stripping naked who didn't know he was being watched. I blushed in the dark and didn't know where to move my eyes, and then I crawled hastily out of the nettles and burrs, spun around, and ran off. The last thing I heard was how the watchdog was barking after me. Maybe I shouldn't have run. Maybe they would have let me in.

I thought about it for a long time. They had their little, separate world and they knew the secret of how to live in it. I'd had a chance to figure it out and I'd lost it. If I had had just a little more courage, if I had believed a little more, maybe they would have planted me among them at the table, given me something to eat and drink. And what's worse: maybe they needed me as much as I needed them, but I betrayed them. Maybe they were waiting for something like that, maybe they wouldn't have left us forever then. Maybe I could have saved them.

For soon after that the Pavlićes all died off, and they were gone. Maybe it was a contagion of some sort, maybe somebody slipped something into their well.

We counted them off, one by one, and we felt nothing, it didn't feel as if anyone was missing from the village, they way we would have felt if one of our own had died. We didn't lose them because we had never had them; they didn't leave because they never had been there. The house stood empty, and children, out of remnants of hatred, broke the windows with stones. When a fire broke out one day and the house burned down, everybody looked on indifferently, no one even tried to put it out. Little by little, the glare of the fire subsided, just as the light that surrounded the Pavlićes went out.

Not long after that what was coming across the hills came, and villages disappeared, people were scattered, got lost, died. The darkness that covered the plain spread out as far as the eye could see, across this whole world where now one had to find one's place. The secret of how you find your place, how you live in such a world, was gone now that the Pavlićes had died off, now that they had disappeared and with them those who'd known them. If they were alive now, maybe they could tell me, but as it is, whom can I ask who won't laugh at me?

»»» «««

Special Envoys

It's been ages since I've been to this café, I said. As far as I can tell I never have been here, said Mili. It's not bad here, not bad. Both of us may have said that. We were thinking it, more or less. It rarely happens that we say what we think. But this time it didn't matter—it didn't change a thing.

We felt like children who have embarked on a strange adventure. We were a little excited that no one knew what we were up to, no one had the slightest notion of its importance. We hadn't told anyone that tonight we wouldn't be going where they were expecting us, where we were expected every evening. People will wonder where those two went. No one will be able to say, because no one will know. Gee, we don't know, the ones who know so much will say.

We haven't told anyone that we don't feel like going to see them, that we will be who knows where this evening, and that it is none of their business. We wouldn't be so crazy as to say such a thing. What is the point of useless explanation? The two of us simply went somewhere where they weren't expecting us and where they didn't notice that we had arrived, just as they wouldn't have noticed if we hadn't arrived. They wouldn't wonder: now where are those two? If they did wonder, they'd be wondering in vain—where would they know us from, who are we to them? Things weren't bad for us: so much freedom and so easy to achieve. No one asked us anything, and there was nothing to ask. That was good.

Next to us in the café was a large window and by the window passed people. In this part of town we didn't know anyone and that was why none of the people who passed by the window were familiar. All of them were some other people. This is a nice, peaceful café, where people sit and sip black coffee or a latte or café au lait. Very few were drinking wine or brandy.

We said, two brandies and a slice of lemon. We liked it that the waiter didn't comment on our order. If we had said two brandies and a slice of lemon in our usual place, the waiter would have asked, lemon? because we never have ordered two brandies with a slice of lemon there before. Here everything is different, because here we never have ordered anything. How easy it is to change your life! Two brandies and a slice of lemon. Coming right up. With a little sugar, please. Just a little, all you need is a little.

Outdoors it was pretty cold and blustery. A woman pulled a scarf from her handbag. We couldn't see whether she wrapped it around her neck or not, because she had already passed by the window. I leaned a bit more toward the windowpane to keep her in sight, but she had gone too far. The great sycamores growing in a row in front of the window released their leaves to the wind. I was glad I didn't have to say anything, because Mili had been looking at what I was looking at. She's pretty, said Mili. I don't know, I said, look at that nasty wind. That is what I was looking at, too, said Mili, what weather we are having for this time of year! Aren't we the weathermen, I said, you bet she was pretty.

We laughed and began feeling really great. We clinked our glasses of brandy together and drank them down halfway and sucked our lemon slices with a little sugar and then we sipped a bit more brandy and sank deeply into the chairs staring into nothing, thinking into nothing, distant, apart, and opaque like those thoughts. We laughed opaquely to one another and we didn't exactly know what we were talking about, because these were extraordinary circumstances and none of the things we usually talked about until now belonged here. We sank into the opaque distances feeling good in that opacity, uncertainly interwoven in a fine network of spaces where we didn't actually belong, not here, not fitting in at any one of these tables, yet somehow present, taking part in everything, but without mingling in the essence of the thing. While they are waiting for us somewhere else where we should fit in, where, truth be told, we don't always fit in even when we need to know that we belong somewhere. Here, temporarily present, aware of everything, judging the circumstances and interactions better than all the others, brimming with confidence at our own independence, not belonging.

You couldn't say that other people weren't in the café. There are always other people everywhere. There were two couples sitting here, for example, and two empty tables further over. Then there was one guy who was drinking mulled wine. Then there was a guy reading a newspaper. Then there were a few wearing gray suits and white shirts who were drinking black coffee and conversing. One of them was writing something in a large black diary, talking a little, and then writing again: these were not young men. Then there was a woman who looked as if she weren't waiting for anyone, and she wasn't very pretty. There were other people there, too, in the further corners of the café. We didn't watch them, they were too far away, they interested us even less.

Give us two more brandies, said Mili. Warmed or regular? We hesitated a moment. Warmed, said Mili at the last moment. I'd rather not get drunk, I said. That's OK, said Mili, just a sip. Two more warmed brandies, shouted the waiter toward the door to the kitchen. I assume that was the door that led to the kitchen. Somebody else must have been drinking warmed brandy; we are not alone, we are not alone. I'd rather not get drunk because I have to work later; I still have a whole pile of work to do, I said. No call to apologize, said Mili. No, I said, it's just I don't like working when I'm feeling swell. Me neither, said Mili, but I never do feel really swell. Never have. Ah, go to hell, Mili, I said. That's no way to talk. I know, said Mili, what can I do? I hurried to salvage the situation, I said: one might conclude from that that you, the greatest procrastinator of all time, actually like working. My father told me that he knew this guy who liked to work, answered Mili hurriedly, but that the guy died before the war from too much work. There's a conversation.

There sure are a lot of people in this café, said Mili. Still, a pretty nice, quiet little café. Here are your warmed brandies. Thanks, to your health. The waiter was quite pleasant, though he had no face. Or maybe precisely because of that. A good waiter. And the warmed brandy isn't bad either, I said. Actually the café is too small for so many people. Sure, it is comfortable, but if two or three more people come, there will be too many. We carefully observed the café in which, there they were, people. The problem was whether there were too many or not. There are too many people in general, said Mili, the statistics have it that Earth is not going to be able to feed them all by the year 1975, or maybe it was 1992. Then two or three more will be born and that will do it, there will be too many of us. What do you mean, too many, I said, there are exactly as many as there should be. Doesn't matter, shrugged Mili. Of course it doesn't matter, I said. Or so we thought, but then again maybe we didn't. It really didn't matter.

For no matter how many people there were in the café, for us the numbers would have been meaningless. The two of us sat in a corner by the window and thought our thoughts and we were a small yet completely independent community and no one had the right to penetrate our living space, which belonged to us by some higher law. For we are foreign here, strangers from another land, and around us are other people for whom we are strangers, the two of us observers from the side, who would stand on the side and, for instance, were something to happen we would stand there peacefully and observe with interest how the events were unfolding, without getting involved in them. Of course it doesn't matter. For no matter how many of them there are, all the people around us are locals, natives, and they would be foreigners if they were to come to us, just as we are foreigners who have come to them, just as everybody is a foreigner who ends up in one place when expected somewhere else. We sat there peacefully in the corner feeling profound respect toward the land we had come to, curiously observing local customs, we, transit travelers from a distant unknown homeland. We sat there peacefully, distanced in a foggy isolation but brimming with secret self-confidence, untouchable, conscious of their special position, conscious that somewhere our report is awaited from our distant journey, conscious that we will soon leave this land and go home, confident, distant, protected by other laws. No matter what happens here, we will be mere witnesses with no responsibility, mere observers, politely smiling, mildly interested, but never overstepping the boundaries of courtesy, watching and taking notes but not interfering, not allowing ourselves to be provoked, entirely independent, apparently alone, but with the knowledge that behind us stands somebody else, that we are being taken care of somewhere, that they are counting on us and that somewhere they will be glad when we return; eternally cautious, restrained, never rushing headlong into things, never uttering a single extraneous word, always careful, apart, incomprehensible to the natives, benevolent to them from on high, cautiously catering to their national sentiments, applauding their life as if we are at the theater, moderately approving their acts and decisions, smiling at crudeness, observing crime with cold interest, tolerating it as we would tolerate crime on a theater stage, precisely as tolerant as we have to be, alone, the two of us, who silently, without commentary, without indignation, look from on high through half-lowered eyelids, noting

*everything, getting involved in nothing, the two of us foreigners in some
other land, among other people.*

The café now seemed pretty nice. It wasn't that there were fewer
people. There were more people because dinnertime was
approaching, and new guests kept coming in and taking all the
chairs around the tables. We watched them without thinking anything, sunken deep in our seats, feeling more and more cozy.
There were lots more people and many of them knew each other,
and they went over to each other and sat at the tables, soon all
the tables were occupied. A dozen or so had gathered around one
of the tables—they were drinking wine and began to sing. They
sang out of tune, drunkenly, songs we weren't familiar with.
The café turned to look at them a few times, but then it left
them alone—they were feeling fine. We didn't care much, either;
those weren't our songs, and it meant nothing to us what or how
they sang.

More and more people were arriving. Now they were approaching all the tables regardless of whether they knew the people sitting
there or not, because there weren't many seats left, but everybody
wanted to be in the cozy little café, and they expected everyone to
let the newcomers sit at their tables, because no one had permanent
rights to any of the seats in that cozy little sheltered café. If they
weren't already acquainted, people got to know each other
quickly—most of them were from this part of town anyway—and
the buzz of conversation filled the room.

People approached all the tables but ours. We sat there and
grinned and looked around us and no one came over, because for
them we were some other people, who, it could clearly be seen,
didn't belong, had come from someplace else, maybe by mistake,
and if they were to come over to us, we would speak in some
strange, incomprehensible language.

We sat there and grinned, feeling either insulted or flattered I can't say, and we ordered a couple more brandies and clinked glasses. I'd like to stay here a while longer, said Mili. Fine, said I, let's stay here and let's drink as the good Lord commands. Great, said Mili, let's have two more brandies. Should we keep on drinking brandy or should we drink something different and finish sooner? How much money do you have? I asked him. Some. I have some, too, I said. Then that means we can drink as long as we feel like it. How much do you have exactly? I'm not quite sure, he said, probing his pockets, but I'll find enough. Of course, then I didn't say how much money I had, either.

But I looked at the people around us in the little café and forgot all about it. We had to stick together. We had set aside all internal squabbles, though there was no point in thinking there weren't any. Each of us was our own man, but now we were in a foreign country where we were drinking out of nostalgia, and we had to stick together, preserve semblances of harmony and unity, we had to look as if we were two of a kind.

We each downed a brandy and now we were acting like two peas in a pod, we tried thinking alike, smiling alike, twins. We distanced ourselves from them in our unity, now purposefully more and more foreign, more cold, more polite, tolerating their noisy conversation, their songs, and even them, these people who in their own way set us apart, who allowed us to set ourselves apart more and more, and who now expected of us, foreigners, that we would study them with interest, and who wanted to leave as favorable an impression on us as possible, and that was why they performed so that we would watch them, that we would create a vivid picture of them, their customs, their qualities, their way of life. As if they are only here to show themselves to us, to talk to us, to sing to us; everything until now was purely for our sake, and we sat there watching them with expressionless faces, opaque, distant, hiding certain

thoughts and judgments known only to us, impressions and observations
behind a fake smile which they did their best to turn to their own ben-
efit, courting us just as we for our part were courting them, their clan-
nish pride, their childish wish to seem better to us than they really were,
and we did not offer any commentary; rather, we attentively watched
the performance, silently shaking our heads, showing only restrained
sympathy, politely conveying that we are honored by their effort and
that all this is quite interesting, delightful really, and that we are grate-
ful for the heartfelt attention. All of this was for our sake and we knew
it and we knew that they were doing it unconsciously, led by instinct, a
sense of local pride, and that was why we felt superior, because we were
the ones who understood the situation from a broader perspective, we
were aware of all aspects of those things they saw only from one side,
and we were prepared at any moment to return to our own country,
which they did not know and which they could only visit as foreigners,
even though they were not even aware of that. Burdened with these
amazing possibilities and variants, but utterly composed under the bur-
den of our many-faceted insights, objective observers who under no cir-
cumstances become personally engaged in the momentary drama for they
are participating in a far larger and more encompassing drama, supe-
rior, closed in ourselves, inaccessible to them, we, people from faraway
islands with eyes full of the blue skies of warmer climes and exotic seas
which they have never navigated, whose fragrance has never touched
their nostrils, and that is why they do not think as we do, that is why
they are not like us, that is why they do not know why we are differ-
ent to them, different for them and different for ourselves.

No one came over to our table. All the tables around us were
packed with people, but no one came over to ours. There were several women and only one man sitting at the table that stood right
next to ours, between us and the middle of the room. They were
talking loudly, they laughed a lot: the women, while laughing, kept

glancing over at us. We returned their glances, of course. At first the looks were curious, then more welcoming, warmer, a little silly, then they were openly beckoning and promising boldly, showing that we would, if we got up and went over there, be received with hospitality. But we were aware of the delicacy of our situation on foreign territory, we knew that caution was the watchword, and we returned with looks that were, though genuinely kind, nonetheless full of restraint, apology. We looked at them because good behavior clearly demanded it, for one ought to respect the rituals of others, we had to subject ourselves to the rules of decency and be tolerant to an extreme degree, but one must constantly keep in mind one's obligations and duties, one's commitments and oaths, and we must never even for a moment overstep the permitted line which always had separated us and probably always would from the people of this region.

That woman looks as if she has a mustache, I said. Yes, said Mili, the other one looks a bit like Faruk. People are always looking like somebody else to you, I said. What can I do, said Mili, just look at her, if you please, Faruk's spitting image. You are forever noticing women who look like men, I said, and men who look like animals. Animals look like nothing, said Mili, as if he were apologizing that animals didn't look like anything to him, they simply were what they were.

The women noticed that we were talking about them and smiled and started whispering among themselves; they were obviously flattered. For a while longer we watched their giggling, very courteously, inclined favorably, but nothing more, nothing more, and then we got tired of that. Forget them, said Mili. You've got it, I said, who cares. We didn't care about them, we didn't care about anything.

Without drawing excessive attention to ourselves, as if against our own better judgment, we shifted our gaze in a different direction. On the other side, sitting around a table, were several elderly natives who were drinking spritzers, smoking, occasionally muttering a few words through clenched teeth. One of them was a larger man, his hair was gray, and he had a large mustache. You probably think that one looks like Kraljević Marko, I said to Mili. He looks old enough, said Mili, besides they say Kraljević Marko is still alive. Maybe it really is him, I said, he always had more luck than brains. The vermin of history had better have luck, said Mili, if they want to survive. Kraljević Marko at the next table was sitting there vacant as a cow, chewing his cud, stingily nursing his spritzer. Clearly nothing in this world bothered him. What could eat him, after all, the old wino, when he was already so legendary? Musa Kesedžija was long gone. He was another guy who didn't have a lot to worry about, I said. For a minute I thought maybe Mili said it.

We sat staring into nothing, thinking into nothing. Hollow, we sat in empty space, a little too lonely, a little too bound by promises, we were beginning to feel the beginnings of weariness of our own heights. But we had to see it through, see it through to the end. I tried to remember why, but nothing occurred to me. Why? I asked Mili. For what? For whom? But questions like that didn't make a lot of headway with old Mili. Cut it out, he said, Why, what? Nothing, nothing, I said. Maybe we did not have to see this through to the end. Maybe we could not see it through. Maybe there was no reason to do that in the whole wide world.

That kind of thinking was way too defeatist for my taste. You shouldn't think things you don't want to say out loud. We didn't dare say them to one another because we were protecting each other from such things. If only something were to come, if something were to happen, everything would be easier. We were getting tired of the isolation. There was nothing a person could do. Nothing. What should we do? I asked Mili. Mili didn't know and shrugged his shoulders. I don't care. I don't care either. There is absolutely nothing I care about.

Without knowing what we are doing in that snug little café, or maybe in general isolated in our corner, lonely, too bound by promises, feeling the burden of foreign laws we must obey here, in a foreign country, and the burden of our own laws, which we must obey in this same foreign country, acutely aware of our double existence, burdened with the awareness of this double existence, at first glance independent but in fact far less free than anyone else, the two of us too foreign, in suits of a foreign make, in shoes of a foreign last, half grinning, half confused, a degree too polite, too courteous the way foreigners in a foreign land often are, but therefore all the more distant, all the less accessible, watching colorful local apparel and the surreptitious glances from the murky distances, the performance for our sake, listening to the unknown speech, those unknown songs, artificially accepting that artificial hospitality, the two of us locked up in ourselves, and they, feeling our presence, equally closed toward us, clearly delimited, we courageously bearing it all, not uttering a single word, unsure what would be remembered and what not, what was an insult and what a compliment, and in spite of the mutual desire to bridge the gap, to overcome the coldness with heartfelt, human words, a gesture from the soul, and despite the fact that we were tired and that we no longer cared for many things, we remained in our places like the rock of Gibraltar, sending around greetings full of respect, a little from above but perfectly polite, within the limits of age-old rules of decorum.

Why, I asked Mili, what is the point of it all? Mili dismissed this with a flick of his hand. You have to be practical, he said. What do you mean by that? I asked him. I don't know, he said, but admit that it would really make the most sense for a person to be practical. I admit it, I said. But I knew that this way out had long been closed to us.

Again, we turned to look at the café, seeking a solution there, or who knows what. It seemed as if the whole little café had turned to stare at us, as if they were expecting something of us. We felt awkward, on the one hand because we were the center of attention, and on the other because again they were expecting something of us. What are these people looking at? asked Mili. Should I tell them to stop looking? What do they want? Should I tell them not to expect anything, because we aren't going to do a thing? At least nothing special. After all, of course, what would we do anyway? I said. Should I tell them? asked Mili. Don't, I said, don't. OK, so I won't, he said. I know you wouldn't, I said, I was only saying. We were very pleased to have something to talk about—that made it seem less awkward. Now the others could think that we didn't notice that all of them were looking at us. Let them look, let them go to the devil. Let them look as long as they want. We really ought do something, I said to Mili. We don't have to do anything at all, he said, we don't care. Exactly, I said, two more brandies, nothing on the side.

Now we looked around ourselves much more freely. We looked people straight in the eyes and one by one they quit staring at us. We didn't look at them rudely or in provocation, oh no, heaven forbid, we looked at them calmly, decently, but without fear, with the implacable dignity our particular situation required of us. Not quarreling but deliberate and with heartfelt attention, as if seeking in their eyes certain meaning, a message, a warning. Our position and the laws that protect us found perfect expression in our bearing, gave us a sense of security. We continued to remain apart from them, not inclined to get tangled up with them, knowing that we had to respond to entirely different questions, posed with a different language, in some other place.

You ordered two more brandies? Yes, here. I'll bring them right out, I'm sorry. Oh, it's nothing. How many have we had altogether? Twelve. Twelve? Then two more. I already counted them in the twelve. Fine. I'll bring them right out. A person needs to be practical, like I said, said Mili, looking at the woman with whiskers. They stared at one another straight in the eyes. Mili wasn't looking provocatively, he wouldn't betray our cause so lightly—his gaze was coldly evaluating, like a judge in a beauty contest, judging according to the criteria from the distant land from whence we have come, the distorted beauty of a domestic star which has, no doubt, a charm all its own, but it would be odd if even here somebody thought it beautiful.

The woman with whiskers was quite pretty in her own way, nonetheless. She's pretty, I said. And the other one is nice-look-ing, too, said Mili. Mili was always the supportive type. All the same, it doesn't matter, I said. Why would it matter? said Mili. Actually, between the two of them there is hardly any real dif-ference, I said. One dame is like another, said Mili, but I have to admit that she is a looker. Sure is, I said. And she was, don't think that she wasn't. The more I watched her, the prettier she got, and I began to feel bad about how I wasn't in a position to do any-thing, I couldn't abandon my special mission because of some passing fling with a woman like her. By that time I had already gotten tired of looking, and our exchanged glances were pretty boring, I was tired of wearing my flirting face.

I'm getting tired, I said to Mili. Me, too, he said, they can all go to the devil. Then the two of us kept looking around the café wear-ing our stern official expressions. Have you got a light? some guy asked. He wasn't asking with his voice, because he was sitting too far off, but rather with his cigarette and a gesture, and that was how I noted down his question. He had the face of a rat, and when Mili nodded to him, fumbling with matches on the table, he padded over to us like a rat, his head drawn in between his shoulders, darting looks around the room. With an unexpected movement he slid into the free chair by our table and reached for the matches, but Mili was already holding them and lit his cigarette. Would you like a cigarette? asked the man and opened his cigarette holder. There weren't very many cigarettes in the holder, let's say maybe seven. I never liked smokers who carried their cigarettes around in holders, especially in those cheap tin holders. No, thanks, said Mili. You? asked the man. No, thanks, I said. It seemed as if all the cigarettes in his holder were crumpled and slimy. Thanks, said the man to Mili's match, planted his elbows on the table, and started smoking. Clearly he didn't feel like leaving.

The waiter brought us our two brandies. The man leaned his rat-like face over the little glasses. What are you drinking, boys? he asked. Brandy? We didn't say anything. Bring me one, too, he said to the waiter. Will you join me with another round? he asked. A man who drinks alone dies alone. We declined, as if we'd agreed to in advance. Then bring just one, please, he said to the waiter. To that table, said Mili. The man didn't say anything, as if he hadn't even heard. The waiter stopped. To that table, said Mili once more. All right, said the waiter. The man kept sitting there. So where are you boys from? he asked. Forget it, said Mili, maybe next time. Too bad, said the man, now don't get touchy about it. Understood, said Mili. Maybe it would be a good idea for me to join you, said the man desperately. It would not be a good idea, said Mili firmly. Too bad, said the man, then I'll be going. He left without turning to look back at us, and there was no way to repair it anymore.

Mili wiped the ashes off the table with his hand. The meeting will resume, he said. That old guy could hardly wait to find a victim whom he could tell all about how his wife is torturing him, how his director is a sadist, and how he hasn't got his own place to live, that he is all by his lonesome, alone, alone. You are trying to justify yourself to me, I said. No, said Mili, that's just the way it is. Sentimentality, I said, more likely the guy is the local busybody. That settled the issue for the time being. The man sat back down at the table he'd been sitting at before and turned his back to us. By his back you couldn't tell if that was the same guy with the rat face and desperate voice—you couldn't see what we had done to him.

So we were alone again in our little realm, having repelled the interloper, a little isolated community with its own special laws, just the two of us, an island in a foreign sea which keeps trying to erode the island's shores from all sides; again we managed to resist temptation, to repulse the charge on the boundaries of our integrity, completely aware that we had defended them, proud not so much for our own sakes as much as for the sake of the large foreign country we were representing and to which we would return unsullied, without the taint of suspicion or indecisiveness, having completely accomplished the special mission we had been sent to do, thoroughly completing the delicate tasks, by all accounts maintaining dignity, awareness of belonging, immune to foreign influences and interventions, never lowering ourselves to the level of the native inhabitants, having enough pride and strength to resist submitting to the snare of curiosity, weary of the heights and personal drives, completely focused on completing our mission, ridding ourselves of all that was not in our interests and in the interests of those who stood behind us, shedding our own lives in this foreign land, we the special envoys, with self-sacrifice and denial, forgetting all questions, above suspicion, the perfect ambassadors.

Pardon me, said the waiter, but . . . Mili looked out the window into the semi-darkness of the row of trees where the occasional street-lamp was lighting. We will pay now, he said darkly through the window. No, that's not what I meant, said the waiter full of respect. What, then, said Mili. The two ladies, said the waiter, leaning over us confidentially, the two ladies sitting at that table send you these

flowers. The waiter was awkwardly holding a little bouquet of violets. The flower vendor appeared from behind the waiter's back
holding a huge basket full of violets. The fragrance of violets mingled with the smell of tobacco and spilled brandy. Apparently we
already have some, thank you, I said to the flower vendor.

The waiter put the bouquet on the table, not knowing what else
to do with it. There you go, he said, it is for both of you. I have
to give him credit for the fact that he did not even smile. What
is that for? asked Mili partially of the bouquet, partially of the
waiter. Those ladies sent them to you, said the waiter patiently. I
mean, why did they send them? asked Mili. I didn't say anything,
though Mili was grating a little on my nerves: why all the pointless questions? I don't know why, said the waiter, I thought that
you probably could figure that out for yourselves. Please convey
our gratitude, said Mili. Are they really for us? I asked, just to be
sure. The waiter looked at both of us.

Mili was reclining in his chair, squinting at the light, his hair
and his shirt were rumpled, and he looked as if he didn't understand anything. Now I knew that I probably looked as if I couldn't
understand anything, too. The waiter measured us very carefully
and slowly, first one and then the other, and clearly he came to
some sort of waiter's conclusion. What is he thinking, I raged in
myself, what the devil is he waiting for? Oh yes, the flowers.
Those girls sent these to us, Mili, the whiskered one and Faruk.
Seriously? Mili asked. Is that a local custom around here? No, it
is not, said the waiter, only a trace of insult in his voice. It is not
the custom? I asked. Listen, Mili, he says that this isn't the custom around here. I was getting pretty dizzy. I was having trouble
pronouncing words. You mean they really sent us these flowers?
asked Mili. As you can see, said the waiter. I gave him a tip.
Apparently that was what he had been waiting for.

∞

So, this means that it is not a custom around here and this procedure toward us was entirely exceptional, unexpected. We do not know of their customs; after all, we are strangers here. But we must honor their gesture of attention and respect, their concessions, their courtesy. This means they have recognized us, they have recognized what we are. Our persistence was not in vain, our courage and reliability did not vanish into thin air. And these flowers were not sent to us, and they were not sent by those girls, but rather this is an honor being shown by one state to another. They are greeting the envoys in us who are on a special mission, showing them hospitality, giving a sign that they understand the weight, responsibility, delicacy, maybe even the tragedy of the position. They have recognized us, they have accepted us for what we are.

Mili, I ask him, do you get this? No, says Mili. Me neither, I said. The two of us rose and turned to face the table where the girls were. The girls looked at us with polite smiles, just a little embarrassed by their own courtesy. They were startled that we had stood up from the table, they exchanged glances, but then they, too, stood up. We stood there facing one another. None of us stepped forward first. None of us stepped forward at all. The two of us bowed deeply, each holding part of the bouquet of violets carefully, as if they were huge, ceremonial bouquets. The girls laughed, a little confused, standing one next to the other, as if encouraging one another. There was nothing here to laugh at really, but they were laughing. We bowed deeply and with respect,

we bowed with deep respect, grateful for the undeserved love of the foreign women, suddenly ourselves feeling full of love for that foreign land where we will never belong, where girls send foreigners flowers as a sign of hospitable attention; full of love for those foreign people who nonetheless do understand our mission, they understand the laws that bind us, the promises we must not break; they will make do with this small amount of participation, which is all that we, special envoys, our hands tied by countless obligations, can offer. We, who are living here among them only our own lives, not theirs, never mingling with them, and though we have deserved nothing as ourselves, we have deserved love and hospitality and respect as envoys from the country from which we came to this land. And the two of them, those girls who feel that they belong here while we belong there, have thrown up between us this floral bridge, obliging us with love, unselfish human pure love, which seeks nothing in return for it knows that it will go unrequited. They have scattered us with the violets of their love, with the mild rain of femininity, believing that we are not, essentially, different, that we are human, that we are obliged by higher and more powerful laws. For otherwise how can one interpret the way that they broke with the customs of their country, approached the forbidden border? We never showed with a single sign any indication of relenting, any tendency that we would betray our mission, we did not seek familiarity, we did not ask them to receive or embrace us. And that is why we deeply believe that this gesture is an expression of their total understanding of our position, their love for people who have a mission, who are committed to it unshakable to the very end.

We felt pride that we belong to a homeland that is shown such an honor, such love to the people who sent us, and it was reward enough for us that we prevailed, that we did not succumb, that we were not lured away. We were prouder and more inaccessible than ever, fortified, reinforced, certain of the trueness of our path, knowing the rewards that await us at its end. We were foreigners in this land, I repeat, and the love shown to us was shown to our homeland. And taken in proportion we felt very small, very insignificant, but at the same time more important, powerful, upright, for we were part of a whole that was far larger than our little private world. We felt now as if we were standing before a sacrificial altar and taking part in a mystical ritual of union.

∞

The entire café was staring at us. We stood there as if nailed to the floor and we didn't move forward, full of tumultuous feelings, solemn, and the two girls stood by their table and waited for us to do something. They, also, did not step forward, expecting our initiative. The café fell silent and waited. Holding on to the table's edge, Mili stood and swayed in place like a mainmast. I raised my eyes airward, moved by the solemn feelings that filled me, and rolled them as if in a trance, watching the smoke that was swirling over the tables.

That was the smoke of the sacrificial altar that was swaying upward, describing a mystical curve toward the ceiling, announcing the final catharsis. The two girls stood there like priestesses. I, the chief magi, was making the sacrifice to the invisible god. I raised my hands in the air. The smoke wafted more and more crazily, the ceiling rocked. I bring you this sacrifice for the glory of the foreign land which has acknowledged that I have a homeland, which has shown that I belong there.

All of us stood and waited. The café had fallen silent. The waiters had stopped stiffly, holding trays with glasses. There was nothing to be done but stand and wait. We could not do anything. We were special envoys who had been explicitly banned from establishing contacts, from embracing the foreign way of life, from mingling. We had no other choice. You must understand us, people, we could do no more. We stood among the hushed people, arms raised, and waited.

The Tour

Following you undetected, from afar, I see how similar were your later destinies. And when one by one these twenty years have passed since we were separated, I think more and more often that whether we like it or not, in the natural course of things all of us will be buried in the same cemetery. Sometimes it almost seems to me that we are buried there now. And I know which cemetery it is. The entire chorus.

I can no longer resist the similarity of our fates nor our common cemetery. I no longer have the strength. The company isn't bad, after all. Weary, as if I am already there, I pass sometimes in my spirit along imaginary twilit avenues and read the timeworn names on the overgrown stones: in some spots a whole first and last name, in others a nickname, in some places there is only a pale, blurred smile on a half-forgotten face. I remember all of you so poorly, my fellow singers! But despite my feeble memory, I feel right at home. Here is my place, I say, among you. The cemetery seems to have the smell and the warmth of the old rehearsal hall where, for so long and so together, we sang.

Singing we earned our whole shared, pathetically short, hysterically happy life. In the name of that life forgive me, friends, that already now (oh, how quickly!) I am thinking and speaking of you as if you are already the deceased. But that was the life! One cannot speak of it except as something that has passed, it was so perfect. To those singers who replaced us secretly, almost as an afterthought, sometimes I'd like to say: that was real singing!

I have the impression that in those first years after the war we were the only chorus. In the city, or the country, or in the world? Who didn't think we were the only ones? We were. Assembled from all sides, after the war that had scattered everything, passionate amateurs, only singing joined us: we sang self-effacingly, fervent, enthusiastic. We sang the way volunteers in those days gave blood plasma. We felt that we were making necessary sacrifices and we gave of ourselves as if we were plasma to the lifeblood of the country.

In parades on the main square, at ceremonial occasions in grand, old theaters, to high school students in their sports gyms, to work brigades under the open sky, we sang wherever we were needed. Singing was badly needed in those days, and we sang without stopping.

We sang without rest, tirelessly, even when we needn't have. In the brief intervals when we rested between concerts, before performances, after performances, between rehearsals, all together or with our arms around each other in smaller groups, in the makeshift quarters where we slept, in the trains we traveled in, in the morning, in the evening, wherever we arrived, we kept singing. We sang as if the hours of song were already ticking by. And it seemed to us that we would never stop.

Sometimes I'd almost go so far as to say that it wasn't us singing: enthusiasm was singing instead of us. Everybody in those days was enthusiastic, the singers and the audience; the song echoed a hundredfold among them, nourished by its own echo. Time frothed like young wine. Maybe the audience was actually sipping the foaming champagne of fervor that poured from the stage instead of just singing. And maybe we really were good.

We always traveled everywhere together. And more than that: wherever we arrived, we were together with the people we sang to. The trains barely crawled from town to town in those days, off schedule and packed with passengers, and we would ride for hours in the cattle cars; sometimes we walked, sometimes we stepped out of the cattle cars into the luxury of a bus, but nothing could stop us: we got where we were going! We slept in schools, on the black, grimy floor where we had to get up in the morning an hour before morning classes began, or in brigade quarters, on straw, mingling with some sort of village work brigade, or other times in military barracks, with the fumes of Lysol, or under tents, on the wooden benches of some train station waiting room, but we took whatever came to us as part of the giving, a necessary part of the world, just as we ourselves were. All of it was shared like the land. We sang.

We would sing with full throat, throwing back our heads so that our neck veins bulged out, our faces turned purple, our eyes closed in ecstasy, and we saw nothing around ourselves. It was better that way, I know. There was no need to look. To stay that way, blind with happiness. That may well be why I remember you so poorly as individuals, my friends, I remember you as the chorus. That is probably why I recall so few things from that time, except the foaming shared sung happiness—I was blind to all else.

In my feeble memory all those long years of travel and singing melted into a single vast tour of the entire country, from Lake Ohrid in the south to Mount Triglav in the north, and all our performances, successes, awards, festivals, parades, all this merged into one single fantastic gesture in which one can no longer distinguish what I did, what we did as a chorus, and what the people to whom we sang did. In one uninterrupted, long floral tour that completely swept us away, like a river—it seems to me that at that time we lived nothing else, there was nothing else.

In a town whose name I have since forgotten, in a jam-packed hall where people were sitting on top of one another so crammed together that you couldn't see the walls for the sweaty human bodies, where there was hardly enough air to breathe, for two straight hours, the length of the concert, from the first song we sang, from the balconies and from the mezzanine, before and behind us, beyond the stage, flowers rained down on us from all sides. For two hours they fell constantly; larger bouquets from the dark depths of the hall, smaller nosegays from all sides, they scattered in flight like fireworks, while the petals, like snowflakes, fluttered through the thick smoky air. The flowers fell on the hair of our girls, so that they looked like happy brides; on us who started the second half of the concert in our shirts, having taken off the jackets of our uniforms; flowers fell on our white shirts, on the heads of the people sitting in the audience, on the ground, every which way, a shower, an abundance, a luxury of flowers, and the ground was soft like a rug when we entered the second half; flowers got tangled in Egon's frizzy hair and petals slid down his forehead with droplets of perspiration, for it was hellishly hot in the dense mass of people who pushed closer and closer in on us in the shower of blossoms, there were members of the audience sitting between us and the conductor, among our legs and behind our backs; they stood with us as if they were themselves singers, so that we felt their hot breath mingling with ours. Egon Košut, the bedecked conductor, and all of us were crazed by the floral festivities, and we sang as if our souls were ringing from our lips, the conductor howled right along with us with all his strength— nothing short of howling could have been heard in all the commotion. Never in my life have I seen so many flowers. We looked at one another, red in the face from howling and the heat, not even brushing the flowers from our faces and shoulders, and we sang. At one moment I suddenly wanted to spread my arms and take, embrace, accept the flowers that were raining down on us like a blessing from the heavens.

Maybe after that we traveled in cattle cars, maybe we walked to the next town. Maybe we performed there only two, three hours later—sometimes we held concerts five times a day—or maybe it was a year or two later. In my memory there are almost no gaps between events on that unending tour.

To the next town, as I was saying, where at the edge of some marsh, under the open sky, we performed on an improvised wooden podium while before us sat several exhausted work brigades, in the warm summer twilight while a storm was brewing and it was so muggy that we could barely breathe, and the members of the work brigade who were sitting before us in scraggly rows on the grass, stripped naked to the waist, killing mosquitoes on each other's backs to the rhythm of our song, and where applause broke out, on their bare backs, their strong dark arms, their calves, which we joined in with, because the mosquitoes from the marsh were unbearable, there were thousands of them, and killing the mosquitoes turned into a song with rhythmic slapping and chanting in which everybody joined in, wholeheartedly, joyously.

We sang there until late into the night, drunken from the heat, stung all over by the mosquitoes, stripping off our shirts so that we could be barebacked as our audience was, until finally lightning began to flash around us, and we sang on in the wind which abruptly rose, suddenly refreshed with the fragrance of ozone, and then a dense summer shower descended upon all of us, and we stood in it singing while the rain streamed down our faces, and the brigaders stood up from the ground and stood, barebacked, in the rain, upright, singing with us a hymn to, I don't know, to the masses, the sky, the clouds, Lord, how we sang! No one thought of leaving. We slept that night soaked in the straw, all of us together, men and women, an entire genderless chorus in one leaking room.

We sang for farmers, for the army, for student work brigades, for the citizens of small towns and large towns. We believed in all of them equally: we probably believed that all of them one day might start singing as we were singing, endlessly happy, merged into one. Just as we were happy and merged. Now, of course, we swore when we had to walk endlessly along roads, we swore at the bad food in the poor villages when we got there, we cursed the rain, the bedbugs, the cattle cars, the organizers. But we did not confess to feeling tired. I thought that we would never confess to it. We would never surrender. Even when we ranted and raved, and felt the most exhausted, we still believed.

We wept sometimes with our audience. They were moved by themselves, I know now, not by our song. But they did weep. All of us wept together, I remember, in a city which had been under the Italians before the war, where people welcomed us with such ovations from the very start that we could barely start singing. And then, when the concert finally did begin and when we had sung about half of our program, such frenzied applause broke out and such pounding of feet that we could not go on. It lasted literally several hours, much longer than the whole concert would have: we stood there wordless, not singing, surrounded by uninterrupted applause, clapping ourselves, until finally, our palms stinging, drained by emotion, we all burst into tears together and white handkerchiefs appeared in the hall like signals for surrender. Our girls were sobbing. Our large, broad-browed basses wept like children, with little voices. Only the tenors were not moved. But the man has yet to be born who can move a tenor. We laughed and cried at the same time. Three full hours. I don't know what got into us. When it was finally time for us to leave and go off to the next town to perform, we could not leave the hall. The people must have thought that Italy or the war would come back if we left. We stood there surrounded by a dense mass of bodies and couldn't budge. If I had only stayed there. I might still be there still today, surrounded by people. If we had stayed there, my friends. But we left, finally, after a quarter of an hour, scratched, in tatters, from the multitude that was pushing to touch us.

Half blind with happiness, feeble with exhaustion, we staggered on, ever on. We never seemed to have enough.

Sometimes we no longer knew what to do, to outdo ourselves, join our audience, merge with them to the end, destroy ourselves in them. I remember a concert in some army compound where the contact with the audience was rather cool, when, during a pause between two songs, precisely when Egon began to give intonations, somewhere fifty-odd paces behind us, by the barracks building, an invisible bugler played taps with crystal clarity. He probably hadn't been informed that there was a concert on or he thought it was over, his notes were so pure, so poignant, and the sound of the bugle undulated through the twilight like the hair of some elegant fairy, measured, precise, clean, and yet silky soft and warm in the air, and when the bugler finished the entire phrase, Egon repeated it almost soundlessly, in a muted voice, and then, as if we'd agreed to it in advance, yet without a word of preparation, the entire chorus sang taps like some sort of angelic horde of buglers, surprising ourselves, and an inexplicable chill shivered through all of us, and suddenly the soldiers with their shaved heads came alive before us to a man and harmony was found, and we had to repeat the phrase I don't know how many times, until finally the whole army was singing it with us.

Or what about when, do you remember, we were in some nameless little town which all of us had heard of for the first time where those dignified peasants were sitting on benches in the little hall with the earthen floor, only men in the front rows, and only women toward the back, the mirror image of us. Straight in front of us sat serious mustached men, elderly, who didn't take the black hats off their heads and held their umbrellas in front of them, leaning on them as if they were sword handles, and stared at us, silently, steadily, and coldly. We had already sung a dozen songs and hadn't heard a peep from anyone in the hall, no one applauded, and Egon began looking at us questioningly, in panic, not knowing what was going on behind his back. He didn't dare turn around to look. No one could guess what was wrong. One of our trip leaders, who was sitting, as always, in a place of honor in the front row, began to fidget, worried. No one in the hall moved an inch. We had lost all hope.

Then our director stood up and exchanged some whispered words with one of the local town authorities, and said in a firm, quiet voice to the whole hall: "If you like one of the songs that our friends in the chorus sing for you, then show them you liked it. Like this," and he clapped, standing all alone between us and the audience, clapping with all his strength, a grotesque, lone enthusiast. "Whatever is he doing that for?" somebody said next to me. "Are we going to beg them for their applause?" I, too, was a little embarrassed, I have to admit.

And then, once we had sung the next song, several people in the hall began to clap cautiously, first the younger men in the middle, then the women, and only then the town fathers in the first rows, who probably were the most anxious about looking silly. First softly, with restraint, then louder and louder, more and more in unison, and when after the next songs their exuberance surfaced, a frenzy erupted which you couldn't describe with words. So this is what had happened. They simply hadn't known that people applaud. They didn't know how to clap. Never had anyone among them seen a choral concert, or anything else for that matter. Afterward they told us that they had been sitting there stunned with elation, tears in their eyes, and that their hearts had wanted to leap from their chests with helplessness, it was so beautiful. With this first, by now timeworn, vocabulary. And then, in the end, I don't know what delighted them more, the singing or their newfound knowledge, and the solemn town fathers clapped with their heavy great hands, which resounded like cymbals, and their umbrellas and canes tumbled to the floor, the handles banging on the packed dirt floor as if on some muted drum that has been echoing ever since, all the way to where I am today.

So that is how it was. But the tour went on, growing before our eyes like some legendary dragon, it couldn't stop, many things were repeated, but they could not be avoided, and finally we reached that threshold when we felt that the tour had gotten the better of us. We were no longer doing things of our own free will: we were not the ones extending the tour, but rather the tour was driving us on, more and more mercilessly.

I can't say for certain whether it was all those kilometers of the country we had traversed, all those crowds of people we merged with, to whom we gave of ourselves, all that frenzied sea of enthusiasm we stirred up and which intoxicated us, whether all that began to give us the feeling that we were less and less important to it all, less indispensable to the common festivities, as if all of it could have happened just as well without us, as if other singers could have been there in our stead, and as if we were not, indeed, the one and only singers, but that we were some paltry, insignificant part of everything, maybe a mere catalyst, and that the earth could easily live on without us, maybe precisely as it had been before, and that people would be delighted without us, maybe even more, and that we felt at that moment that our self-sacrifice, self-denial, our fervor had become less necessary, I don't know. Anyway, suddenly, by the end of that tour, a sense of weariness began to creep into us, a herald of the end. A weariness I don't precisely know how to describe. Maybe we had had enough. Maybe the fervor had all been spent. Maybe the moment comes when you had better start singing as you should or stop. I don't know. Something happened. The dense undergrowth of exhaustion flourished in us, apparently of its own accord.

There would be concerts when the welcome wasn't quite warm enough, for instance, the local politicos would be off at some more pressing meeting, or we wouldn't be invited to a reception after the concert at the local factory. Now and then we had concerts with no audience to speak of—except some children ushered in by force during school hours. There were towns where a soccer game was going on at the same time, and the clamor and applause from the game would filter into the concert hall from the nearby playing field, mid-song; on the abandoned summer stage where we performed, the only people in the audience were a few art lovers.

The concert organizers began apologizing to us more often, with less awkwardness, because of the poor response of the audience: "you know, a poorly developed effort for culture and education in this town . . . ," or, "well, you know, they are rather elitist in that city . . . it isn't that . . ." More articles began appearing about us in the cultural section of various newspapers.

Some of our women wanted to get married, some of us wanted to enroll in courses of study of this and that.

Talk had begun of going home.

And then, I remember, we found ourselves one evening on a small tiled square of some apparently abandoned town where we were supposed to perform. The first two rows of the chorus stood on the pavement of the square, where grass was growing up among the cracks, while the second two rows stood on a two-foot-high stone wall which closed the square on the one side that had no houses, and when we climbed up on the wall and looked behind us, we saw that we were standing, in fact, on the wall of a cemetery. Behind us stretched a small, neglected cemetery where cypresses and sycamores grew, and the sycamores were rustling over our heads in the evening breeze, which was beginning to pick up, and we who had arrived full of chatter and talk, glowing, ready to perform, cracking jokes at first, fell silent after moving in closer to one another, exchanging glances in the gathering gloom.

We turned toward the square where darkness was already falling, where we were expecting any minute now that members of the audience would start chattering, schoolchildren at least, people, our daily folk. But aside from a few elderly people wearing black suits and women in black kerchiefs, no one else appeared for ages, until finally we realized that no one else was coming. The handful of people stood some ways off, in the shadow of the houses, so that we couldn't see their faces. They showed no inclination of coming any closer, although our choral director went from one to another to try and talk them into approaching us. Apparently, we had arrived late in this town, he told us later on, late, and they hadn't informed the surrounding villages, and in this town there were hardly any inhabitants left. The town was almost completely vacated. All the young people had moved away to the bigger cities. These people had no idea what was going on, said the director. Apparently they were under the impression that we had come to promote peasant collectives or tax collection, that is what they told him.

The wind was picking up briskly now, and it seemed as if the darkness was falling too fast. There was no likelihood of lights. We stood in the dark prepared to hold our program—as always—while around us on the square shutters banged and squeaked spectrally in the wind, the sycamores rustled, and somewhere in the cypresses pygmy owls hooted.

"I guess no one has made it this far except for us," said the director.

"Damn it, is this the end of the world?" somebody asked from the chorus.

"I don't know how we will leave here after the concert," worried the director. "There are no trains or buses of any sort, nothing."

And for the first time the question was posed, clearly and succinctly, of when and how we would ever get home.

But we couldn't not sing, and sing we did, standing on the cemetery wall, in the dark depth of the earth, in this overgrown, uninhabited town, lost, left to our own resources, without the possibility of returning, a small clutch of anxious people.

When we sang, we sang for ourselves alone, very softly yet dramatically, growing bolder with the song, leaning on each other, touching each other's bodies literally with our hands, feeling that we were all that each of us had left, that now at last we needed to get to know each other better, and we stood there, touching the hair of our women in front of us, which was fluttering in the darkness, in the gusty breeze.

I believe we never sang as well as we did that night, with voices trembling full of repressed intensity, permeated with a chill, while the cemetery lay there at our backs, waiting for us to sing our fill. There, where we did our finest job of singing, there was no one to hear us. We sang for ourselves. Nothing echoed. The song was carried off toward the cemetery by the wind. The shadows of those people who had stood close together by the walls of the houses vanished as if they had suddenly melted into the dense darkness. We were completely alone. Egon was standing in front of us with his hands dropped, he wasn't even conducting. There was no point, we couldn't have seen his hands. He sang with us, just as downhearted as we were. We were alone, abandoned, lost in a country that no longer needed us.

Here, it was here, after we completed our regular concert program, that we fell silent for the first time, sitting long and glumly on the little wall, in exhausted poses, wordless, not knowing where we should sleep or how we could travel out of there. Here we stopped singing, although we may have gone on and performed after that, though we gradually dropped out of the chorus, one by one, each headed in his own direction, until not a single one of us was left, although we went on for a long time doing that same or similar work, some of us even professionally; though, I hear, some of us are doing it still today, it was here that we ended our song. We didn't end it badly: Egon, if you hadn't been so grief-stricken, like all of us, if you had been able to hear us from the side, you would have congratulated us, believe me. But it doesn't matter. You probably didn't have the strength to say anything then. None of us did. We had already squandered it, scattered it unparsimoniously, and now we were standing here helpless, staring into the darkness.

That is where they buried us. Now we are all lying somewhere in the same grave, a neatly ordered chorus under the dark cypress trees, a phantom choir without an audience, and around us the shutters are squealing in the dark like wounded creatures.

p. 3: The last two lines in A. B. Šimić's poem "Otkupljenje" ("Redemption") are:

> U Boga mi se uvijek natrag povraćamo
> Zemlja: kratki izlet

> [To God we keep returning
> Earth: a brief excursion]

p. 24: Kraljević Marko—a hero from folk epics of battles between the Serbian feudal lords and the Ottoman army, famed for his late appearance at the Battle of Kosovo.

p. 24: Veli Jože—the Paul Bunyan of Istrian folk tales.

p. 27: Ohrid—a town and lake in Macedonia along the Albanian border.

p. 27: Triglav—a mountain in the Slovene Alps near the Austrian border.

p. 61: The poet quoted is Ivan Goran Kovačić:

> Ima li većeg bogatstva i sreće
> nego što je škrinja i klupa i stol?
> ("Jama—The Pit," verse 10)

p. 61: Osor—a small island and town on the northern Adriatic.

p. 129: *ćevapčići*—a dish of small, grilled, ground-meat patties.

p. 229: Musa Kesedžija—a hero from folk epics who was Marko Kraljević's arch nemesis, fabled to have three hearts.